# Undateables

## The Collection

# L. MOONE

ISBN-13: 9781913930158

# CONTENTS

# THE

# REBOUND LIST

# VIRGIN

# CHAPTER ONE

The first real warning sign that our relationship was doomed came a few weeks prior to our fourth anniversary. During a chat with Sally—arguably my best friend as well as colleague—she speculated whether or not Jeff might propose to me. The thought filled me with dread. Don't get me wrong, I didn't hate him. I actually kind of still loved him but the idea that this was all that life had in store for me depressed me greatly. There was more I had to do; more experiences I was yet to have.

Was he really planning to propose? I certainly hoped not because I couldn't accept. No way. And I have always hated confrontations, so having to say 'no' was an extremely unpleasant prospect.

In a way, finding the inappropriate emails from him to an old lover had been a relief. A chance to make a relatively clean break without having to confess uncomfortable truths. I moved out within the month and found myself free but also apprehensive about what might be in store for me next. Would I find what I had been missing?

I wouldn't make the same mistakes again. Starting a new relationship on the rebound, not fully celebrating my newfound freedom were definite 'no-no's. I needed a plan to figure out when I would be ready to settle down. A means of measuring whether I had lived single life to the fullest.

That's how *the list* was born. While it mentions only the highlights, between the lines I intended to not just vary who with, but also how or where I would *get it on*.

*To Do:*

*Virgin*

*Silver fox*

*Stranger*

*Threesome*

Actually I'm omitting a few steps taken to get to this point; the depressing realisation that I was—for the first time in my adult life—alone in this world. The resulting evening spent with Sally, drinking wine, crying and complaining about how unfair life is, until a few glasses later her eyes lit up with the best idea ever.

Unlike most drunken ideas, this one was pretty workable. She asked me about my deepest, darkest sexual fantasies. She encouraged me to let my inner slut out and enjoy myself in ways I hadn't been able to while playing the squeaky-clean committed girlfriend.

While we spoke our minds, our combined imagination or the wine, probably more the wine actually, awoke something in me. I could feel myself getting excited, blushing feverishly while listening to anecdotes of some of her less responsible exploits. She didn't hold back on the details and I felt an urge grow inside me.

I wanted to be that girl: the one who walks into a room and causes heads to turn in her direction. She made me feel like I had this potential, in the way she described how she saw me. Not boring and average as I had felt all my life, but a rare and exotic beauty who could wield immense power over the male of the species. It was a revelation.

Playing with another girl was never meant to make *the list*, which is just as well because it happened way too quickly. The exact details of how that night ended are beyond my grasp; all I know is we woke up fuzzy-headed and half-dressed in my bed, with one of Sally's arms draped across my chest.

This fact alone should probably have been a lot more awkward than it was. Instead of dwelling on blurry memories, we simply agreed that the night had served its purpose and that *'we should do this again sometime'*.

＊＊＊

Anyway, back to the list. Some additions were clear choices I had thought about for a long time: hooking up with a virgin and an older guy for example. Other details came to mind after drunkenly bouncing ideas off of each other. These usually started with the phrase *'wouldn't it be awesome if...'*

In the cold light of day, some of the excitement still lingered, however I had also lost a little confidence and started to doubt whether I could pull this off. Indeed Jeff was only the second guy I had slept with, and I'd be lying if I said that baring all in front of various men wasn't at least a bit unnerving.

But I would cross that bridge in time, so I set about executing the initial stages of the plan. Sally had shown me a site she had used to hook up before, like a social network for dirty minds. To avoid any risk of early commitment issues, my backstory was decided to be that of a bored wife, looking for fun on the side.

I set up my profile with a suitably disguised photo, sparse personal details mentioning my supposed marriage and a well-filled list of sexual interests and kinks. The opening line was simply my newly adopted motto: *No commitment, only pleasure.*

The possibilities were mind-boggling. What kind of man would I like? Who would I look at in the street? I couldn't form a clear answer; I don't have a "type" only a long list of potentials, so I wrote down all I could think of. Long hair, short hair, beard, clean-shaven, fat, athletic, older, younger, black, white, anything in between. The whole point of this exercise was that I didn't have to settle for just one; I could have them all.

Despite not showing any flesh in my photograph, it didn't take long for friend requests and messages to start coming in. Among the inevitable stream of creepiness I had braced myself for, there were also more thoughtful messages than simply '*show me ur tits*'. Perhaps I would indeed find kindred spirits, to share my body with in addition to good conversation but without the expectations of monogamy hanging above my head.

When I logged back on after work on Friday, my

inbox was full and my friend list had grown considerably as well. I felt empowered to explore more of the site, to join a few groups and read through some message boards. It surprised me how extensive the site's membership was. I even found a group with local personal ads, which would keep me occupied for quite a while.

# CHAPTER TWO

The ad titled '*sick of being a virgin*' captures my attention immediately. It's written by a guy in his twenties who explains in the understatement of the century that he's never had much luck with relationships: he's never been with anyone. I have trouble focusing on the entire text because his profile picture keeps inviting me to stare.

His eyes hold me like a deer caught in headlights. He's got a bit of a hipster thing going with slightly too long, light brown hair and a goatee. How the hell did he make it this far without so much as a date? Not even a kiss. What's the catch?

I've no choice: this ad, the timing. It's all a sign, I was meant to find his profile. I nearly forget to breathe when I see his location, barely twenty minutes away from me. Perfect; I must try to pursue him.

It looks like he has spent quite some time fleshing out his profile; he's trying to give this site a good go while also remaining anonymous beyond his picture and location. His name isn't mentioned anywhere and that suits me just fine. To me he's a concept: a few pictures and an assortment of likes, dislikes and worries, but not quite yet a fully formed person.

Supply and demand; he wants a certain experience, as do I. Really, the less I know the better, if I'm going to be successful and avoid emotional entanglement along the way.

He writes that he worries he'd disappoint and has considered visiting an escort, but so far not gone through with that plan. His fear is that all other guys are experienced, whereas he so obviously isn't. *That can change, sweetheart, and no payment will be needed.* He blames his lack of *game* on his larger physique which practically breaks my heart. Whoever led him to believe that was not just cruel, but mistaken as far as I'm concerned.

I keep hovering over the message button. Or should I just send him a friend request? I wish I knew what would be the right way of handling this, but I doubt anyone's ever written a self-help book on this topic. *'How to hook up with a virgin on Fetlife'.* Too bad, I'd love to read it.

Instead of acting on my impulses straightaway, I decide to grab myself a glass of wine and think. Willing and nearby virgins don't grow on trees I imagine, not of this calibre anyway. I can't afford to fuck this up.

Finally I take a deep breath and type out a message to him. Perhaps it would be best to just be honest. The wine is starting to give me a pleasant buzz by now, which definitely helps.

Hi, I read your personal ad and felt compelled to respond. Just as many men would love to be someone's first, the opposite can be true as well. And frankly I'm surprised you've not had more luck so far, because I think you're very attractive. If you like, send me a friend request and perhaps we could see where this goes?

Too forward or not enough? I can't decide if I come across as an idiot and decide to just send it before heading to the kitchen for a refill. Chilled white wine isn't the best drink for this cold weather. Or perhaps it's the nerves giving me shivers.

Sitting back down with the full glass in hand, I notice one notification: a request. I guess maybe he doesn't think I'm that much of an idiot after all. Although my heart is racing, my nerves are dulled just enough to transform my earlier anxiety into excitement.

When I hit 'accept', his name appears in the little chat box to the side of the page, but I don't get the chance to think about it too much. His profile reveals extra photographs which weren't available before and I'm hopelessly distracted. Oh my, I can see why he would've set them to be hidden from his public profile because by the end, nothing is left to the imagination.

They say women are less visual than men, and while that may be true, I can certainly appreciate the view. He's beautiful in a way that an airbrushed underwear model could never be. My wish of wanting something new and totally unlike Jeff may just turn into reality. Jeff was skinnier than average and very boyish and hairless, this guy looks more towards the other end of the spectrum on both counts. If he were gay, I guess he might be referred to as a bear.

It hits me that I've spent years being very naive about my sexuality. I never looked at anyone with quite the same mind-set as what I'm doing now and it surprises me how aroused I'm becoming.

Taking a sip from my glass, I'm having a hard time looking away. Not only could I imagine myself having sex with him—which in itself is out of character for me—I am already obsessively fantasising about it. Merely the thought of what it might feel like to touch his chest is starting to make me wet.

I'm done for; I've found my first mark.

A chat window pops up with just one solitary word in it. "Hi."

Before I know it, the wine is set down and my fingers are moving over the keyboard in crazed excitement. Must remember the cover story and not be a cow. It would be a crying shame if this one got away.

"Hey, handsome! Thanks for friending me, I'm finding it impossible to stop looking at your pic, you're insanely cute..."

"Yeah right. Bet you haven't seen any beyond my profile pic or you wouldn't be saying that."

"Oh no, I've seen 'em. Believe me, you're gorgeous. All over."

There is a pause before he starts to type again.

"Your shot, is that really you?"

"Yeah. Just you know, wearing a mask so I don't get myself in trouble... Why?"

"Despite that, I didn't expect to be complimented by someone like you. Am half expecting you to turn out to be a guy..."

"No way. I'm going to assume that's a good thing."

"Definitely."

After the initial flurry of words exchanged between us, I suddenly struggle to think of any small talk at all.

"Have you had a lot of responses to that ad?" It's the best I could come up with.

"I've only put it up last week, but no, not really. I mean there were a couple of messages but nothing serious. Dunno what I was expecting."

"Don't take this wrong, but I'm relieved not to have competition..."

My heartbeat shows no signs of slowing. Really, I would've been quite disappointed if someone else had gotten to him before me. I'm not sure what fuels my fascination, but the thought of being a first for someone consumes me. I've never had that opportunity; my first time was with a guy who was quite a bit more experienced. And I probably wouldn't have known what to do anyway.

But I would know this time. I want to show him things he hasn't experienced before. Hopefully the opportunity will be mine if all goes well.

"Have you been married long?" He's read the profile, suppose that's a good sign...

"A few years." Sally had advised me to stick to a story as close to the truth as possible so I'd be modelling my fake marriage on the near-four-year relationship with Jeff.

"I hope you don't think I'm a bitch for talking to you while married. I'm fine with the way things are between us, but physically I just need more... I've been playing with the idea for a while and finally decided to sign up on here to experiment a bit."

"Actually, the fact that it's so secret and forbidden is... interesting. A turn on. He doesn't know what you're up to at all?"

"No, this is just for me. He won't find out, his job takes him on the road a lot." I hope we can move past this topic soon so I don't need to keep track of tons of backstory.

"Right."

"So tell me about yourself, what are you looking for?"

"I guess same as everyone else. Just to not be alone. I mean I've got plenty of friends, including girls. But somehow..."

"Ah, the dreaded friend zone. I can see how that would be frustrating."

"You can only hear '*I don't think of you that way*' so many times before giving up."

"Yeah, it's hard to change friendship into something more, but it does happen. It did for me."

"I dunno."

"The problem is you start off over familiar, there is no mystery."

"Or, since all of 'em tend to date jocks, there just isn't any demand for guys like me."

It hurts to admit it to myself but I know he's right, at least as far as society as a whole is concerned. I want to tell him that's only true for shallow girls, but that would be hypocritical since I'm equally picky. Though I honestly am attracted to him just as he is, it was his face that drew me in. I'm a total sucker for a handsome face, or so I've discovered just now. Had he not had that, would I have given his ad a second look? I like to think it would not have made a difference but I may be deluding myself.

"Bullshit. It's all about attitude," I finally write.

"I've always been shy. Not sure that can change." I hope it can, for my own sake as well as his.

"We shall see…"

"Hey, I just realised I was meant to go out tonight. My friends will be waiting. Nice chatting to you, perhaps we can pick this up again soon?"

*Did I scare him away? I certainly hope not.*

"Oh, sure. Don't let me keep you. See you around."

"Later." He goes offline straightaway.

I'm left alone in front of the PC, wondering if it's pervy to keep going back to his photos in between reading his blog posts. He bares all, his worries and fears as well as obviously his clothes. It is just about attitude, I'm sure of it now. Most girls don't want to date a needy guy, they don't want to pick up the pieces after years of rejection and put them back together, over and over again. They can sense desperation from a mile away.

But I'm not looking for a relationship, just an experience. And I'm not most girls either. Actually yes, I'd love to make a difference and show him that he can instil at least as much passion in someone as any gym nut. I want to convince him he's desirable, so we both get something out of this hook-up. I will have had my virgin. Hopefully he will gain a new outlook in his love life, or at least learn a few tricks in bed to help his confidence.

All this seems like a win-win to me. I just hope he feels the same way. Just one last look at his photographs before bedtime. And another. I want him, badly. My hand has a mind of its own and I decide not to worry about whether I'm acting like a crazy online stalker.

I bring myself to orgasm swiftly with my fingers.

Fantasies of his naked flesh pressed up against me stay with me even beyond my release. Wonder if his chest hair would tickle me, or not. I'm sure other than that he'd be pretty soft all over, it would be a nice change. I think I'd prefer a bit of padding after four years of skinny, bony Jeff.

The next morning, I wake up still a bit fuzzy from excesses past. Too much wine, I'm such a lightweight. I've nothing planned for this entire weekend, so the first thing I do is listen to my inner longing and turn on the PC. Surely he wouldn't have been *that* interested, would he? It's just me who's obsessed.

When I log in, I'm greeted by a message. I've been getting a lot of those lately from random men wanting to befriend me. But not this time, *he* sent it around two a.m.


Hi,

Sorry to just run off on you earlier. I just reached back home, hoping that perhaps you'd be up late too. I apologise if this is weird, but I kept thinking about you all night. Maybe you were just being nice, but it's driving me crazy that you could actually be interested. It's unexpected. Your photo is very beautiful, wish I could see the rest of your face but even so, you seem way out of my league. Again, sorry if this is inappropriate. I may have had a few...
P.S. thanks for the lovely comments you left.

I'm thrilled. I didn't misread our chat, I didn't put him off. But, what comments? As I've done so many times before, I open up his profile and attempt to retrace my obsessive actions from last night.

Oh fuck, there it is. A gushing message sprawling over multiple paragraphs right underneath one of his most recent blog posts. I wrote (again and again) that he's beautiful. That if someone took the time to really see who he is, they'd be lucky to have him. *And that I want his virginity, delivered to me on a silver platter.*

Right, how drunk was I? I suppose he will have been too, or this whole thing may have gone down differently. This is embarrassing, and yet I can't deny that I still feel the same.

Before I'm able to continue analysing myself or his message, he appears in chat. Damn, where do I even start?

"Hey :)" he starts.

"Oh hi, what's up?"

"Nothing much, bit of a headache."

"Yeah I can relate. So what did you get up to last night?" I ask.

"Just went out. Open mic night where one of my mates was performing with his band."

"That sounds awesome." I wonder if it would be weird to bring up his message, or my drunken comments. Should I make some sort of apology?

"Yeah. I found it a little hard to focus though..."

"Why's that?" I tease.

There's a bit of a pause before he answers.

"Well, our little chat earlier had me... distracted."

"I have to admit, I've been distracted as well... So, I should ask, what are you hoping to get out of this whole ad thing?"

"Umm, honestly? Maybe not so different from what you seem to want. Experiences. I feel like I should've you know... *done it* by now. If I end up dating someone, how the hell do I explain? I'd need to know what to do, know what I mean?"

"Yeah, experiences sound about right. So in short you're after some instruction as well?" I ask.

"I guess, yeah. I get that most people would be nervous the first time round, but maybe I've been obsessing about it so much over the years, I'd be an absolute basket case."

"Somehow I doubt that. It'd be totally fine." *Yeah, because I'd be pretty fucking nervous as well.*

"Would you be into that, like with someone who's pretty much clueless?"

"I think I'd welcome the chance to feel all knowledgeable. That looks pretty stupid now that I've typed it out..." It feels stupid too.

"Not at all."

I can see him typing and stopping a few times, so I decide to wait and see what he's trying to say before responding myself. After about a minute, the next message shows up and it nearly makes me choke on my own breath.

"Would you like to meet up?"

I stare at the text on the screen for a while, my heart pounding in my throat. *Yes, yes I do! But I don't even know you. What if...*

When I put my fingers back onto the keyboard, they visibly tremble.

"I'd like to, but I'm a bit scared. What if my husband finds out?" My cover story provides a convenient excuse, but actually I am just terrified that things might go wrong. I suddenly feel like I have a lot to lose; that I can't be the confident temptress I had pretended to be online and all would fall apart if we meet.

Almost straightaway a response arrives.

"I knew it. Never mind then."

Hang on, this isn't what I wanted. I need some kind of encouragement that things would turn out OK, not for him to give up.

"That's not what I meant, I'm just apprehensive. Suddenly it seems it's not all that simple."

"You don't have to sugar coat it. I understand. It's not the first time and I don't even know why I thought this would turn out differently. Just forget it." No sooner does the message arrive, than he goes offline.

*Oh fuck, now I've done it.*

I sit around for a while, feeling incredibly torn and upset. The sensible part of my brain is telling me that it's all for the best if this goes no further. Yet I feel so frustrated, that I could happily throw my laptop out of the window. I'm furious at myself for cowardly backing down, and guilt-ridden for making him feel like I'd rejected him. This isn't how I had planned to celebrate my singledom, is it? None of the things on the list stood out as much as this one and yet I fail at the first hurdle?

No. I won't accept defeat. After a few deep breaths, I open up his profile and compose a new private message. Time to take back control of the situation.

I know how my messages came across and I'm sorry, but your assumptions are wrong. If you're free on Saturday, please let me know where & when and I'll be there, bearing in mind the following:

1. There will be no obligations for either of us; we can say no at any time if we're not feeling it.

2. I don't just sleep with strangers, so I expect to be taken on a date first. I'll have a hotel room booked so we have a relatively neutral place to retreat to in case things go well.

3. Be clean and well groomed; I expect you to make an effort to look nice for me. (To avoid any confusion, I mean common-sense stuff like taking a shower, clipping your nails and brushing your teeth

etc. No need to worry about body hair.)

4. I like for a man to make the first move. To help you along, remember that I won't make ANY physical contact unless I am open to more.

5. You're bringing the condoms.

Send.

A cold chill travels down my spine when I realise that there is no turning back now. Time to put my money where my mouth is; I told him I want him, it's only fair that I show it. And to ensure I don't screw things up, I'll only keep an eye on messages but stay away from the chat until the deed is done.

It's Sunday morning and the chat and resulting message are still very much on my mind. Worried that he might not take me seriously, I'm apprehensive about checking my inbox where his response awaits.

Wow, OK. I clearly overreacted, the conversation just seemed to be going in a direction I had seen a few too many times lately, how embarrassing! Please accept my apologies.

How about 2pm at Cineworld?

Damn I'm nervous already (excited too though!), hope you were truthful on your profile about liking shy guys because I'm afraid that's pretty much exactly what you're going to get... And I'll do my best to follow your instructions but might struggle with point 4.

He has no idea I'm going to be equally terrified, which is kind of sweet. I can only hope that he's as easy to talk to in person as online, and things will somehow naturally progress without too much awkwardness. In any case I'm pleased he's proposing to meet at a cinema, if the conversation stalls at least we'll have a movie to talk about.

I respond straight to the point with simply '*See you then x*' and log off again after having a last nose around his profile page. He really is bloody cute, no matter what other girls have led him to believe. The last thing I see before closing my browser is his most recent status update; '*Date on Saturday, wish me luck!*' My heart skips a few beats.

The week passes in a blur, though I try not to obsess too much. Seeing Sally at work helps, because I get the chance to spill all that's happened so far and she seems more excited than I am. This fear is hard to overcome.

We both agree that what's needed is some retail therapy to calm me down. After demanding that he makes an effort for me, it's only fair that I do the same. A new outfit is required: new clothes for a new *me*. I must make a good impression; it's not every day that one tries to live out a near lifelong fantasy.

# CHAPTER THREE

Throughout my train journey I keep running through different potential outcomes. What if it's a disaster? What will I say to him when we meet? Shaking hands would be an odd greeting, wouldn't it? I should move in for a hug. But what if I don't like him in person? Crap, he hasn't even seen a proper, picture; what if *he* doesn't like *me*? I'd call Sally for a much needed confidence boost but typically, I've no network.

I feel like a cigarette even though I don't smoke and I know that'll make things worse. Damn, if I'm this freaked out, how scared must *he* be right now. We're surely doomed if I don't get myself under control. I'm the one in charge, I tell myself. *I've got this. Ugh.*

The hotel looks just like every other Etap I've ever visited, which isn't necessarily a bad thing. At least it's impersonal and clean and not so small that we'd feel too overlooked.

The short walk to the cinema feels like it lasts forever and yet not long enough. I'm five minutes late according to my watch. Stupid public transport. And of course in my efforts to keep things simple and anonymous, we didn't exchange mobile numbers and as such I couldn't let him know of the delay.

It suddenly hits me that we don't even know each other's names. Should we?

With jelly for knees I walk into the bright, glass-covered entrance and spot him immediately standing off to one side. He's looking at the floor and hasn't noticed me, giving me the chance to check him out first. Wow, I really do like what I'm seeing.

Clearly he has been paying attention to my instructions. He looks great, a crisp white shirt, not too formal dark trousers. He's big, yes, but I already knew that and I still don't understand why others consider that a negative; it's different but not in a bad way. I do adore a bit of facial hair and am pleased that he's kept it like in his pictures, carefully trimmed. Fashionably unruly hair completes his style. Yes, this is what effort looks like and it suits him wonderfully.

I am already imagining what the fabric of his shirt might feel like under my touch... *Fuck*. He's looking right at me.

Immediately I can feel my face burn up as I hurry towards him, already late and now caught staring shamelessly without even doing the decent thing of saying hello first. God, this is embarrassing.

"Uhh, hi." I try my best to straighten my shoulders and look at him, but the urge to inspect the floor is almost impossible to fight.

He gives me a strange, vacant look.

"You're...?"

I just nod, forcing myself to look into his eyes momentarily. He has really nice, greenish eyes.

"I'm sorry for... you know..." Clearly my vague hand gesture isn't doing the job of completing my apology for me. "Being late, staring rudely, that sort of thing."

I can't read him and it's driving me insane. How do people do this without falling to pieces?

"OK.. this is awkward," he says finally, taking the words right of my mouth.

I let out a sigh in an attempt to sound agreeable. So much for my plan of greeting him with a hug, things are already way too weird as they are.

"Anyway, you look great!" I say with a smile. He shrugs and suddenly I can detect a glimmer of emotion in his eyes when he looks back at me. It's not positive.

*Shit, he hates me.*

"Kind of odd to say that now."

"What do you mean?"

"If I hadn't noticed you, you'd have just turned around and walked back out again," he says.

His interpretation of events is unexpected.

"No way! I mean seriously that's what you think just happened here?"

I put my hand on his arm and feel the intensity of my heartbeat surge instantly; a sensation not lost on him because he twitches slightly as if I've just given him a static shock.

"I was just nervous, is all," I say.

"*You're* nervous?" he asks. I nod slowly in response, feeling my lips tense together and eyes widen significantly.

"OK, fuck it. Let's start over." I take a deep breath. "Hi! I'm really sorry I'm late, my train was delayed."

"Hi..." A hint of a smile plays on his lips as he plays along and stretches out his hand as if to greet me.

Still thinking that's a very weird way to start a date, I instead put both my hands on his shoulders, tiptoe and give him a light kiss on the cheek. I'm intoxicated. Don't think I've ever been one to swoon before but here we are.

"You smell lovely," I whisper, before letting go of him and stepping back to where I started off.

After a few seconds of shyly grinning at each other he clears his throat and produces two cinema tickets from his trouser pocket.

"I think we should probably head upstairs or they'll start without us," he says.

It's a relief to walk off towards the escalator together where he shows the attendant our tickets. He gestures at me to go up ahead of him. I hadn't realised how much of a sucker I am for simple gestures like that; Jeff never gave a shit. *I have got to stop thinking of Jeff!*

Rushing to the correct floor and finding our seats in the last row of the theatre, he suddenly turns towards me.

"Totally forgot to ask, would you like me to get you anything, a drink, snack, whatever?" He looks so apologetic it makes me chuckle.

"Don't worry, I never go to the cinema unprepared," I respond, patting my handbag. Indeed, I do have a compulsive need to keep sweets in my purse whenever I go out for the day. I don't necessarily end up eating them but it's nice to know they're there.

We get comfortable in our seats and immediately the lights dim and the movie starts after a few obligatory trailers. I can't decide whether he's chosen a horror film because he suspects I'd enjoy it, he's trying the classic 'scare the girl in order to get cosy on a date' move or he likes the genre himself, but I'm probably going to find out soon enough.

The opening credits pass and we're only into the first scene when I remember the one thing I dislike about cinemas. They keep them too cold and my lack of comfort certainly isn't helped by the dress and heels I chose to wear today. In my efforts to impress, I chose an outfit not suited to the late autumn climate. My hands previously clammy and cold due to nerves, are now practically frozen, sending chills up my arms and around my back.

Rubbing the skin on my arms through the light sleeves, I try desperately to fight the onslaught of goose bumps without drawing too much attention to myself. I fail on both counts and he leans towards me, asking if I'm cold.

Oh my, I do love his scent even though being this close to him is making the shivers worse. Even so, I decide to fold away the armrest between us and wait to see what he'll do. Neither of us are paying much attention to the movie at all, completely ignoring the gasps some of our fellow audience members let out at something undoubtedly scary happening on screen.

I subtly scoot a bit closer to him and he does eventually put his arm around me. He's blissfully warm and I'm so excited to feel him against me, I have to fight every impulse to not start cuddling. It's way too soon for that, isn't it?

Not long after, the physical closeness between us starts to melt away all sorts of worries and obstacles. Trying our best to keep our voices hushed, we start to pass commentary on what's happening in front of us; the vast majority of which isn't complimentary and makes me giggle under my breath until a very stern looking man a few rows ahead of us turns around and shushes me.

I press my lips together in a desperate attempt to keep quiet and stare at... well I don't know his name. He gives me an equally helpless look, almost causing me to burst into loud laughter. Luckily I manage to save us from certain disapproval and embarrassment by covering my mouth with my hand and cuddling against his chest.

Something changes immediately, in his breathing as well as body language. He's tense, which affects me instantly, making me forget what we had just been giggling about and serves as a reminder of why we're both here. It's no longer terrifying, at least not to me. Excitement inside me is growing and I'm happy to hold back and see if he picks up on my willingness.

Feeling his short, quick breaths against my hair, I pretend to watch the film again and wait. He doesn't move a muscle; is he worried I'll move away if he does or am I making him uncomfortable? I can't be sure.

Minute after minute passes and nothing happens. I adjust myself to a more comfortable position, causing his hand to slip off my shoulder and brush my side. He freezes mid-breath and although I really want to act, I pretend not to notice when he quickly puts it back where it was before.

It is obvious that my whole body has noticed though, I'm buzzing inside-out and starting to feel a deep, delicious warmth develop in my lower abdomen, together with a definite moistness further down. This has never happened to me, not in the company of someone else and certainly not in public. I can count how many times I've been turned on enough to get wet on one hand; invariably happening when alone in my thoughts and fantasies but not once because of a man.

Obviously I've fallen in lust with him, from the moment I saw his picture, his profile, his messages. Everything I've learnt about him has heightened this sensation, and it almost made me mess everything up because it felt so alien that it threw me off.

But I'm in control now. I've identified what I'm feeling; I know what to do about it and I'll gladly let him in on the secret eventually.

In a seemingly absentminded gesture, I reach up and take his hand which has been resting on my shoulder. His fingers thread through mine, heat travels from his skin and into mine to force my excitement to another level. I feel my own breathing turn erratic and wait again.

Gently at first, he squeezes my hand and I respond by snuggling against him more closely. I'm about ready to lose patience when I feel his other hand caress my hair. My eyes close and I raise my head after taking a few seconds to enjoy the moment.

Looking at him, despite the dimmed light of the theatre, still I feel a jolt run through me when our eyes meet. He runs his fingers through my hair again. Hoping this is going where I want it to, I look at his lips, so tempting. I want to taste him, right here and immediately.

His hand cups my cheek but he continues to just look as if asking for permission. Over-eager and impatient, of course I jump the gun and reach for him, planting a soft kiss on his lips. I feel his breath against me, his arms drawing me towards him closer.

He kisses me back. It's a bit awkward at first but then our lips, tongues, our beings seem to be in tune. Every inch of me appears to sing with excitement. My eyes flick open and find his staring into me, smiling as I am.

I wrap my arm around his neck, my hand reaching for his hair now. It's hard not to get carried away, after all, a cinema does not afford all that much privacy. But I suppose there's no harm in indulging my impulses just a little.

Running my fingertips over his shirt, I enjoy the outlines of what I know to be underneath. Mystery is overrated. I have spent enough time looking at, no, studying his naked photographs to know what awaits me and frankly, that's reassuring as well as arousing.

He doesn't have this advantage though, until today he had only seen the bottom half of my face and my eyes, and that too in black and white instead of colour. I kiss him with more energy, more passion and feel a moan travel over my lips. Was it mine or his? Does it even matter?

Suddenly aware of angry stares burning into us, I pause, biting my bottom lip and try to signal to make him aware of the grumpy man ahead of us. He continues to hold me, grinning back at me until I decide to turn and use him as a backrest; his arm draped across my front in a similar position as you'd keep a seatbelt in a car.

He seems to be enjoying this changed dynamic as much as I am, because he starts to nuzzle my neck, where all the little hairs at the back stand right up. His hand, fingertips soft and careful, running up and down on the fabric of my dress, just over where my ribs end and the soft part of my waist starts. It's beautiful, the slow progress we're making towards the inevitable.

The movie, although kind of gory and scary, passes by quickly and largely unnoticed. His face remains comfortably resting in the crook of my neck and I'm hanging onto his arm, my hand travelled up his sleeve just enough to hold him. There should be no mistaking that I want him here, this close and even closer to me.

His confidence grows and he wraps his other arm around me too, caressing my arm which is still pretty cold in the unnaturally chilled cinema air. By the time the credits start, I can't wait to get out, away from grumpy man who interrupted our first, tentative kisses.

"I think I want to go..." I say.

He sits up, letting go as I turn towards him.

"Thought it was going well..." he says, his gaze lingers on my lips just a bit.

"Oh yeah, I meant both of us, somewhere more private... if you want to." I smile at him. "You didn't think that I want to leave? No, not at all."

He gets up and offers me his arm, the relief quite evident in his face when he smiles back at me.

"As you wish, my lady. You lead the way."

My face is burning up again; the thought of what's to come is both a bit scary and yet incredibly exciting. I can feel my heart pound, I fear if he wasn't holding on to me I'd have to sit down and catch my breath.

He's quiet while we go downstairs and exit the cinema. I wonder if this is going too fast for him, but our previous interactions didn't make me think he was the patient type.

The bright sunlight makes me squint and somehow manages to increase the goose bumps all over my body. I direct him towards the hotel and our walking speed intensifies the closer we get. Neither of us seem to want to delay things any further.

# CHAPTER FOUR

Closing the door behind me, I turn to face him. He looks lost, standing in the middle of the room, eyeing the bed momentarily but not making a move either towards or away from it.

"Do you know why I came out and met you?" I ask.

"Because I suggested it?" He shrugs and puts his hands in his pockets. His eyes are fixed on the floor.

"You think I'm doing this as a favour to you? That you guilt-tripped me into it?" I feel my confidence grow in this newfound role.

He nods silently.

"Well you're wrong," I say, greeting his confused expression with a subtle smile. "I'm not a charity, and I'm here because I want to be, because I knew I'd enjoy this."

He blinks a few times, frowning slightly and still refuses to make eye contact.

"You wrote that you want to experience, learn, meaning I'd have to guide you. Is that still what you want?" I take a step towards him and place my hand on his cheek to guide his face upwards until he's looking right at me.

He's clearly beyond nervous, I just want to hold him, to make it better somehow but that would just give the impression like I'm patronising him.

"Yes." His voice is only barely audible.

"Well then. I promise I will do just that if you're unsure. I won't ever judge or laugh at you. Understand that it'll please me to see you succeed, not fail... Do you trust me?"

He nods.

"Stand up straight," I whisper and place my hand on his shoulder, "and try to look at me when we talk. It'll help you in future if you make a habit of it."

When his eyes meet mine, I feel my heart jump.

"You're not the only one who's nervous..."

He attempts to push his shoulders back, raising his height by an inch or so and looks at me for a split second before letting his gaze wander into the distance.

"You could've fooled me," he says.

"Exactly. Body language can be faked." I let my fingers run over the side of his face, down his neck and pause on his shoulder.

His eyes are drawn downwards towards my chest, nipples visibly hard underneath my dress, then back up lingering on my lips. He leans in, hesitating slightly before I respond by putting both arms around his neck. Our lips brush against each other, the soft tickle of his breath leaves me helpless in his arms and swept away in the kisses that follow.

"You're a great kisser; strong yet not too rough. I like that," I whisper.

It surprises me just how much I like it. I don't want to let him go actually... *No!* I should stop these thoughts before they take hold.

His hands explore the small of my back, the muscles

running alongside my spine. I hang on to him, encouraging him with further kisses and nibbles, letting my fingers run through his hair. Although I didn't even know of his existence until about a week ago, I feel like I've had to wait ages for this moment and what's yet to come.

He's pressed up tightly against me. Warm, glorious skin hidden beneath that shirt. I'm not sure what's gotten into me but I can't help wanting to make further demands. He must be made to realise that he's here for my pleasure: this isn't a sympathy fuck.

"Take it off," I say, tugging at the bottom corner of his shirt.

He takes a step back, clearly conflicted between obeying me or his instincts which seem to be half driven by fear. For a moment I'm not sure whether to repeat my instruction, but that turns out to be unnecessary.

Slowly he starts to unbutton and while I watch, I worry that my growing impatience will make my chest explode. *Deep breaths, collect yourself.* More of him comes into view when he rids himself of the shirt, then his vest as well. I'm starting to realise how lucky I am.

"And that." I point at his trousers, fully aware of how terrifying this situation must be. His blog had already revealed how guarded he is: he's not one for trips to the beach and I'm the first in years to even see him shirtless up close.

While he fumbles with his belt I can make out that his hands are shaking.

"Remember what I said earlier?" I try my best to

speak with a calm, soothing voice, despite feeling utterly on edge and on the verge of panic myself. "I want you. It's obvious that your pictures didn't do you justice."

He swallows away any remaining reluctance and strips down completely before giving me a sheepish look.

"You don't have to lie, you know."

"I'm not nice enough to lie about this. Stand up straight." I give him a stern look and he immediately obeys.

When I start to caress his chest, he does his best to remain still and sucks in his stomach which is unnecessary as well as ineffective. He does have quite a bit of hair, unlike Jeff who was almost boy-like in appearance. It's kind of soft, straight and irresistible; I love it already. His nipples tighten under my touch, but really I am under his spell, not the other way around.

Knowing that a lot of women nowadays prefer the clean look, I especially mentioned body hair in my email. My hopes of getting him au naturel today have been answered, beautifully.

My fingers travel south, following the same path as some of the stretch marks on the side of his belly. A quick look up reveals that although he has remained upright, his eyes are now shut. I take the opportunity to bend down, kissing and sucking on any skin in my path. He lets out a gasp and grabs my hair.

"Am I tickling you?" I ask, looking up from his right nipple.

He shakes his head but doesn't let go.

"Do you want me to stop?"

He looks helpless, making me want him even more.

"Why are you doing this?" he asks finally.

"Because your body is begging to be touched. Do you not like it?" I say.

His grasp on my hair loosens and he shrugs. His cock is a more reliable indicator, seemingly unaffected by any awkwardness and hardening even without any direct stimulation.

"I don't know. I wasn't expecting... this."

"Do you still want to please me?"

He nods, and I get up, facing him for a second before turning around and presenting the back zip of my dress to him.

"Open it," I say.

The fabric loosens around me and I shrug it off. I wait for a reaction, looking back for only a moment and finding him quite preoccupied and unable to decide what to do.

"Do you like what you see?" I turn around once more.

He nods.

"Why?"

"You're.. my God, you're stunning."

I quickly open my bra and take off my panties, leaving both on the floor beside us. He's breathing heavily and his eyes look glazed, feverish. Being naked in front of him turns out to be easier than expected.

"Show me," I say, while brushing my fingertips over my nipples, savouring the chills this sends down my entire back.

Then I reach out for his hand, putting it on the small of my waist. Leaning in for more kisses, he eagerly reciprocates and only stops when I interrupt him.

"Keep touching, caressing. And most girls love it when you kiss their necks, some like it rougher, some gentler, so experiment a bit." Immediately he does and I have to use all self-control to not throw him onto the bed and pounce.

"Ohhh..." My fingers cringe and dig into his shoulder while he sucks on my neck and finally lets his hands roam freely over my back.

Throughout our previous kisses he had craned his neck forward, trying to keep a bit of distance between us. Whether through my desperate attempts of clawing at his back to get him closer, or the knowledge that he is truly turning me on, he's not so reluctant anymore. I wonder whether to draw attention to how amazing he feels against me, or if that'll make things weird again.

I decide to just show him by touch, exploring the outline of his shoulder blades and curvature of his back all the way down. His lips pause when I reach his ass, the resulting groan tickles my neck. He is as ready as I am, more foreplay seems unnecessary.

"Where are the condoms?" I nibble on his ear as I reach for him and loosely close my hand around his impressive girth. He flinches slightly but doesn't pull away yet.

After catching his breath, he pulls back and looks through the pile of clothes, finding half a dozen wrappers in his trouser pocket. Sitting down on the bed, he struggles to open the first one, nerves unsettling his movements. For a few moments I manage a bit of patience, watching him without interfering.

It's slippery, unmanageable and he's getting more irate by the second. Kneeling down in front of him, I take the condom. I answer his apologetic expression with a smile.

"You might want to practice this on your own later," I say, while rushing to put it on.

His intense focus returns and he seemingly can't take his eyes off my chest. But I can't cope with any more delays and direct him further back onto the bed, before straddling him.

"I can't believe this is actually going to happen," he says.

I kiss him deeply, guide his hand over my breast and hear his sharp intake of breath when I touch his cock again. He is so sensitive, so tightly strung. I hold him in place and lower myself down slowly. His eyes close; my God he's beautiful. Everything about this is perfect.

His hand squeezes me gently at first, but twitches erratically when I start to move. He's out of breath, looking at me with drunk eyes. I rest my hand in the centre of his wonderfully furry chest. I've been missing out. From now on, I prefer men with a bit of hair on them.

I'm dripping, unable to feel much friction, increase my movements gradually but do not reach the desired rhythm. He groans, freezes and digs his fingers almost painfully into my thigh. He shudders and grits his teeth. *That was quick.*

Leaning down, I kiss him, everywhere within reach. His skin feels hot, slightly damp with sweat but not unpleasantly so.

"I'm so sorry," he says in between gasps of air.

"Don't be."

I'm still aching for more, and I know I will get it. I'll get anything I want today, because I don't intend to let him leave until I do.

Getting off him, I lie down on my side and watch as he tries to remove the rubber. He's gone softer but not fully so. The embarrassment is written all over him, his face, his shoulders deflated as he's sitting there with his back towards me, trying to clean himself up.

It strikes me how broad and masculine he looks from behind, but slouching doesn't suit. I put my hand on his shoulder, pulling him back and inviting him under the covers with me. Refusing to look me in the eye, he hesitates at first but soon realises how much I crave his touch. This is far from over.

"You're wet," he notes when his hand reaches between my legs for the first time. "So soft."

I moan, enjoying the tentative exploration of his fingers. He leans up onto his elbow, and stares. My chest rises and falls in rapid succession, spurred on by every touch of his fingertips. He's careful, gentle, gaining focus.

Writhing against the sheets, I savour the moment. So much pent up tension inside me, raring to escape. What

I want most is for him to complete me.

Getting up on all fours beside me, he scatters soft kisses over my chest. Each one I meet with a gasp, before holding my breath.

"You like this?" he asks, rhetorically, I should hope.

I can't form the words to answer, instead gripping his wrist tightly, aiming to get him to finger me again. He has other ideas, letting his lips travel down my skin. His goatee tickles me, worsening my impatience.

There is a pause when he finishes kissing me around my bellybutton. I'm close to losing my mind.

"May I..." He has lowered himself onto his elbows to allow his hands to grip my hips.

I lean up off the pillows to meet his uncertain gaze.

"If you're asking what I think you're asking—" I nod downwards and smile before continuing, "Yeah, absolutely!"

The moment he dives downwards for more kisses, I let myself drop back again. His hands have found the inside of my thighs, caressing my skin. His tongue, shy at first, must've decided it likes the taste of my arousal.

Warm, wet lips close around my clit while the tip of his tongue spreads fire inside my folds.

"Oh my," I pant.

"Yes, right there. See if you can go deeper..." I lean up on both elbows, too restless to simply submit.

His hands tighten their grip on me and what was meant to be a quick glance downwards at him gets drawn out into a stare. Smooth, relaxed forehead; eyes nearly shut until he catches me looking.

Even if he could, there is no need for words, his eyes speak for him. They say that this is as good for him as it is for me. That my pleasure means everything right now. We've broken the ice and with it some of his earlier worries.

He finds my clit again, running his tongue around it in a circular motion. It feels so good, soothing the ache I've felt ever since our first kiss.

"God, you're good!" I say, finally falling back on the pillow again.

Kneeling up between my legs, he lets his fingers travel over my slick pussy. Every part of me gets touched, while he studies my reaction in an attempt to learn to read me.

It's not difficult to, considering the almost violent reaction he causes when he slips first one and then two fingers inside. So good, but not quite what I'm holding out for.

Up on my elbows again, I allow myself the chance to watch him exactly how I had done when he was just a picture on a computer screen. Between his thighs I can just about make out that his earlier orgasm hasn't affected him all that much. Hard, no doubt aching as I am, I want him inside me again. And this time it shouldn't be over that soon.

"Another condom?" I breathe.

He stops what he's doing and looks up. His eyes reach into my soul and make my entire core vibrate with further tension. I can't explain why, but somehow I know he feels it too.

"Am I not doing it right?" he asks. His uncertainty despite all that's in front of him makes me smile.

"You're perfect, just too far away."

He understands. Another awkward packet, another struggle with a slippery rubber. But he's more focused now and I need not interfere.

While he's on all fours above me, mostly I can just see his face because my eyes refuse to look anywhere else. My hands similarly single-minded, are on his chest again. Warm, inviting, irresistible. As is the rest of him.

He pauses and I realise some input will be needed to make this work. Guiding him toward my entrance, my hand threatens to get trapped when he lowers himself.

This feels right, how I had hoped.

His arms surround me, hands scooping me up under my shoulders. He starts to move, slowly at first. When he grinds down, I'm in heaven. My hands hang on tight, digging into his side. There is so much to touch, so much to feel. He was made for this moment with me. I wouldn't change a thing.

For a moment he stops and we're both still except for our lips and tongues which merge with a need I've never felt before. Am I picking up on his feelings? Though I have had sex numerous times, is it better because I know for him this has been so long awaited that he is overflowing with urges to catch up on? The moment is so intense, I'm not sure how to react.

He starts to move again, trying to figure out what it is the best way.

"Fast or slow?" His voice sounds so strained, I'm

compelled to hug him and caress his back.

"Do what you feel, you'll know what's right."

And he does, speeding up a little and taking care to try and push deeper. My insides are on fire, a certain sweetness spreading through me and collecting around my pelvic bone. Like syrup, the sensation builds up, pools together, threatens to explode until it makes me scream.

"Faaast—" I can't speak anymore and scratch at him instead.

He does his best to respond and within moments all the pent up energy inside me erupts. I try my best not to claw, not to hurt him. I nearly fail.

I thought I'd orgasmed before: with Jeff, on my own; with my fingers or a vibrator. All of those memories pale in comparison with what I'm still feeling the aftershocks of.

Pausing with his forehead against mine, his short breaths tickle my face. We're both slippery with sweat, his and mine indistinguishable from one another. And strangely, I don't even mind. And he's still hard; I don't mind that either.

Picking up the pace again, he tries to hide that he's getting tired. I can only imagine how amazing he'd be with a bit more practice. Not that I'm complaining as is.

His solid length still fills me just right and continues to hit the special spot nobody's ever reached quite like this before. Could that even be? Or was it just that I had been more turned on than I'd ever been with a man?

"That was the best," I say, just before kissing and

biting softly into his neck.

He groans in response and speeds up, re-energised.

"I've never cum that hard." This second encouragement causes an even better response. Who says flattery doesn't work, especially when it's true.

Meeting his thrusts with my hips, I shift slightly until my feet find grip on the mattress beside his knees. He's close and following an intensifying rhythm which I try to emulate. Faster and wilder, and more erratic than before.

Lips meet for sloppy kisses, until he closes his eyes and shudders to a halt. If his expression is anything to go by, he is enjoying his climax as much as I did mine earlier. And his voice; primal, devoid of shyness or hesitation.

We don't move for a while, not sure how long. But it feels right. When he has caught his breath, he leans up on his elbows and smiles down at me. It's infectious.

"I'm starving. Get off," I tease.

***

Neither of us wish to waste any more time on than necessary, making the junk food place opposite the hotel the perfect dinner destination. It's one of those brightly lit and unromantic joints that serves fish and chips as well as crappy pizza and mystery meat presented as lamb doner kebab.

We need not wait long for our order.

"They're staring," he says, putting his burger down.

"Are they?"

I finish chewing my slice of pizza and get up from my side of the table to join him. Indeed the group of teenage boys who are the only others in here this early on in the evening seem unusually interested in us. Looks alternate with whispers and laughs.

He scoots over to allow me space on the bench, still much too concerned with our random observers. But not for long.

When I cup his face and move in for a kiss, cheers erupt from the bunch of kids behind me.

"They don't matter," I whisper, "this does."

His face is in the process of turning red, and his pupils dilate. I'm in half a mind to straddle him right there on the bench seat for a lengthy make-out session, but worry about the state we'd be in on our way back to the hotel.

He leans forward, lips seeking me out again. I can't resist and cling on to him. When our tongues finish their feverish dance, I pull back slightly and look into his eyes. *I like you. A lot more than I should.*

We rush through our leftovers, knowing exactly where we'd rather be. Upon getting up and heading out the door, his hand snakes around the small of my back until it rests on my ass. He's claimed me, in front of the overly hormonal audience who are now talking amongst themselves in hushed voices.

Still staring, but not to ridicule. They wish they were the ones getting laid tonight.

I look over to my right to find him with a little smile forming on his lips. *Mission accomplished.*

***

Back in our room, we cuddle up on the bed. I rest my head on his lap, trying but failing to shake off the laziness dinner has caused in me.

"Tell me, if you had met me for the first time out somewhere..." he starts, "like if we hadn't spoken online. Would you have noticed me at all?"

His eyes fill me with all sorts of feelings I can't find the willingness to identify. I look up at him, carefully considering the question while shamelessly studying his gorgeous face.

"Honestly—" I pause again, distracted by his lips which I know to be so talented. "Yes. There's something about you that spoke to me just from your profile shot. Before I knew anything about you, you awoke something in me. Would you have?"

A fleeting smile later, he seems to want to look anywhere but at my face.

"Of course, but I would've never approached you."

"Why not?" My question causes him to glance into my eyes momentarily and sigh.

"Too shy." He shrugs. "I wouldn't have expected you to be interested anyway, so why bother..."

"I'll bet there have been girls who would've loved for you to talk to them, but been equally shy."

He lets out a laugh and threads his fingers through my hair.

"Why can't women come with neon signs in their foreheads, telling us guys what we need to know?"

"The whole point is that you're meant to take the risk. That's what makes it valuable. If everything were a sure thing beforehand, there'd be no meaning in it," I say.

He picks up my hand and kisses it lightly.

"OK, say you didn't know me, but I've been looking at you from across the room, quite similar to how I'm looking at you now. Our eyes met and I glanced away for a moment before continuing to stare. What should you do?" I ask.

"I suppose, come over and talk to you?"

"Say I'm with a few friends, and it would be embarrassing if it went wrong, how would you test that I'm really interested from a distance?"

"Dunno, perhaps smile at you, see what you'd do?" he speculates.

Good. We're getting somewhere.

"I'd smile back at you, because I like you already. And then?"

"Walk over?"

I nod.

"I'd have to say something..." he says.

"Honesty is best, unless it's rude."

"In that case, I'd have to say to you..." He plays with a lock of my hair, thinking.

"That standing across the room, I thought you were the most beautiful girl I'd ever seen." Finally, he makes eye contact again and I'm done for. My heart is pounding, my breathing gone crazy... "Yet that did nothing to prepare me for feeling as lost as I do now, looking into your eyes up close. That if you asked anything of me right now, refusal would not be an option."

I'm not one to swoon, and surely this is just roleplay, but his words got to me more than anything else that happened so far. Butterflies, fireworks, the lot. Surely, we're just getting caught up in the moment?

"Assuming that totally swept me off my feet, I let you buy me a drink or two, we head back to yours or mine and it's time to make a move..." I lift myself and sit up straight next to him.

"This would so never play out the same—" he says, "but..."

He leans in, running the back of his fingers over my cheek and letting his gaze linger over my lips. I catch his scent, sweet and tempting, and instinctively get drawn in closer.

"It would, because I'd want it the same," I say.

The moment our lips touch, a lot feels the same and yet something has changed between us. The same passion, desire, but we've reached a new level of comfort. All this is no longer strange and tense, rather it's effortless.

I start unbuttoning his shirt, only pausing to allow him access to my back zip. We're unwrapping each other as if we were gifts. Much desired, even if we already know what's inside.

Once again allowed access to his gloriously warm skin, I feel at home. I push him back onto the bed before he can argue, but then why would he. My fingers move swiftly to open his belt and trouser, tugging playfully until he lets me take them off.

My dress meanwhile has slipped off my shoulders, so I rid myself of it completely.

He leans up, but I don't let him move. Kneeling beside him, I experiment: kissing, licking and sucking. He likes his nipples played with, of course.

His vigour impresses me; despite two earlier orgasms, he's already growing again. I close my fingers around his shaft, and he hardens further immediately. My lips surround the tip of his beautiful cock and I take as much of his length as I can. He tastes of condom, but I'm sure that'll pass.

Panting heavily, he no longer tries to move. Indeed he is as erect as he's ever going to be, after only a few attempts at sucking him deeply. I let my tongue flick the tip, clearing away the slightly salty precum which has appeared.

He moans, tries to grab the sheet beside him, but it's too smooth. One of his hands finds my hair but he does not interfere with what I'm doing.

Meanwhile I'm back to deep, satisfying movements. Starting slow, but speeding up little by little. My fingers steady him before I'm able to get fast enough. My other hand has moved up towards his belly, though I suspect that does more for me than it does for him.

His grip on my hair tightens. I can tell that he wants to push my head down, like most men try at one point or other. But he catches himself, lets go and folds his arm behind his head. From the corner of my eye I see him watching me, inspiring me to adjust my technique to make it more visually pleasing.

"Fuck, yes!" he grunts.

In keeping with the rhythm, I pump his cock with my hand, while sucking on the head, swirling my tongue around it and changing angle just enough so I can try to make eye contact. Men love that view as much as women, don't they?

His eyes close in a frown. It's the good kind of frown, the one I saw earlier. There isn't any more warning; the spasming, groaning and this time, pulsating has begun. I suck one last time; hard and slow, and he loses all restraint.

"That was... damn, I didn't expect it'd be that good," he says.

Still on his back, he nods for me to come closer. How could I resist?

His satisfaction is contagious. When he turns and puts his arm around me, I feel equally at peace and my eyes get heavy. I'd forgotten how nice it can be to just be held.

In my resulting slumber, I dream of him. Of us. Of something poking me in the hip. I wriggle free of his embrace, so I can reach it with my hand.

I dream of the resulting gasp in my ear when my fingers feel the veiny result of his permanent arousal. I'm wet, tingly.

He rolls over onto his back. Deep, regular breaths. Mine are not so regular.

In my dream I crawl on top, clumsily. He closes his

arms and keeps me tightly pressed against his chest. I'm unwilling to fight it.

His flesh moulds to mine. Everything about him is soft, except one thing. If we merged and became one, I would not mind.

I don't want to move, and yet... Grinding feels so good but also burny. I must scratch this itch, even if it's starting to hurt. But then, it hurts no more.

I open my eyes, momentarily disturbed by the wetness between us and the chest hair tickling my nose. It was just a dream, but when I half-wake, he's still inside me.

# CHAPTER FIVE

Throughout our night together, I had tried my best to not dwell on its end. With light streaming through the curtains, flooding the room, I don't have that luxury anymore. I'm aching all over with a delicious reminder of everything we've done, over and over.

The whole experience had been way better than my most optimistic hopes. He's talented, eager, and the appeal has certainly not worn off. If anything, I could imagine myself getting addicted to this. I have to remind myself not to even entertain the idea. This is meant to be the beginning of my journey and it would be such a failure to give up now.

He stirs next to me, turning around and pulling me closer against him. His face looks so still, no nerves, no worries left. The more I look at him the more I feel like he could be my downfall.

I've been his first, and second, third; I don't even know for sure. Not only do I have more stuff to experience, he does too. Plus, we hardly know each other. The few details I've told him about me were lies.

Leaning in, I kiss his lips softly and attempt to slip out of bed, but he doesn't let go. Instead his arm locks around my waist even tighter. His body pressed up against my side threatens to get me excited all over again, if only the burn between my legs makes me wonder if another round would draw blood. I've never had this much sex in a twenty-four-hour period, so it's impossible to predict for sure. But I suppose it's possible; I'm quite sore already.

"Morning, beautiful," he whispers in my ear, before nibbling softly on my neck.

He's been an excellent learner.

"Hey..." I respond, trying to fight the shivers he's sent down my back.

"Don't go yet," he says.

I decide to give in to him, as well as part of myself and rest my arm on his side. I love how soft his skin is there. *No, I should stop this line of thinking immediately!*

"It smells of sex in here," I say. It really does.

He lets out a short laugh. "It bloody well should after everything we've been up to."

I want him again, but I really don't think I'm physically up to the task. The muffled groan that escapes him as he stretches betrays he may be in a similar predicament.

"I don't think I've had this much exercise since... forever," he laughs.

Same here.

"I've had fun though. This really has been great." My voice trails off. Why is it I am feeling so conflicted this morning? I really do not want this to end, and yet I know it must.

"Do you think, perhaps, we could meet up again sometime?" he asks.

Shit.

"You remember I'm married," I say.

"I know, it's just... I really liked this, you."

"I wasn't after an affair, no commitment. You know that," I remind him. He sighs, continues to run his fingertips over my hip, and side, and back down again repeatedly.

"We can be friends, talk online, that sort of thing? But if we keep seeing each other like this, it will just get messy."

"You're probably right." He moves back, the look in his eyes reminding me of when we first spoke, less than twenty-four hours ago, at Cineworld. Withdrawn and guarded once more.

Goodbye has come sooner than I wanted it to. I kiss him on the lips one last time.

"You're a great guy, which is what makes this so difficult."

"If you say so."

He gets out of bed and gathers up his clothes. What was I thinking? That I could find someone whom I connected with so well and just make a clean break in the morning? All things considered, this is for the best.

There is no more conversation, no more eye contact while he gets dressed. I sit up in the bed, watching him with the duvet pulled up to my shoulders.

"Bye," I whisper, when he shuts the door behind him.

After waking just minutes ago with someone I've started to feel such closeness with, I'm now alone. It hurts a lot more than I thought it would. Damn, is every encounter going to turn out like this? Why does something so beautiful have to end so horribly?

I stretch out my achy back and get up to retrieve my handbag. On the way, I peek through a crack in the curtains to see the dreary November skies opening. Even the weather feels like crying.

Back on the bed, I rummage through my possessions to find the notepad. *The list.* Crossing out the first line, I take a deep breath. I shouldn't be upset, last night we made some of the most amazing memories of my life.

One down, three to go.

# Silver Fox

# CHAPTER ONE

Commuting by bus can be a pain in the ass. This winter morning it's cold, drizzly, and I missed the first two because they were full. There is hardly anything more disillusioning than standing at the bus stop, shivering uncontrollably and watching a full, steamed-up bus drive right past you without even slowing. We're only two people at this stop, surely the driver could've fitted us in!

It takes another five minutes for the next one to arrive which thankfully does have a bit of room inside. A seat is too much to ask for the first few minutes, so I'm forced to stand, hanging on to a grab handle and trying not to get ill while at the mercy of the world's most erratic bus driver.

The heated air is finally starting to penetrate my woollen coat, allowing me to open my muffler a bit. At the next stop, someone gets off, freeing up a seat which I am all too eager to take. This gives me another ten minutes or so to find my diary and write.

'Dear Diary,

It has been a month since I started my journey: a quest towards sexual enlightenment sparked by my breakup with Jeff. I'm not sure it's going brilliantly, in fact, I haven't a clue how to move it along. Seemingly everything on my list, although tempting, has some kind of drawback or obstacle. But I did by some stroke of immense luck already manage to find myself a virgin to fuck, which was pretty great. The thing that isn't so brilliant is that I'm having a hard time sticking to the first half of 'casual sex' as a concept. I can do sex, not sure I'm casual enough about it.

As a result, I've been thinking a lot about him, despite not knowing him at all, not even his name. This is not a situation where I'm fondly remembering just one of the items on my sexual wish list, but rather an inconvenient obsession with the guy. I liked him. And with where I'm at in my life right now, I can't have that. I'm not sure I like myself anymore, and surely that should be a priority.

We ended our time together with the suggestion (from my side) to perhaps stay friends. I've shied away from making contact though. My worry is that I'll get even more lost in this fixation.

I had planned for more experiences and I'd better get on with it all. But for some reason I feel a bit blocked, like something drastic needs to happen for me to finally consider the rest of my options, or I may just give up. The truth of the matter is, I'm in the mood for more experiences; I just happen to want a few reruns with him.

I should definitely put that idea out of my head now. This wasn't what I had signed up for. I didn't want all this what-if bullshit going on in my thoughts; all I was after was just a bit of fun…'

Something needs to happen soon, or my plan will be doomed. I remind myself with my original list, written on a little notepad kept with me pretty much all the time.

*To Do:*

*~~Virgin~~*

*Silver Fox*

*Stranger*

*Threesome*

A glance at my watch tells me there's little hope of still making it on time. Not that that matters, most of my colleagues work flexi-time. As long as I'm there the eight hours they've hired me for, it's irrelevant if I'm a little late coming in. Plus in the four years that I've been there, Craig has never given me any grief about little stuff like that. He's never given me any grief at all.

The moment I reach work, I'm greeted by Sally's radiant grin.

"Hey, Becks, don't you look grumpy and miserable this morning! No matter, allow me to change that," Sally says.

"Morning, Sal," I say while taking off my soggy coat.

"You know that guy, the one I told you about?" she continues.

"The one you were doing last weekend, or the week before?" I tease.

"Shut up, slag. Last I checked you were the one making a name as the corrupter of innocents, not me."

"Fair point. So yeah, the guy. What about him?"

"Well, so he's managing the sales team over at Aspect. I sent over our CVs and he's just called me to say they'd be willing to hire both of us!" Sally has a hard time keeping her voice down, she's that excited.

"No shit, that's awesome!"

"I know, no offence to Craig and all, but this place is kind of a sinking ship. Over there we'd get better pay, and I hear they've got their own on-site gym. How cool is that?"

"Wow, thanks so much for putting in a good word for me. I've been getting really sick of the endless austerity bullshit around here. Not even a raise in two years..."

"Totally. It's going to be great. New surroundings, new people, but we'd still have each other."

Sally wanders off again, chatting to some other colleagues who have come in. What an amazing opportunity. She was right; this news has indeed cheered me up to no end.

"Morning," Craig says, steamy tea in hand.

I often wonder if he uses his *The Boss* mug ironically, or because he can't be bothered looking for a different one after a bunch of us gave it to him two years ago. The whole image is hilarious because he's the sharpest dressed at the office as well as the supposedly mature one in charge of a horde of twenty-somethings. And yet he keeps using that ridiculous mug.

"Happy Monday." I grin.

He makes a face at me and starts talking about the Christmas party. In support of further cost cutting, the one event we've all been looking forward to—no, gagging for—has been affected.

"So rather than cancel the whole thing, which would inspire nothing short of a revolution and a bloody coup, I managed to convince them to let us organise it in-house," Craig explains.

I sigh. He's a nice guy and I'll miss him when Sal and I leave, but she's right. This is a sinking ship.

"I guess, so long as there is booze and halfway decent food. No, strike the food. So long as there is lots of booze, it'll be fine."

"That's what I thought." Craig gives me a half smile.

"I know you're busy, but would you be able to get a couple of people together and help organise this thing? Caterers, drinks, whatever."

Way to over-simplify it. Just because it's going to happen at the office, doesn't mean it shouldn't be a proper Christmas party.

"Yeah, alright."

"Brilliant. Please pick two or three people to work with and get them into Meeting Room One at ten."

★★★

"Let's begin. Becky will have told you this meeting is about the Christmas party…" Craig starts.

Sally has the chair next to mine, and has started doodling on her notepad. Holly and candy canes, how appropriate. Next to her sits Lesley, who I only asked because I needed another person after Sheila didn't want anything to do with this extra work, the lazy cow.

"So as you might imagine, the budget is limited, as is time. Ordinarily by now things would have been fully organised already. The truth is, they wanted to cancel. But we can't have that, can we?"

We shake our heads in unison, failing to mirror Craig's faux excitement. Too much to do, too little time, no money. *Awesome.*

"What about dates?" I ask.

Craig opens his planner and leafs through the pages until he finds December.

"Thirteenth?"

"Friday, the thirteenth, you're kidding, right?" Sally says.

Craig shrugs. "Well I suppose the following week would be suitable as well, but we'd be without those who've booked early holidays."

"Or it would have to be a weekday, which kind of sucks," I remark.

"The thirteenth it is then." Sally sighs and sits back with her arms folded behind her head.

"Right, the budget..." Craig continues.

The meeting takes the best part of an hour. A lot of ideas are thrown around; things like theme and decor, which I imagine Craig would never have brought up on his own. We may have a catering service shortlisted, run by a friend of a friend. It's going to be a ton of work to pull this off, but we might just manage it.

As everyone scatters to head back to their workstations, I'm in dire need of caffeine. Craig joins me in the kitchenette. For the both of us the kitchen area serves the added purpose that the proverbial water cooler does for most people. We do have one of those as well, but who wants cold water in the middle of winter? This is our little space to chat.

"Normal tea, none of this new-fangled organic, green stuff, yeah?" I ask, putting the 'healthier' option back into the cupboard unopened.

He nods and puts his mug on the counter next to mine. We've always had a pretty informal atmosphere around the office. All the coffee drinkers hang out together for regular refills, as do Craig and I, the only tea drinkers on the floor. The pleasant thing is: in this room, salary scales, job titles and even age gaps mean nothing.

"Had a good weekend?" I ask.

Craig shrugs and is about to answer in the affirmative, out of habit. But something seems not quite right.

"Yeah... No, actually I'm pretty glad it's over."

"How come?"

"Just, personal stuff. I'm sure you don't want me going on about that..."

"Your call. Hope it sorts itself out," I say, meaning every word. Wish he'd say what's wrong though, it's unlike him to be reserved.

The resulting silence between us becomes even more striking when the kettle's click startles me. I pour the water and watch the swirls of reddish brown fill the mugs until the colour is just right.

He takes his, gives me a fleeting smile and walks off toward his office.

That was weird.

***

"Hey, Sal." I wave her over as she comes back in after her cigarette break.

We sit together at our adjoining desks for a quick catch up session before choosing to be productive again.

"The weirdest thing just happened in the kitchen. So I asked Craig about his weekend…" I tell her what he said; first a summary, then a detailed report including slow motion replay of every shred of body language I can remember or invent.

Sally leans forward, a knowing look on her face. Her smoking buddies have filled her in already on what is now the department's number one talking point: Craig's wife left with their children and is apparently intent on making the split as difficult and painful as possible. We both can't help but sympathise with him, our perception no doubt biased by how he is at work. I just can't imagine him ever doing anything to deserve that kind of treatment. She sounds like quite a piece of work.

Just when we're speculating about what might've gone on, his office door opens. Silenced by his presence as he walks straight past our desks on the way to the stairs, I try to focus on work rather than noticeably stare. We still need to confirm with the caterers today.

✳✳✳

Five o'clock comes and goes, and I'm still at my desk. Most of the floor is now vacated; Sally left especially early saying she has a date. Who the hell has a date on Monday?

I, meanwhile, do not have a date. Only my empty flat awaits me and I'm in no hurry. On my way out, I make a quick detour to stick my head through the entrance of Craig's office.

"Night, Craig," I say.

He momentarily looks up from the paperwork avalanche he seems to still be working on and nods. Guess now he'd rather stay late here than go home as well. How depressing.

In all my naivety I always assumed that by the time I'd hit forty-five, or however old he is, I'd have my life sorted. Married, perhaps with a kid or two, a house somewhere on a nice suburban cul-de-sac which we'd choose for the school district and low crime rate. I'd work until retirement and come home to the person I'd like to grow old with. Definitely not Jeff though, he never fitted into that dream for as long as I can remember.

Perhaps that's exactly the kind of plan Craig had.

As I walk downstairs, out the main entrance and towards the bus stop, I think about him some more. He reminds me of a teacher I had in school who stood out among the stricter ones. Mr. Robertson would let me get away with anything. Not doing my homework: forgiven. Getting late or skipping entire classes: at most a dejected headshake and a sigh. Not that I wanted to skip his class often, I had a particular liking for him. I suppose you could call it a crush, though it was platonic.

Skipping class inevitably meant something absolutely unmissable was going on. Like a rare get-together with a friend from another school. An ill-advised plan to hang out at a kids' playground and have a few drinks or worse. We'd cycle to our respective homes still high as kites, but in the back of my mind I always wondered if Mr. Robertson had noticed my absence.

Craig was exactly like Mr. Robertson that way. He didn't get upset if I was late, early, or particularly mouthy after a few drinks during one of the rare work events the company still paid for. If I one day decided not to do my job at all anymore and just sit there playing *Angry Birds*, I'm certain he wouldn't be upset: only disappointed.

But perhaps there's one difference between the two: I could possibly imagine something much naughtier happening with Craig than I ever considered with Mr. Robertson. *Could this be?*

His stylish dress sense covers up what looks like an athletic build in perfect proportion with his six-foot-one frame, plus his salt and pepper hair and face made all the more handsome by the subtle depth of his features. Craig appears to be the exact definition of a silver fox, one who had been out of reach and as such out of the picture until now. With my departure from the company nearly set in stone, and his marriage already in tatters, could Craig become number two on my list?

Only this morning I was despairing about how to proceed with *the list*. Now I seem to have a cunning plan, one which might do the both of us some good. Funny, how much can change in just one day…

# CHAPTER TWO

Glass of wine to hand, I let the mouse pointer hover over His profile: my nameless partner for one sizzling night that is impossible to forget and remains the inspiration of many a resulting fantasy. My defences are down and I'm weak tonight, alone. Easily tempted by a glimpse of him and a reminder of what we shared just weeks ago. It seems like only yesterday. Despite trying my utmost to swallow any lingering emotions, a sense of loss tries to claw its way out of me.

The chat window in the corner of my eye alerts me to the fact that he is also online. Inevitably, I cave and send him a message.

"Hi!"

I immediately feel stupid for making contact because my mind is empty. All I've got to follow that up with is *what's going on*. Blegh.

"Hey there, stranger," he responds.

"Strange but also weirdly familiar…"

"How've you been? I've been wondering whether to message you, since—but wasn't sure if you'd prefer it if I kept my distance?"

"Oh no, not at all. I did say we could be friends. I meant it." I didn't. I'm not sure we can be friends, at least at my end. But just the fact that he responded so enthusiastically, is doing wonders for my mood.

This is a dangerous game.

"I'm glad to hear it."

"Things have been fine, same old really. Though for some reason I'm now officially in charge of the office Christmas party. It's a bit of a pain, to be honest."

"Sounds it. Still, at least you've got a job. I've been looking and not had much luck."

"Oh that sucks. What are you looking for?"

"Honestly, anything. I don't know. While still in university, I worked in a shop. Now that I'm done, I was looking for something a bit more… grown-up, an office job of some sort. Must've sent out hundreds of applications and nothing."

I feel for him and wonder if I could help. But the last thing I need right now is to get us into a situation where we'd actually see each other at work.

"It's tough out there. I've heard similar stories from friends who are looking. In any case, people won't be keen to hire before the holidays."

From there, I ask about his studies. English Lit, apparently, though now he wonders if he should've done something a bit more "real world".

"OK so this is going to come out weird, but I wanted to say thanks…" he writes.

He's still typing, so I wait. Yep, this is definitely already weird.

"For meeting me…"

"I did say then, it wasn't a favour. I was being totally selfish."

"Well mainly for not leaving me there at Cineworld, like a mug, waiting for an hour or more, before realising nobody was going to turn up."

"Standing you up would've not served my own, selfish purposes either. ;)"

"Still."

How does he get to be that sweet? It's entirely unfair. I sigh and just stare at the screen for a while before gathering my thoughts enough to be able to put them into words.

"I'm just glad you're not mad at me. I thought, for sure, you won't want to speak to me after you left that morning," I write.

"Guess I just thought that maybe there was a chance… I'm not mad though."

This conversation, these little confessions, they make me smile but scare me at the same time. I'm digging a deeper hole for myself just by being online. The urge to run overcomes me: it's what's best for both of us.

"Oops, you know what, my phone's ringing. It'll be my husband so I'd better take it. Talk later?" I type. It's a complete lie of course; my entire backstory with him was designed to avoid emotional entanglements. But I can't go down the path of what-if's right now.

I shut down the laptop to stop myself from staring at his photographs. It would be so much easier, had I not messaged him at all. That's also a lie; nothing about this could be easy. I should move on. Perhaps if I complete the list, it'll be possible for me to keep emotions and lust separate.

* * *

"What do you think?" I ask under my breath, motioning across the office floor.

Sally leans back in her chair in a much too obvious fashion and checks Craig out head to toe until he notices her. She—unfazed—gives him the thumbs up, to which he simply shakes his head like one would about a crazy person. At this rate she will totally blow this for me.

"Yeah, I see what you mean. He's pretty doable," she responds, "for an old guy…"

"We won't have much time after your fuck-buddy in Aspect sends us the contracts. One weeks' notice, that's it. It's going to have to happen soon."

"I concur." She grins at me. I detect a hint of pride: thanks to her expert tutelage, I may yet turn into a confident seductress after all.

Wouldn't it be really weird though, hitting on someone you've worked with for years? And oh my God, how do I make it clear I want to leave it at just a hook-up? It was a lot easier getting all that awkward stuff out of the way online with—whatever his name is. And even then it was difficult to stick to the plan. It still is, if last night's chat was any indication.

I decide that this kind of thing requires the kind of finesse that can only be achieved by mutual inebriation. It's going to have to wait until the thirteenth of December. The Christmas party we're in the process of planning. The last thing either of us needs is misplaced expectations.

***

Time passes quickly with so many arrangements to be made in addition to the regular old work. By the time the second week of December rolls around, what started off almost a lost cause, is turning into an event everyone is looking forward to.

Meanwhile, I've started putting my killer outfit together. Theme, anyone? Am I going to end up shopping anew for every encounter? If so, this is going to be an expensive pastime. I've justified this latest spend as an investment to ensure my *game plan* works. I need to be able to drop a few not-so-subtle hints to figure out if he's interested.

The message has to be spot-on, but still allow for an *out*. What better way to get his attention than with a strategically flashed stocking-top… So the dress has to be the right length, yet not too clingy; matching underwear. These are all essentials.

"Becky, tea?" Craig holds up his mug and raises his eyebrows a few times in quick succession.

God, he's hilarious.

"What do I look like to you, a dog? Next you'll start whistling every time you need a hot beverage," I grumble.

He laughs, knowing my faux-offended routine all too well by now. "Whatever works."

We head to the kitchenette, where I grudgingly agree it's my turn to actually make it.

"Things are looking good for Friday then," Craig

remarks.

"It'll be great."

"I was thinking, nobody will want to work 'til five, so we might as well call it a day a bit early and start the festivities then."

That suits me just fine.

"Setting up won't take too long, if we clear away some of the unused desks aside already near the stairs," I suggest.

"I probably should've had that done a while ago. Seeing those empty workstations every day, can't have helped morale."

He's right, remembering that the colleagues who used to sit there were let go has impacted everyone. Knowing that further cutbacks are inevitable and seeing Craig wander around the office looking like a former shadow of himself has further worsened the overall mood. He may not have totally lost his sense of humour, but it's obvious he also needs a good cheering up.

"So just don't put them back after the party. Or it could be turned into a break area for everyone?" I suggest, handing him his tea.

He nods and accepts it and we're both quiet and lost in thought while taking our first sips. My thoughts focus on the upcoming plan. It has been hard to stay on track, but I'm on day seven of not logging on to Fetlife, and not looking at anything to do with *Him*. Daily efforts to imagine how exactly my encounter with Craig will go down have helped a lot. However those same activities are making it slightly weird standing next to him now in this everyday, innocent context.

I wonder what he's thinking about.

"Christmas is going to be a nightmare," he remarks.

"Yep."

My response seems to surprise him.

"Aren't you going home to see your folks?"

"Nah, Dad's spending time with his new girlfriend and Mom has decided to go travel the world. She's off on some organised tour of Egypt or whatever." I give him a bleak smile.

"We always used to take Gem and Adam to see their grandparents. This year I don't even know if they'll get their gifts on time or at all. I had to send parcels, can you believe that..." He shrugs as if to direct his thoughts into another direction.

Yep, he definitely needs cheering up.

We share one of those pity smiles before carrying the remainders of our tea back to our desks.

# CHAPTER THREE

"I fucked up, Sal," I whisper, handing her one of the last bits of decoration. The party is going to start in mere moments and I'm freaking out.

She raises an eyebrow waiting for me to spill everything, staring downwards from halfway up a stepladder.

"Well, you know how I said I was going to stay away from that guy…"

"The one from Fetlife?"

"The former virgin, yeah. Well… I was kind of bored, alone. Desperate."

"Oh for fuck's sake, Becky! What did I tell you?" Sally climbs down the steps after hanging up the obligatory bunch of mistletoe from a hook in the ceiling.

"I mean we just talked, but I just feel so… I dunno."

"You're such a loser. You're free, can do whatever you like. You have this great opportunity here to figure yourself out and instead… Jeez."

"He's so easy to talk to, we get on really well. Last time I spoke to him was over a week ago, but then last night again…"

"You know what you need? You need to get laid. And fuck me, you look bloody amazing. You should put that brilliant plan of yours into action." Sally turns around just when Craig walks out of his office, fixing his tie.

"I mean, damn, look at him!" she whispers.

"What if he's not into it?"

"What if— Bitch, give it a rest. He's fucking lucky *you're* into it. You have to stop taking things so seriously." She gives me a whack on my ass and walks off towards the "bar"; a makeshift cluster of tables with an impressive array of bottles lined up on top.

Smoothing down my 'little black dress', I can feel the straps of the garter belt through the fabric, though I know they would only show to the most perceptive observer. I suppose she's right. If it all works out, tonight ought to cheer me up about everything. And I totally hadn't foreseen how sexy I'd feel just by wearing a pair of stockings underneath my otherwise fairly conservative, classic dress.

I give her a thorough once-over as well from across the space. Sally looks great, her little red number shows off a bit more tits 'n' ass than mine, but she so has the attitude for it. The blonde curls piled on top of her head in a messy bun and matching red lipstick with otherwise understated make-up tie it all together. She looks like she walked right off the cover of *Vogue*.

She'll undoubtedly have her own plan for tonight. I wonder who the lucky guy is…

"Wow, all this looks splendid," Craig says, walking up behind me.

He's right. In mere hours, what was once an empty office space has been turned into a venue fit for a bunch of soon-to-be beyond drunken office workers. Amazing what a few metres of organza fabric and assorted Christmas trinkets can do.

"It's going to be fun," I say, trying to convince myself as much as him.

He smiles briefly and walks off towards his office again, not to be seen again until the festivities officially start.

∗∗∗

By seven, the party is in full swing. The caterers have brought in an impressive range of tapas-style finger foods, the booze is flowing freely, and the music is appropriately loud and terrible. Luckily it does look like our preparations have gone down well, and Sally and I, the *'official Christmas Committee'*, as we are now known, can finally abandon our posts to let our proverbial hair down.

Across the room, Sally's gaze meets mine. She subtly gestures over towards the strategically positioned mistletoe where an unaware Craig is standing around holding a pint glass. She grins and I nod subtly and we close in.

"Mistletoe!" Sally and I shout, a split second before attacking and leaving lipstick marks on either side of his face.

"Bloody hell, didn't realise we had one of them!" He looks up sheepishly at the small green bunch hanging from the ceiling by a piece of red ribbon.

Sally gives me a knowing look and leaves us behind.

"We do indeed. Sal's idea, of course."

"Of course," Craig says.

He wipes off the lipstick from his cheek before taking another sip of beer.

"You might want to move if you don't want that to happen again…" My eyes focus on the side of his face where I can still make out a distinct pink smudge.

"You've still got a bit—" I motion at my own face and he tries to mirror where I'm showing him, to no avail.

It's quite hilarious, and I can't stop myself from giggling. Must be the wine.

"Well you're no use," Craig says, picking up a napkin from a nearby table and trying again.

He has a lovely smile, warm and genuine. All the more so whenever he truly does look happy—something that has been rare lately. *I think I'm staring, am I staring?*

"Thanks so much for taking care of all of this," he says, gesturing at nothing in particular in our surroundings.

"Mmhm."

I'm staring at how the corners of his eyes crinkle when he smiles. And he smells rather nice, must've put on fresh aftershave not too long ago, because I don't recall him smelling this good before. *Can I do this? Fuck yeah, I can do this! I think...*

Finishing what's left in my wineglass in one go, I lean forward, tiptoeing slightly.

"Can we talk?" I whisper in his ear.

Across the room in my direct line of sight I see Sally grinning and nodding at me furiously. She seems almost more excited than I am.

"Sure," Craig says. He looks around and focuses on the familiar door some ways away from where we are now.

"My office?"

I agree with a smile and put my glass down on the nearest table.

For a moment I wonder if we ought to be more careful about who sees us heading to his office like this, but I decide that I really don't give a shit. Plus, everyone seems very much preoccupied with whatever they're doing; eating, drinking, dancing, chatting each other up… The only person who is paying attention is Sally, and she was already in on the plan anyway.

He closes the door behind him and I lean back against his desk, watching his every move.

"So," he starts.

"So." I lift myself on both hands and slide back until I'm sitting down properly on the desk and cross my legs.

His attention is momentarily drawn to my thigh, specifically the bit of black lace which has made an appearance just below the hem of my dress. It takes him a moment to focus back on my face. So far so good.

"What did you want to discuss?"

"Aren't you being all formal…" I look down and start tracing my finger along the stitching on the bottom hem of the dress. Back and forth, making no effort to adjust my dress to hide the stocking.

"This was meant to be *in*formal?" He is once more distracted by the goings on lower down than what could be deemed appropriate.

"I consider us friends, not just colleagues. You know that, right?" I ask.

He gives me a questioning look.

"Well, yes." His voice sounds tentative.

"It's obvious you haven't been having the best time lately…"

"Obvious, eh? But yeah, that would be a fair observation to make."

"I was just wondering if there was anything I could do to help." I uncross my legs, letting them just dangle down off the desk with my hand now resting right at the top of my thigh.

Looking back up from under my lashes, I study him carefully. I'm pretty sure that whatever's hidden underneath the stylish grey three-piece suit and shirt, would be quite the sight to behold. On those rare days that he comes to work minus the tie and with his collar unbuttoned, I've spied a little glimpse of dark brown hair which I wish to see more of tonight.

He shoots a quick glance out towards the party and closes the blind, then takes a couple of steps in my direction. I feel floaty, nervous beyond belief but excited as well. The wine acts as a convenient buffer, enabling me to override any worries, while still being painfully aware of their existence.

"Becky, how much have you had to drink?"

"Oh for fuck's sake!" I blurt out, slipping off the desk and onto my two feet again.

"What is it with you men, whenever someone takes initiative, you've got to try and blame it on some bullshit excuse…"

"What? I didn't mean—" He looks quite startled at my outburst, which despite my frustration is still kind of endearing.

"No, let me finish. I may not have the slightest clue how to go about this, and I may have had a couple of glasses of wine tonight. But last I checked, neither of those things are a crime. All I'm trying to say is, if you've ever wanted to… you know. We're both unattached, it's a party, stuff happens, and it need not leave this room." I take a deep breath and stare him right in the face, despite increasingly feeling like this was the stupidest idea ever.

He steps up right in front of me, forcing me to crane my head back quite a lot to keep looking into his eyes. Wish I knew what's going on in there right now.

Finally, a glimmer of a smile plays on his lips, but it doesn't linger long enough for me to be certain. Perhaps I imagined it.

"Fine. I just had to make sure…" He runs his finger along my jaw and my airways seem to snap shut with a new, yet already familiar sensation. Things are heading in the right direction, and I want *more.*

"Plus you know how *we, men,* rather prefer a level of subtlety akin to being run over by a freight train… I didn't expect it to be you." Now, he's definitely smiling.

I'm panting slightly, not sure whether it started when I got annoyed, or more likely, because I'm enjoying our changed dynamic

"We're only following tradition," I whisper.

"What tradition is that? The one where the attractive female employee tempts her boss with sexual favours until the whole situation escalates into a lawsuit?" He grins at me. He has the best smile.

"Actually I was thinking of the other great tradition where you drunkenly hook up with a random colleague at the Christmas party. But, whatever works for you." I bat my eyelashes a few times, before returning a grin of my own.

"So it's *random* now, is it?"

He's so near to me I'm lost in the intoxicating scent of his aftershave, or him generally. Yet with the edge of the desk pressing into my half-seated behind, and him stood up straight, he's just too far off for comfort.

I place my hand on his shoulder and straighten myself, while he leans down just enough for us to be nearly equal.

"Perhaps not entirely random." Finding it hard to focus, I'm not certain where to look. His eyes, which seem pitch black even if I know they aren't. Or his sensual full lips.

His hands rest on my hips, waiting patiently for my permission or my first move. I want him to kiss me now, need him to have his way with me. It's pathetic, but having him this close to me has a calming influence. Like for a moment we won't be alone. For all the shit I keep thinking about Jeff, at least he was there when I got home in the evening, mostly.

It's that moment, just before something happens, but you can already taste it. I imagine someone braver and totally unlike me would feel this way just before bungee jumping. Or before diving off the highest board at the pool. What do I know, I'm a chicken-shit that way. But I now know this moment, just before you kiss someone you've thought about kissing but never had the chance before.

I breathe in his scent once more and hold, and while I want this ticklish, brewing excitement to last, I also want it to erupt and be expressed without further delay. His lips touch mine. It's exhilarating. Soft, tentative, exploration of two tongues, which in a perfect world shouldn't have met. In a perfect world, both of us would still be happy with our significant others...

# CHAPTER FOUR

During this first, careful kiss, a switch flips in us. A fuse blows. This was a daft idea, and a moment of genius at the same time.

He pushes me back onto the desk, and down. I don't fight it. This is what I've wanted.

A pen holder gets knocked over and its contents clatter onto the floor, along with sheets of paper that glide downwards, zig-zagging through the air.

My legs spread around him, his hand cups my cheek and he eagerly takes what's on offer. My kisses, as many as I'm willing to give, for starters. Though he isn't rough, he's confident. Weaving his fingers through the hair at the back of my neck, he secures me where he wants me. His other hand explores my thigh, squeezing and stroking the skin left exposed by my stocking.

He's a force to be reckoned with. A caged predator, who, upon being let back out, remembers his primal instinct. Fumbling with his jacket first, then the buttons on his waistcoat, I do my best to keep up. It's impossible to when you can hardly get enough air.

I didn't expect it to be this wild, which was silly of me because we've been skirting around the issue for years. In our lonely tea-drinking sanctum, away from the coffee folks, I've taken many an opportunity to tease him. We've had our inappropriate banter, our *in jokes* which often escalated firmly into the realms of innuendo.

All that was before, though. Before circumstance made *this, us,* possible. I see now that it would've been almost inevitable. But not while he was married and I was committed to Jeff. That had always been a deal breaker.

"You're beautiful," he whispers in my ear.

When his lips—and teeth—find my neck, I can't help moaning.

"You're not so bad yourself," I gasp, in a last attempt to seem in control of my faculties.

The wood surface of the desk cools the naked skin on my arms and just above the neckline. The rest of me burns up inside the dress which suddenly surrounds me like a trap, suffocating me. I need it off, as much as I need his shirt off. The buttons seem to be fighting me as I struggle on without much progress.

"Unzip me," I say and he retreats just far enough for me to make headway on the shirt. With it being halfway open now, I can see enough of what awaits me to drive my senses further into muddled, confused bliss. He *is* gorgeous.

After taking half a second to realise there is no zip within reach, he flips me over onto my front and opens the whole thing top to bottom in one swoop. My face is pressed against the wood and finding sweet relief from all this heat inside me, his hands burn into the muscles beside my spine. Up and down, over my shoulder blades, unhooking my bra, then grazing downwards over my hips.

I lift up on both elbows, allowing the dress to fall free and taking my bra with it. When I look back, I see he has also dropped his trousers. One hand on my ass, the other is already working on his cock. My attempt to turn fully is met with a determined push on my shoulder and whisper in my ear.

"Not yet. The view from here is magnificent."

Skilled fingers slip past my thong and caress and play with my pussy in a way only an experienced man would know how. Perfection.

I sigh and lower myself again, enjoying the heat of his kisses down my back in beautiful contrast with the cold shiny surface of the desk against my bare nipples. I'm dripping, aching for more than just a finger.

His hand snakes around my waist until he's able to lift me slightly and pull down the thong, allowing me to step out of it. The hot, slick tip of his member pushes against me and I moan, catching myself before I get too loud. Thankfully whoever's in control of the stereo on the main floor has gone crazy with the volume, so we're unlikely to be heard while the music plays.

I wiggle backwards, making it known exactly what I want and he responds by entering me. It's been over a month since my last encounter, and despite plenty of solo activities, I'm noticeably tight. Or perhaps he's larger than expected. He leans over again, I can sense his breath against my shoulder as he groans with each push. Slow at first, but soon ramping up to a pace I'm surprised to be enjoying this much. *Jeff certainly never tried it like this!*

He has one hand on my hip, the other all the way on my shoulder, anchoring himself for optimum control in his movements. Despite being mostly incapacitated against the desk, ticklish sweat is starting to form on my back and down my spine. I am on fire, taking his whole length gratefully, savouring the hard pounding.

The only thing missing is that I can't see. Can't reach to touch him from here. From time to time I turn to look back. His face betrays extreme focus, dampness starting to glisten on his features. Tonight I'm unmistakably his, he has claimed me. The feverish rhythm and intensity of his movements forces me to straighten again for fear of pulling a muscle.

His harsh technique seems just the thing to drive out lingering demons and thoughts. I blank out, focusing only on the in-out-in-out, which is continuing at a maddening pace. Our bodies seem in tune, breaths synchronised and muscles working in unison, bracing for and welcoming the sting that marks each thrust.

I'm getting close already, surprisingly. The familiar sweet, sticky feeling inside my lower abdomen starts. It's what I've come to recognise as the first sign that I'm on my way to nirvana. It builds, I tense, I gasp. He groans behind me, I close my eyes and shudder and buck against him, aiming for maximum pleasure.

He reads me as if he has known me like this all along, his hand travelling forward around my hip to gain access to my clit. The soft play of his fingertips makes it hard to believe it's performed by the same man who is thrusting into me so hard at the same time. But it is him, and he can see I'm unable to resist.

"More!" I cry out, and he gives it to me.

He fucks me until my backside is tingly. Until fireworks erupt between my legs, beautiful shivers travel the length of my skin and I'm left limp on the desk. My insides quiver and I lose all coordination while my orgasm overwhelms me.

He pulls out and I have to force myself up or I'd drift off into a blissful post-coital nap right now. My eyes focus on his half-naked form, disposing of a condom in the wastebasket. I didn't even realise he'd put one on before everything went a bit crazy. How reckless and stupid of me!

I'm about to ask him what he'd I can do for him in turn, when a knock on the door startles both of us.

"Just a moment please," he calls out loud enough to ensure whoever it is will hear it over the music outside.

Meanwhile I stumble about the place, picking up my dress and underwear and crawl underneath the desk which thankfully has a covered back. I can only hope no part of me will show through the small gap between the wooden edge and the floor. I hear some rummaging around, the swishing sound of paper being straightened and placed on top of a smooth surface above. Finally he sits down, blocking me in.

"Yes?"

The door opens and I hear a female voice, vaguely familiar but somewhat unplaceable in my current state of panic.

"Hi, Craig. I just wanted to say... Merry Christmas

in advance. Great party. Umm…" She sounds reluctant, and I really wish I could see her face from here without being visible myself.

"Thanks, you too." His voice sounds deeper than I'm used to. The sound makes me shiver.

In this dark cave of mine, surrounded by cool wood and his scent, I start to feel safer. Too safe. He may have buttoned up his shirt again and pulled up his trousers, but he has failed to zip up. Tempting.

"I was wondering if you'd received my card…" the woman says. There is something about the way she speaks, a hint of a regional accent. Who the hell is it? Having the answer to this question almost within reach, but not quite accessible, is starting to annoy me. I am starting to forget how close we are to being caught.

Also, this small talk about cards and Christmas wishes is making me impatient. We're not done here yet. Letting my hand travel up his thigh and towards the still visible bulge in his trousers, I note he twitches just enough for me to notice. Rather than bring his legs together to deny me access, he seems to relax...

"Umm no, sorry. What card?"

The woman stammers a few fragmented words before finishing with a 'never mind'. I am encouraged to continue stroking at first through his trousers, then inside. No underwear. I do hope he didn't leave any incriminating evidence on the floor.

Wrapping my fingers around his now freed erection, I'm momentarily distracted by a few noisy things that happen in quick succession: the opening and closing of a door, the creaky strain of a heavy drawer just beside where I am and a clunk of something solid being set down just overhead.

"Well I'll be damned," Craig sighs and leans back in the chair.

He glances down at me, and my puzzled frown while I wait for some sort of additional explanation.

"I thought you left that card."

One eyebrow raised, I wait with his cock still in my hand.

"What card? Who was that anyway? I knew the voice but couldn't quite place it just now," I say.

"Sarah."

*Oh, HR-Sarah. That makes sense, I recognise the voice now.*

Craig takes a swig from a glass that must have appeared from his desk drawer just now and stares at nothing in particular while running his hand through his hair.

"You don't think she's going to come back, do you?" I ask. As if he'd know the answer to that. "Fucking hell, you don't think she noticed it smells of sex in here?"

He shrugs and tries to roll his chair back to let me up, but I hang on to his thigh and shake my head.

"Not yet, the view is magnificent from down here."

We both laugh, probably mostly due to relief because we're alone again. I adjust myself until I'm kneeling properly, rather than being slumped down on the cold floor and gratefully accept the glass he hands me. Scotch.

As I take a sip, he's looking at something right above

me in what sounds like the stack of paper. Then he hands me the explanation, a Christmas card written in gold ink. Feminine handwriting much neater than my own, *Wishing for a naughty Christmas*, and below a blank bit of double-sided tape. Next to that, another as yet wrapped condom.

"Holy shit, Sarah left you this?" I blurt out. It's shocking and yet hilarious. "I'd been thinking what a happy coincidence it was that you had condoms to hand."

"God, this is awkward." Craig sits back again, accepting the glass back from me and refilling it.

"Only if she finds out." I grin.

It takes me painfully long seconds to remember what I had been doing only moments earlier. *We're not done here yet.* I start stroking him again until he grows rock solid in my hand. It doesn't take long for the bizarre condom card incident to seem a lot less important. He relaxes, closing his eyes, only opening them again in surprise when my lips surround him.

The cold of the floor has started creeping in through my stockings, making my knees numb. His reactions are worth the discomfort though. He never fully tucked in his shirt, so it's easy to slip in underneath, to caress his chest while sucking deeply. As good as he made me feel, I hope to top it for him.

I've always had this strange fantasy, the one of the below-the-desk blow job which risks exposure at any moment. It only seems fitting that I get to cross off an item from *the list*, while doing it in surroundings I've fantasised about. For Sarah's sake, I hope she doesn't come back.

He groans and writhes in the chair when I take him in as deeply as I can manage, massaging his balls throughout. When he opens his eyes, I decide to increase pace. Certainly while he was in charge, he favoured a faster, harder rhythm.

His breathing turns strained, faster, catching up and then exceeding the speed of my movements. I decide to alternate and tease him with my tongue for a moment before continuing deeply. His hand finds my hair but he resists the urge to push me down. After being in charge on top of the desk, he's letting me have my turn underneath.

As his movements get more erratic, he starts to tense up. His eyes are glued to the view between his legs. My head bobbing up and down, trying to maintain eye contact with my mouth full.

"I don't want to finish yet," he says in between forced gasps.

Perhaps he's right, we ought to stretch this experience for all its potential. He rolls his chair back, offering me his hand and I stand up in front of him. My clothes are still on the floor and after the cave-like surroundings under the desk, the air elsewhere in the room seems cooler. It stings against my skin.

I lean over him, still on the chair and he finds my lips for a prolonged, passionate kiss. Meanwhile I'm looking for something underneath the seat. *Ah, found it!* A tug on the lever drops his chair down to its lowest level.

Finding Sarah's card on his desk, I remove the last condom packet from it and hand it to him.

He gets right down to it and I observe. When I straddle him, I find the height of the chair to be perfect: with my heels on, I can comfortably reach the ground.

I ride him, enjoying his eyes on me, his flesh against my exposed breasts when I grind forward. His hands rest on the stocking tops with his thumbs where the front straps of the garter try to hang on for dear life. I feel like I've never felt before: confident, seductive and beautiful, and in charge of someone accustomed to authority himself. It's strange and empowering and gets me dripping once more.

Lips nibble at my chest, teeth gently catch my nipple. I run my fingernails through the cropped hair just above his neck. His breath is a shudder against my flesh, which makes my nerves sing with further excitement. We're at one again, for this fleeting moment, before normal life takes over, and inconvenient truths have to be revealed. I'll have to leave this place…

I force away the unpleasantness and focus on this, us. I like the feel of the stockings against me, and keeping my heels on for this experience. It's all so perfect. If there were a hidden camera in this room somewhere, our little show could rival any porn shoot.

His fingers dig into my hips, guiding me to the right speed without being intrusive. All the while, I dive in for more frantic kisses, which he seems to enjoy as much as I do.

He's getting there, I can tell by his movements, and

intense look in his eyes. I want his pleasure, to taste it on his lips and feel the energy erupt between my legs. His eyes close, hands tense up into me, I pour all my reserves into a final sprint towards salvation. When he lets go at last, he takes me with him, and I'm beat.

This is where the porn effect wears off. I haven't the stamina for an elegant dismount, but sort of wilt on top of him instead. We take an age to catch our breaths, without finding appropriate words or actions to fill the silence. Clearly this isn't the time for conversation.

After getting up, I rush to retrieve my clothes to get dressed.

"Let's get back before they start talking." I nod in response and attempt to fix my hair by touch. He wipes a smudge of what I suspect might be mascara off from underneath my eye and smiles to signal we're ready.

# CHAPTER FIVE

On another cold, drizzly Monday morning, I make it into work on time for a change. Actually I'm five minutes early. Sally texted me yesterday to let me know in advance: all the paperwork is ready for our move. Today will be the day we let everyone else know.

Friday was amazing. A boost for my confidence, not least because right up to the moment of truth I couldn't be sure that Craig would be interested. And what a shocking twist about the card! Unwittingly, Sarah had helped me greatly in getting my point across. Wonder if it even would've happened, had he not been put in the right mood in advance. At the same time, I do pity her a bit...

After leaving my stuff on my desk, and noticing Sally isn't in yet, I am craving my first cup of the day. Shall I see if Craig is in? Would it be weird to talk to him now? I'm certainly feeling a strange lump in my throat, one that's telling me to avoid him. How silly and juvenile.

His door is open, so I knock quickly and take a step inside.

My senses might be deceiving me, but it's as if I can still catch our combined scent in the air. The desk is once again covered with papers with a laptop in the centre, Craig sitting behind it, looking all serious and professional. All *looks* normal, but it's hard not to give in to the flashes of naked, lustful memories.

"Morning. Would you like some tea?" I ask, failing to disguise my nerves.

"Sure, give me a moment."

He finishes typing something and pushes his chair back to get up. The leather chair reminds me of more naughtiness yet.

Trying to shake it all off, I stalk off to the kitchen with him on my heels. Once inside I do my best to efficiently prepare our drinks so we can get out as soon as possible, because I've suddenly lost the motivation to actually talk.

"So, Friday…" Craig starts.

The hair on the back of my neck stands up, but I don't turn around and try to play it cool.

"What was that exactly?"

"As I said. A hook-up at a party."

"I just want to make sure I'm not going to be vilified for not acting gentlemanly enough. It's not going to make things awkward between us, I hope?"

"Relax, it won't," I say.

"I've a feeling I should at least offer to buy you dinner."

My mind is racing so much I hardly hear his response. I know what has to happen today, but suddenly when faced with him, I'm not quite sure how to put it. Best if I just fucking say it.

"Actually, I wanted to give my notice today."

He draws a deep breath, pausing for a painful few seconds. I could swear my heartbeat is so loud, it's echoing off the walls.

"Jesus, was it that bad?" His voice is low. Shit.

I turn to hand him his mug, try to offer a reassuring smile.

"No, no. You misunderstand me." I put a hand on his arm and wait for eye contact despite my racing nerves telling me to shut up and run.

"I didn't want you to think that you owe me anything after… Plus I got this offer, which I'm sorry to say is a lot better than what I could hope for here. Honestly I'm done waiting around and finding the next time positions have to go, mine will be one of them."

He sighs, regains his composure. "I would've done everything not to let that happen, but I understand. Things haven't been looking so good here for the last couple of years."

"No hard feelings?" I say.

"Just because I understand, doesn't mean I have to like it."

"Fair enough." Looking at him again, despite his attempts to put a professional face on, I can recognise he's furious. Damnit.

"I'll miss this, you know." Voicing this particular emotion is weird to say the least, but it's true. Our daily chats have been invaluable. Without them I may have left sooner, without a safety net.

"Yeah."

As I walk out of the kitchen, I look back once more to find Craig still frozen in the same place. I had wanted to bring up Sarah and the card, and that I hope there's something there worth exploring, but nothing could be less appropriate right now.

"You'd better make it official. In writing," he calls after me when I'm almost out of view.

★★★

Back at my desk, I'm turmoil. I'm writing my letter of resignation and wondering if I've just messed up terribly with Craig. Friday night was wonderful in its own way, and stupidly I've only just realised how attached I had become to him as a work friend. I feel so guilty. Though I know everyone says you never share your job change plans until things are set in stone, perhaps I should've treated him less as a superior and more like an actual friend and just been honest. Too late for that now...

With no idea if this strange work-based friendship could extend into my personal life, I'm now even less certain how to proceed. Should I ask if he wants to keep in touch? Would he misunderstand it as a willingness to date? Would that just piss him off further?

Bloody great, with my second experience done and over with, I'm finding myself grown closer to both men involved. Unlike what Sally had wanted me to believe, one hook-up didn't override the other. But if anything, my attachment to Craig really does want to stay in the friend zone. Friends with benefits maybe, whereas I had felt something deeper with *what's-his-name*. Damn me and my stupid emotions!

I finish typing the bare minimum for the letter and print it off. After signing my name at the bottom, I sit and stare at it for a while.

Sally is in a meeting this morning, so I can't even talk it through with her. Stuck, with no outlet for the mess in my head, and a sense that all bets are off in this place anyway, I do something risky and stupid: I log onto Fetlife on my phone.

Last Thursday we'd had a wonderful chat, former virgin and I. I'd felt closer to him still than I had done being in the same bed with him. Perhaps he could share some insights if he's around.

After noting he's not online in chat, I look at the updates on his profile instead. What did I miss during the past four days?

'Falling for a friend, once again I don't think I'm really on her radar plus she's with another guy. WTF, not this shit again!'

I stare at those words for five whole minutes, trying to sort out what they mean. He wrote that on Saturday. *A friend of his.*

Fuck!

I thought we'd had a connection, a kind of trust enabling us to share details of our lives with each other. He never mentioned her. Seeing this now hits me like a punch in the gut. And yet, how very hypocritical of me to expect to be kept up-to-date about his love life! I'd made sure he knows there's no chance between us and I sure as hell didn't tell him anything about *the list* or Craig. So really, I'm the last person ever who ought to be jealous and hurt right now.

And yet I am.

Disgusted with myself but mostly with the world, I exit the site and put my phone away again. Finding the familiar little notepad in my bag, I run my fingers over the two crossed-out items on my sexual To Do list. Virgin and Silver Fox—done. Next, a stranger. Sounds doable.

I know what Sal will say, continuing will help. In any case, now that I've burnt two bridges, I shouldn't find it so hard to keep my stupid emotions in check about my previous exploits.

Perhaps she'll be right this time...

# Stranger

# CHAPTER ONE

I'm having one of *those* evenings. The ones that stretch on forever. Can't sleep but can't face sitting around on my own for much longer either. It's because I'm troubled by everything that's happened lately, which I've been unwilling to deal with. At this rate I'll never get to sleep.

A dejected sigh later, I find my diary and decide to expose all and confess my sins, even if nobody will see them but me.


'Dear Diary,

Today was my last day at work. And with it, perhaps the last time I see Craig, ever. He's been acting weird since our crazy hook-up at the Christmas party a couple of weeks ago. That's not even a fair assessment. Ever since I quit the Monday after the Friday that we hooked up, he's been cold and indifferent. I hadn't handled it well, not at all. Not only did I have the worst timing ever, I'd been way too blunt. Sal later wondered if he was about to ask me out a mere moment before I told him, so perhaps he was hoping for more as well. Could that even be? I'd made it abundantly clear beforehand that it was going to be just sex. Not that that plan had gone well the first time around.

Meanwhile, my first list-based lay, the ex-virgin, has

been posting a lot about his latest tragic love interest. Apparently she's great, and perfect, and cute, and God knows what else. And taken.
We've talked off and on, but I've taken care not to broach the subject of his crush in conversation. I'm curious, but I'm also still pissed off about it, but realise I have no right to feel that way.'

I put the diary and pen down and take a deep breath. None of this is helping; rather than having a calming effect, my rant is just getting me more and more upset. I hate how things have ended with Craig. And I hate even more how the ex-virgin has seemingly breezed past our night together as if it meant nothing to him.

'Sally meanwhile has set the wheels in motion for item 3 on my list. I am to pick up a stranger at a New Year's Eve party, with her support (in case I get the urge to fuck it up with my now-legendary bluntness). God knows why I ever decided I'd wanted to do a stranger, it's a scary prospect. But Sally's idea of doing it at a party seems solid. Yet the plan does not excite me. Perhaps I should try internet dating and just act normal. Boring.
I'm not sure how you're meant to feel after a breakup, but it's been a big, stinking river of shit so far. And I'm not sure the occasional list-inspired highlight has made up for any of it.'

Snapping the diary shut and throwing it away from me

onto the coffee table, I rest my head in my hands. There's no option but to try and stick to the plan. I've crossed out two items on my list, meaning I'm halfway through. It doesn't feel like halfway, more like the easy part is over and the real struggle will begin now: a stranger, and a threesome. So first I need to find one random guy to sleep with and then two of them?! What was I thinking?

A stranger. It seemed like a good idea back when I wrote *the list*. Now it seems stupid. But I set these tasks for myself and would hate it if I gave up now. Sally will be there with me. She even joked that if a particularly cute guy comes along, we might end up killing two birds with one stone. I didn't have the heart to tell her I was after a threesome with two men, not just one and her.

So indeed today was my—our—last day. It was also the last day before the Christmas holidays start for most people, so the new job doesn't begin until January. Which reminds me of another thing I'd been dreading: Christmas.

Christmas by myself. No family, no boyfriend and no turkey. The dreariness never ends.

The only positive that's come out of the entire previous week was bittersweet as well. Our departure at work opened up a vacancy in the internal system, the details of which I was able to send to the ex-virgin. I haven't heard back from him yet, but I assumed he's still hunting for work. I'd recommend him to Craig myself, but at this point, that might have the opposite effect.

A glance at the clock reveals it's three a.m. and I still

can't sleep. Wonder what's on TV.

***

Ding. *What a strange noise he just made.* Ding.

Ding, ding, ding.

*From there his gorgeous face morphs into Craig, but not the one I remember working with before. Rather he looks like the version of Craig that I'd just quit on with a stare that cuts right through me and chills me to my core. His tense lips hardly move as he continues to make the weird sound. Ding, ding.*

I blink a few times, trying to shake that overwhelming lethargy you experience when you're woken at the wrong time. Within seconds, I'd gone from being bedded by the guy this whole list debacle started with, to being bombarded by strange noises and seeing guilt impersonated in front of me. Where's that god-awful noise coming from?

My phone lights up, presumably for the tenth time at least, and dings again. Argh, my head. Facebook Messenger is merciless.

"Hey, where the fuck are you?" Sal writes. "I've got something to run past you. Wake up, sleepyhead!"

Stretching my arms fails to loosen my shoulders which are suffering the consequences of sleeping on the couch.

"What?" I type.

Sally appears to be writing furiously on the other end and I decide to make myself a cup of tea. This morning has started all wrong. That dream. I won't forgive her for interrupting that dream. It had felt like the guy wasn't just doing me, but rather we were making love. The way he was looking at me… I'm still on edge because of it. But now that glorious moment has passed.

Ding.

Goddamnit, *I'm coming, woman!*

The kettle starts bubbling in the background and I check the message that's just arrived.

"Change of plans for Xmas, you still around on the 25th?"

"Yep."

"OK, awesome. Looks like I'll be as well. Let's do something."

Sal to the rescue, to save me from a lonely Christmas without even any roasted poultry to look forward to? Why not?

"Call me in 10." I hit send and slump down at the breakfast bar in the kitchen, rubbing my forehead with the palm of my hand. Caffeine. Need caffeine.

A few sips of tea and a biscuit later, the phone rings.

"Morning!" Sally cheers at the other end.

"Meh."

"Oh you're such a grouch, you know that? It's fucking eleven in the morning, not like I'm calling you at an ungodly hour or anything." She chuckles. Her excitement is making me even grumpier.

"I slept at like five. Or seven. God, I dunno. Had someone else been around, I'd be accusing them of bashing me over the head with something after I finally did fall asleep. Bloody headache."

"You've got to go easy on the wine,"

"I wasn't dr—"

"Anyway, stop changing the subject. Christmas Day. You, me, turkey, roasties, and all that stuff. What do you say?"

"Alright."

"I may ask around if anyone else is free as well, for those of us not visiting family that day, we might as well make our own fun."

"Fine."

"Since you're the only one I know who can actually cook, you'll be in charge of the food. We'll pool together to buy everything, but it'd be nice if it was edible."

"OK."

"Awesome. Talk later." With that, she hangs up and I'm left wondering what exactly I just agreed to.

*I'm in charge of the food.* Suddenly I wonder if sitting at home by myself without the hassle would have been preferable to this new plan. Still, she had a point. We might as well have something edible on the table that day and I know what her cooking is like. Finding my notepad and pen, I make a quick list of ingredients to hunt for. Five days to find a suitable bird. That ought to be doable.

✳✳✳

Turns out, time flies when you're planning a feast. Sally's main contribution, beyond the initial idea, came in the form of a few more attendees, and a ridiculous email inviting us all to her place for her proposed *'Christmas Day for sad, lonely fucks'*. You simply can't make it up.

I've accumulated more food than the average household would eat in a month, while leaving her in charge of the booze. The kitchen is covered with a mountain of dishes I thought I'd need, just in case. I need to give her one credit, a big one. I haven't had time to feel guilty about anything that was bothering me last week.

Hearing Craig greet Sal at the door and thanking her for the invitation comes as quite a shock. Even so, I don't have time for a meltdown, instead I nod at him once he enters and continue to do my best not to burn any of the food.

When we finally sit down at the table; Craig, Sally's two school friends and a neighbour, her and me, I notice everyone else is much cheerier, than I've allowed myself to be. But the food is ready, and I think I've managed reasonably well, despite the constant distractions earlier. Everyone agrees, even Craig, who seems a lot less cold and horrible than I'd remembered him.

By the end of the evening, which drags on a lot later than just lunch, apparently all is forgiven. A huge weight is lifted off my shoulders. He had indeed wondered whether to ask me out the day I quit, but more out of a sense of obligation than anything else. In the meantime, he's been on a first date with Sarah from HR and found they have a lot more in common than expected. We exchange a knowing look and grin, remembering the Condom Card debacle, but keep it to ourselves.

Despite the herculean task of putting together a meal for all of us on my own without much in the way of previous experience, the day leaves me content. It has been a success, and someone I'd worried about turning into an enemy, ends up still being a friend.

*** 

"Merry Christmas," I clumsily type into the Fetlife chat box, excited to see the ex-virgin in my list of online contacts.

After getting home, at a respectable one a.m., it seemed like a simply brilliant idea to unwind from earlier hard work by logging on for a chat.

I don't stop to think why he'd be online at this hour on Christmas Day, it's enough that he's here.

The response is slow, but it does come eventually.

"You too. Did you spend today with family?"

"No, at a friend's house. They put me in charge of the turkey." Although I don't share it with him, Sally's description for today's events finally seems funny to me. *Christmas for sad lonely fucks*, she's such a hoot.

He tells me about his day, spent at his grandparents' house. Three generations under one roof, exactly the sort of squeaky-clean stuff Christmas card illustrations are made of. Now he's back at home and I wonder how different our worlds really are.

"How about New Year's?" he asks.

I remember the plan, but have enough of my

faculties left to decide it would be a bad idea to be too frank about it all.

"Just going to a party, my friend Sally has organised tickets. I think it's in town, but I don't know for sure where."

"Cool, similar for me. Tagging along with my friend, the one with the band. I may have told you about him before. He's got a gig."

We slip into a lengthy discussion about music, and the struggle of the independent musician. Afterwards, I mindlessly change the topic to something that's been keeping me occupied for a while.

"Say, your other friend, the one you've been writing about…" I start, feeling too nosy for comfort, yet not really giving a damn at this point.

"Who?"

"You know, you've been posting status updates about her. The one you're crushing on."

"Yeah?"

"For what it's worth, I hope it works out for you both."

"She's with another guy."

"Yeah, I know that, but things are never set in stone, right? If it's meant to be, it's meant to be. I don't know how serious it is, but I wish you the best."

Suddenly overflowing with the milk of human kindness, I continue along the same trajectory. Tomorrow, I may regret my candour.

"What's she like?"

"Smart, funny, caring, pretty as well. The whole

package."

"If she took a good look at you, she'd realise you're all that and more. And that's not the wine talking, I promise. Having had a very close look myself, I'd like to think I know a few things about it…"

I sit back and stare at the words on screen. My fingers just wrote all of that seemingly on their own. Did I really see him this way? My heart is beating way faster than normal and there's a funny lump in my throat. Though that might be the wine again.

Suddenly I want to cry.

# CHAPTER TWO

The nightclub is packed full of bodies, there's skin everywhere in all colours and different grades of exposure. Music blares from the speakers, the bar is buzzing with activity and I feel like a model strutting down a catwalk with Sally by my side. There's a pulsating, almost collective heartbeat in the place. Like everyone's there for one thing, and we're all willing to do our best to get it.

We're all trying to score. To get lucky before the New Year.

For today's mission, I've opted for something a little less conservative than the office party. A multi-coloured bodycon dress and matching platform heels. No tights. Nobody needs tights with a dress like this. I'm in two minds about whether I should've left my underwear at home too.

Sally's gorgeous as ever, swishing her blonde curls over her shoulder and giving everyone at the bar a good once-over. She's on the look-out for herself as well as for me. We're in this together at first, though I'll be the one making the approach and closing the deal.

We order a couple of drinks, ready to get this party going when the guy next to her starts making a pass already. He's cute too, so she gives him about thirty seconds of undivided attention before checking what I'm up to. I nod at her to go for it, I've got this. The atmosphere of this place seems to contain more pheromones than oxygen. I can sense the underlying heat and desire in the room, the epicentre of which seems to be the dance floor.

If I can't get laid here, I'll fail anywhere.

With my drink in hand, I scan the crowd for faces which stand out. I'm not after the typical *hot guy like all the others*. I want something interesting… something different. A beautiful *stranger*, whose face will stay with me forever. If I never gather up the courage to do this again, I want the memory to be worth it.

I haven't found him yet, although someone seems to have found me. Strong aftershave and gelled hair. He looks in his thirties, dark eyes and olive skin with a slight five o'clock shade. The neutral accent does not give away whether his origins are Southern European or further afield. Does it matter? Probably not. Actually, I'm thinking Sally might really appreciate this one, only she's already dancing with the guy from earlier on.

Her loss, I shrug. *Exotic stranger* offers me a refill and I gladly accept. We sit at the bar for a strained chat over the music. It's all small talk; what do you do, you're so pretty, that kind of thing. Just when he's about to ask for my number, I am hit with tunnel vision. The light touch of his fingers on my arm fades out of my perception and there's just one thing I can focus on: a familiar face in among the crowd near the entrance. A face I'd seen in person just one time, much too long ago, afterwards only in photographs that couldn't quite capture him. The same face that has haunted me in my most intimate dreams and made my heart beat faster with every recalled memory.

Our eyes meet and my heart stops. He's frozen in place too, causing a bit of a traffic jam until one of his companions drags him out of the way, barely.

Number one on *the list*. Number one in lots of ways, I suppose. It's my ex-virgin.

*Exotic stranger* is still talking, or was up to a moment ago. I can't concentrate on him and rummage through my clutch bag to find the solution. "I'm sorry, you seem nice but I can't do this," I say, while putting a fiver on the bar. "That's for the drink earlier."

He's about to protest, but I've already slipped off the barstool and am heading into the crowd towards the general area where I saw *him*. Sally catches me and attempts to bring me out of my trance.

"What's wrong, you look like you've seen a ghost?"

"The guy… I just saw the guy. The first item on my list!" I shake myself loose and continue into the crowd on the dance floor, not entirely sure where I'm headed. I can't see him anymore.

Sal's hand finds my shoulder again.

"Jesus, Becks, are you sure? Where?" I shrug in response, pressing forward while dodging the odd flailing arm belonging to one of the more expressive dancers. She follows, making progress difficult.

"I've got to go talk to him," I say. I'm not quite sure what I'll say, but it's important I go over there.

Sally shakes her head at me, and gives me one of her trademarked pity smiles.

"You've fallen for this guy, huh?"

"Don't be an ass. Go dance with your man there. Or have the one I left at the bar, he was pretty hot too."

She lets out a quick laugh and admits defeat, letting me slip out of her grip and onwards past couples grinding against each other and singles jumping about to the beat.

At the other end of the dance floor, nearer the stage, I see a small group of people unpacking boxes. Of course! He came with the band, just like he said. What an epic coincidence that his friend is playing this particular party.

And there he is, suspiciously eyeing me as I come into view.

"Hi!" It's all I can manage, while still catching my breath from the initial shock, as well as my epic journey through the dancing masses.

"What's up?" After a first glance, he looks off to the side, not really at me, which is both infuriating and really cute in a way.

"Fancy seeing you here." I force a smile through my nerves.

He nods towards the bar, where I had come from.

"Your husband?"

I turn to see Exotic Stranger in the distance, still looking at where I've run off to, and let out an awkward chuckle.

"What, him? No. Just some guy."

Former virgin's face darkens and finally does look me in the eye.

"Some guy, eh. Well don't let me interrupt—whatever…"

"You're not. I…" It occurs to me that perhaps this situation, me showing up with a bunch of his friends around, might be extremely uncomfortable. God knows if his crush will turn up with her current boyfriend. How would he explain who I am? Awkward!

"I can go if you want me to," I mumble. The music drowns me out.

"What?"

"I said, if this is weird, I can go."

"You're the one who didn't want to meet up again, you decide."

"Oh. No, that's fine. I got quite excited seeing you in among all these people. A familiar face."

"So where's your husband? He left you by yourself on New Year's Eve?" He still looks annoyed, but his tone suggests the object of his displeasure has changed.

"Err… it's sort of a long story. How about that special friend of yours?"

"Oh, she's already here."

I look around the group he arrived with and spy the petite girl with the pixie hair who's unpacking a red bass guitar. His eyes never leave me though.

How is it that I was making significant progress with the stranger at the bar, when the mere sight of the ex-virgin became impossible to ignore? Not the stranger and the prospect of ticking another item off *the list*, nor Sal could stop me from coming over here and making a fool of myself.

He seems to not have much to say either, so I just observe. This must be his usual style. Jeans and t-shirt, though in this case with the band logo like everyone else in his group. I realise I like this as much as his slightly less casual look from last time.

His hair is the same, kind of messy, but intentionally so. And the goatee is too. That face. He really is infuriatingly cute, despite his hostility.

"Dude, give us a hand!" shouts a voice from the stage, and ex-virgin startles into action. I hang around nearby, watching him help his friends set up. Why does he have this effect on me? All I can think about are the things we've done, for real in that bland hotel room, as well as in my imagination. I'm terrified, but his presence here is somehow magnetic.

Once everything's unpacked and installed, he looks back to find me still standing in the same place, waiting. Some of the others have also become aware of my lingering around and are giving each other nudges and glances.

I don't really care what anyone thinks, so if it bothers him, he'll be the one to take action.

"So," he starts.

"So."

"What are you really doing here?"

"I'm not stalking you if that's what you mean."

"No, I'm talking about the guy at the bar. Another one of your little just-for-you extra-marital experiences?"

I glance at the floor, shrugging awkwardly, blood

rushing into my cheeks. If I didn't know any better, it sounds like he's jealous. More likely he just thinks I'm a cheating whore and I'm not fond of being judged.

"Can we talk somewhere?" I ask.

# CHAPTER THREE

After a stare that seems to last forever, he nods and gestures to his friends that he'll be a while. We walk off towards the exit, heading for the smoking area outside. It was so hot inside the club that the chilly air feels pleasant against my bare arms. We move past a group of smokers to a quieter part of the street where we'd have some privacy.

It had been hard to keep up appearances the first time around, when I didn't even know him. Now, after revealing bits of our true selves in every conversation since, it's impossible. The truth is gnawing at me, if I don't let it out, it might rip me open from the inside. Despite knowing that pixie-girl inside has already defeated me, he deserves to know, surely.

"I'm not actually married," I blurt out, eyes fixated on the wall just behind him.

His face falls. *Me and my big mouth, when will I learn to work on how I put things?*

"You're not—what?" He grabs me by the arm, forcing eye contact. I want to run, or at the very least close my eyes and wish I'll simply become invisible. And yet, that touch… It's spurring me on to spill everything.

"I'm single."

"Fucking hell." He lets go of me and rubs his temples, then glances at me again with shock written all over his face.

"Why didn't you—"

"When we hooked up, I had literally just come out of a long-term relationship and didn't want any complications. So I pretended. And I didn't want to keep in touch at all."

"Complications, eh?" From the initial surprise, he's back to looking annoyed again. Or perhaps hurt, I'm such a dope when it comes to reading people.

"You know, I didn't want things to become messy. To have some time to figure out what I need to do."

"And have you figured it out?"

I shrug, feeling the prickle of tears in my eyes. Surely everything's ruined now, he's never going to forgive me for lying to him. But I couldn't keep quiet; I couldn't keep up with the charade.

"I didn't plan this, didn't think it would make a difference," I whisper. "I'm scared."

"*You're* scared? What the fuck? What on earth would you be scared of?"

"Ever since… you know, I haven't been able to get you out of my head, and I've fucked it all up and now you've fallen for this other girl and I'm—" I take a deep breath, trying to hold it all in, but a tear escapes and rolls down my cheek anyway. "I fucking hate it!"

He suspiciously eyes me while I half turn away, making a big show of trying to keep my makeup in check. It's no use, tears are falling freely now.

"OK let me recap, to make sure I haven't misunderstood anything."

My response comes in the form of a sniffle.

"You are not and have never been married."

I shake my head.

"You're *single*. And the whole story was just a means of keeping me away after we slept together. To avoid so-called *mess*."

"You make it sound all terrible."

"From where I'm standing, I'm not sure how else to take it?"

"People make idiotic life choices on the rebound. I didn't want to get out of one doomed relationship and go headfirst into another. Jeff and I got together when I was still living at home. I've never been on my own and had to find out what it would be like. To be free. So that when I start dating again, I'd know what I'm looking for."

"And how has that been going for you?"

"It's been a fucking disaster to be honest."

His stare chills me to my core and I suddenly realise it's freezing and the temperature is getting to me as well. Wrapping my arms around myself, I try to control both the shivers and the emotions that continue to overflow.

"Well anyway, that's all I had to say. Not like it matters. As I told you last week, hope it works out with you and that friend of yours." In between shivers, I nod towards the club where pixie-girl must be tuning her oh-so-cool bass guitar by now. *The smug bitch.* She'll probably continue to ignore him while he quietly suffers on the inside.

"You're quite something, you know that? Wow." He laughs, not cheerfully, but rather in that kind of incredulous way people do when they want to hit something. Or someone.

"I've said all I had to say. Now I'm going inside before I freeze to death." Just when I turn, his hand grabs mine, and I pause. Not only because he's so warm it's making the chills worse, but also because I wish he wouldn't let go. "What?"

"Let's just for a moment assume you're telling me the truth now."

"Right." My fingers twitch and weave through his and he lets it happen. He's so warm. How is he so warm despite the weather?

"You're jealous of this friend I mentioned?"

I'm too tired to pretend or hide my real feelings, but also not up for further drama so I just nod in defeat and stare at the glistening pavement.

"And you've been thinking about me, which is why you ignored your brilliant plan of simply cutting off all contact?"

I nod again and am met by painful seconds of silence.

"What if I said that friend was you?"

Just when I'm about to shrug by default, the meaning of his words sinks in. The *friend* is me? Not the girl with the band? I must have misheard that.

"Don't fuck with me, OK. I won't be able to take it if you're just messing me about!" I say, while searching for truth in his eyes.

His frown had gone from confused to hurt to furious previously, but now he mainly looks nervous.

That same look he gave me in the hotel room last month, when he wasn't quite sure what to expect from me.

"It's always been you," he says.

I'm about to cry again and the cold has made my body numb and uncooperative.

"Talk is cheap," I blurt out and take a clumsy step towards him.

He wraps his arms around me and I instinctively hide. Rather than relief, I'm plagued by an array of confusing emotions. Mainly I'm still shocked that there is no other *friend*. I'm also angry at myself for dragging this stupidity out so long. But mostly I feel guilty. I've been selfish and stupid and have hurt everyone this past month.

"I'm so sorry," I whisper.

The tears refuse to stop, so I keep hiding in his arms. His face presses into my hair and we both stand still for what seems like forever.

I really like him, have done from the moment I read his profile, saw his picture. He already had me when I observed him standing at the cinema, waiting for me with that terrified expression on his face. My attachment grew when he put his arm around me during the movie we saw. I was lost by the time our clothes came off and he seemed to bare part of his soul as well as his body. I felt like I knew all I needed to about him then. I mistook it for lust at the time, when actually I felt something else.

"Please don't lie to me again." The vulnerability in

his voice makes me cry again. Despite planning to fulfil both our needs with the initial meeting, I had used him. Shame on me. I don't deserve this chance.

Warmth creeps through our clothes and makes gives me pins and needles. His hands roam my back, leaving trails of burning skin underneath my dress. Through my lingering guilt, I just want to show him I'll try to be good enough. I find his lips with mine, cling onto him tightly and express how much I've thought about him in the only way I know how.

"I wish I could take it back," I breathe.

His goatee tickles my chin, but not in a bad way. He directs me against the wall and I'm trapped between the cold, rough brick and him. Minutes later, he startles with the realisation I was cold earlier. I'd forgotten all about that, but he's right.

***

When we walk back inside, I make a quick escape to the ladies' room to clean up.

I look like a total wreck with black streaks running down both sides of my face. While doing my best with a scrap of toilet paper, I can't help getting distracted by the question of why waterproof mascara never truly ends up being waterproof. The door creaks open and in walks a very confused looking Sally.

"Becky, hey, where've you been— Shit, are you OK?" She rushes to my aid and helps dab some of the mess away from the corner of my eye with another piece of tissue.

129

"Yeah, don't worry about it. Everything's cool."

"What happened? If he hurt you, I'll tear him a new one!"

That makes me chuckle, and she joins in.

"No, I'm just being stupid as usual. Sal, I really like him. He seems to like me."

"Right, so why are you crying?"

"Was. I *was* crying. Well—" Realising we're far from safe yet, I feel my eyeballs stinging once more. But I try to keep it in.

"He's so sweet, and as you might imagine, not exactly a *player*. What if after I explain everything, he thinks I'm a total slut and changes his mind?"

"Becks, there's a simple solution to this. You don't tell him."

"Shouldn't I be honest? About everything that's happened: *the list*, Craig?"

"Be honest about the here and now. You like him, he likes you. That's all you need to focus on. It's none of his business what you've done before. Men love to feel special; telling him how many other guys you've fucked isn't going to achieve that. Especially considering you were his first."

Perhaps she's right. There's a fine line between honesty and over-sharing.

"I guess I can try." I smile at her, while still trying to convince myself she knows what she's talking about. If only I can put a leash on my big mouth.

"So, are you going to introduce me, or what?"

"Where's your guy gone, wouldn't he be waiting?"

Sal waves my question off.

"He was starting to bore me anyways. Becks—" She pats me on the arm and offers another reassuring smile. "Remember: As long as your feelings are genuine, keeping some things to yourself is perfectly acceptable. You're just protecting him, so he doesn't misunderstand your intentions."

While I'm not entirely sure it's all that acceptable, I do believe it's the only solution. After fucking up spectacularly already, I can't risk scaring him away now.

After a last once-over we both decide I'm ready to face the world again. She puts her arm through mine and we leave the facilities together.

# CHAPTER FOUR

He's waiting by the doors, holding two pints, and looks surprised that I'm not alone.

"Hi," he nods at Sally, who is smiling sweetly with her head cocked to one side while shamelessly checking him out head to toe.

"This is Sally…." I say, and then I'm stuck. *Shit.* I don't know his name. He doesn't know my name. This is awkward.

He hands me one of the drinks and greets Sally—who has now let go of me—with a handshake.

"I've heard so much about you," Sal says. "In detail…" That last remark is making me want to smack her over the head with something.

"Alex," he introduces himself. For some reason I forget to breathe. He doesn't look like an Alex, does he? I'm not sure, but something tells me he will redefine the name for me from this moment on.

I nervously take a sip, hoping the beer will provide courage. It doesn't. I wish Sally would go now, she's had her eyeful and it's just getting weird now.

"She's a good one, Alex. Don't make her cry again." Sally winks at me and heads to the bar, signalling we should just get on with it.

"Sorry about that. She can be… Well she's just Sally." My cheeks glow, no doubt they're bright red. Damn her and her embarrassing ways.

He flashes a smile and nods.

"Umm, sorry to be a pain, but could you tell me your name now?"

The surrealism of the moment successfully breaks the ice again and makes me laugh.

"Rebecca. But everyone tends to call me Becky." I briefly forget myself in his eyes, before finding a suitable comeback. "I'm guessing next you'll want my phone number as well, huh?"

"That would be handy, yes."

The music that previously surrounded us stops abruptly in favour of the crackle of a microphone. We turn to see that the band is finally about to start playing. For a while we remain where we are, towards the other end of the venue, away from the stage. I love how he puts one arm around me from behind. Just like that first time. I'm giddy from the butterflies in my stomach and yet strangely relaxed. A soft kiss on my shoulder tries to convince me all will be fine.

By the third song, our drinks are finished, taking with any lingering doubts away with them. I turn around and kiss him again. And again. His embrace is seemingly the only thing stopping me from floating away. He gives the best hugs. My arms wrap around his neck, anchoring myself to him further. I don't want to let him go. Everything in front of me now is the realisation of many a dream. Sparks fly when we kiss. I want to cry again, as well as laugh. I want to run up to the stage, steal the microphone and scream that he's beautiful and I want him. I want him, with every fibre of my being, right now.

And his kisses don't disappoint. I've been horrible to him, yet he still wants me too. The first time I needed to take the lead, but tonight that won't be necessary. He seems to need no reassurance beyond the knowledge that he's been in my thoughts as much as I've been in his. We both know exactly what to do.

While our breaths quicken, our hands are moved by an irresistible greed to catch up on lost time. We're absorbed in our little world, of tactile exploration by fingertip and tongue, with no awareness of how much time goes by. The crowd of bystanders blends into a colourful backdrop for our passion. We keep things decent enough to avoid too much embarrassment, but don't stop tasting each other, holding on so tightly we might merge into one.

When I finally do pull back, I see those lust-drunk eyes again that have stalked my thoughts since the first day we met. I want to go, I can see he wants to as well. We'd had a bunch of firsts together already. From his first kiss to my first deflowering. Right now it's our first night out, our first nightclub make-out session, our first attempt to become a couple rather than simply a shared memory.

"Ladies and gentlemen," the microphone crackles again.

"It is almost time to ring out the boring old year, and welcome the new."

Alex looks at me, and I look at him. Although over a month later than it needed to be, now feels like the perfect time to meet.

The countdown starts in the background. 10, 9, 8—TVs switch on—7, 6, 5—he smiles and I respond - 4, 3, 2, 1 and cheers erupt throughout the crowd. Other couples pair up to kiss, fireworks light up the flickering screens all around us. But I can't look away from him.

"Happy New Year," he mouths.

"Best New Year ever," I respond. Hopefully, this year will be the first of many to belong to us.

✱✱✱

We rush out to find a cab, our hands entwined. I steal glances at him and he at me, but somehow we still manage to flag down one of the few taxis passing by. I give the cabbie my address and we get cosy in the backseat.

"Are you for real?" he asks.

I kiss him, then rest my forehead against his cheek.

"I keep expecting to wake up," he continues.

"I know. I don't want this moment to pass."

He puts his arm around me and I gladly lean against him for the remainder of the journey. We are a picture of calm, while behind the scenes at least I am anything but.

By the time we reach my place, I'm beyond ready to let him into my life and my own bed.

Inside, we discard our coats, wherever they happen to fall. We kiss as though the drive lasted hours, not just minutes and we need to catch up. Just feeling his body pressed up against me so close is turning my desire up to eleven.

"Becky," he whispers against my lips.

"Yes."

"Is this OK?"

I pull back and give him a questioning look.

"Is it OK to want to—" He bites his lip and gives me a smouldering stare.

"I could just tear that dress off you and—"

The rawness in his voice makes every last hair on my body stand up.

"How about, I take off the dress in one piece, and you tear your own clothes off." I grin at him, while unzipping myself much more slowly than necessary. He rushes to pull his t-shirt over his head and starts on his jeans. I watch. It's hard to believe we're here, together. I hope this never gets old.

He gives me a sideways, slightly bemused look while he drops what little remains of his clothes.

"Distracted?"

I realise I'm frozen with my arms reaching behind to unhook my bra, yet not making any progress with it.

"Sorry, yes." I startle into action while continuing to enjoy the view of him, naked, aroused. Shortly, all those things I've only been able to dream about lately will really happen again.

He takes a step forward and hooks me by the elastic of my knickers. I forget to breathe while he pulls them down and they, too, fall to the ground.

"You're even more beautiful than I remembered," he says.

The nibbles on my neck make me weaker still.

I direct him a few steps back to where the sofa is and he sits, pulling me along with him. Straddled on top, I'm unable to resist the unlimited access. Sloppy kisses interrupt feverish caresses. I can't get enough of all that's on offer. If I've learnt anything since I started experimenting, it's that less is not more when it comes to the male form. He's my new ideal. My new definition of sexy going forward. I can't imagine wanting any other guy more than I want him.

It's hard to decide what to fondle, squeeze, run my nails over, or nuzzle my face against. He's all mine and I intend to appreciate every part of him tonight. And tomorrow. And for as much of the foreseeable future as he'll let me.

His hands feel amazing, wherever he chooses to place them. I grind against him, his erection hits me just right. I want him inside me, like I've never wanted anything before. We know how this works now, neither of us needs to worry or be afraid of disappointing the other. We've been through that once, and came out wanting more. That first night didn't relieve our desires, rather, it intensified them.

He massages my ass, really digging his fingers into my flesh and I can't resist any longer. When I lift up to reposition myself, he eyes me, our joining, down below. His face contorts with that first introduction into my wetness. He lies back, bucking his hips just enough to set a rhythm and I do the rest.

I'd been dripping from the moment those first kisses

started, back at the club. My body screams for release, but it's not within reach yet.

In a desperate attempt to scratch that itch deep inside of me, I speed up, riding him hard, hanging on to his shoulders for stability. He's lost in the moment, and watching his enjoyment empowers me to try harder.

Harder. Faster. Better.

I am powerful, like I was made to do this with him or to him now. Pushing myself beyond the limits normally imposed by my lack of stamina seems easy. Like I'm able to rise above it all and allow someone else control over my body.

This dream-like state I've found myself in is momentarily interrupted by his voice. His groans, signalling the build-up towards what I've been working for. My only goal is to push him over the edge. Fingers clamp down on my hips. His eyes flash dark-green at me, but only for a split second. He's ready.

In one final push towards the finish line, I give him all I've got. He fills me, completes me. I grind down and he shudders slightly, though it seemed like every muscle in his body is trying its best to remain rigid.

He cries out one last time before sinking back into the cushioned backrest with a blissful peace washing over his face. Surprised it took that long, I continue to be impressed by him.

I'm momentarily sated as well, exhaustion is creeping in. He pulls me into his arms and I cuddle against him, waiting for my breaths to slow.

"During all that, I forgot," I sigh.

"What?"

"Condom."

He startles. "Shit, now what?"

"If you're safe, I am. I'm sorry, I should've been more careful, this has never happened to me before. Getting this carried away." I should be worried, even regret this recklessness, but my senses seem dulled and woolly.

He blinks a few times, wipes a strand of damp hair out of my face and puts it behind my ear.

"Should be fine then. There's certainly nothing to worry about at my end." His face still sports a slightly puzzled expression, despite his reassuring words.

"In case you're wondering. No, I'm not going to get pregnant or anything."

He smiles, as do I.

"Right. It's weird having to worry about stuff like that all of a sudden."

I can't help but get distracted again. His eyes keep holding mine. His lips invite me to taste. So I give in, with little kisses at first, all the while looking at him looking at me.

Soon, I realise that things are getting sticky, so I force myself to interrupt our little moment.

"I'll be right back."

He nods and stretches leisurely.

"I'll be in the bedroom, if I can find it."

As I pick up the leftovers of tonight's outfit off the floor, he follows and I point him towards the bedroom. He doesn't miss the chance to swat me on my naked backside while I pass by.

"Oi!" He's gone by the time I've turned around.

The last thing I hear before closing the bathroom door is his chuckle. *Cheeky bastard.*

# CHAPTER FIVE

When I enter the bedroom, I'm still ecstatic to have him here, to have moved past all the lies and pretence. Alex, who's made himself comfortable under the covers in the meantime, has gone quiet.

"What are you thinking about?" I ask, then immediately wish I'd bitten my tongue rather than let the most annoying of all questions slip out.

He doesn't answer, just looks around the darkened room. It is all a bit strange now that at least some of our urges have been fulfilled. Neither of us expected the evening to turn out like this.

"Umm, Becky?" He turns, revealing a worried frown.

"Yeah?"

"I don't want to be difficult-"

My pulse starts to quicken, uncertain where this conversation is going.

"What is it?" He's not having second thoughts already, is he? I'm left imagining worst-case scenarios while waiting for his answer.

"I know what it's like to want something so badly, yet never get it. But, that's all. Now, there's a chance of making things work, but I'm worried I'll fuck it up."

"I understand."

"Do you? You've been with the same guy for years before this. You've already learned how relationships work, how to share. I mainly know how to do my own thing while bitching about how unfair life is."

"So? We'll figure it out." Indeed I do understand now. We've both come a long way from our first meeting, but that was just sex. The before and after is still a mystery that needs sorting out.

"Feels like absolutely everything is riding on this. And I'm not sure what happens next."

"What do you want to happen next?"

All of this is close to déjà vu. There was no way this was going to play out smoothly, with both of us instinctively on track. He suspects I have the advantage, but I have plenty of baggage that he has no idea about.

"If I stay, promise you won't change your mind by the morning?"

I shake my head and try to reassure him with a smile.

"You won't either?" I ask.

"No way." He sighs. "Sorry I even brought it up."

"Best to get it all out there," I say and hesitate before continuing. "I need to ask you something too though."

"Shoot."

It's my turn to be scared, because the answer that awaits me, might not be what I want to hear.

"Why do you still want me? I mean, I've been horrible to you. Lied to you."

"You're kidding, right? You gave me hope."

"I guess I just feel like I used you. It was wrong."

He lets out a laugh.

"This must be one of those brilliant male-female perception things people keep talking about. You'd be devastated if someone used you. I was upset it didn't last longer, but was glad that at least someone wanted the sex."

"That last part isn't going to change." I grin and lean into his arms. "I still want the sex too."

He turns serious again and looks into my eyes for a few, endless seconds.

"If you hadn't agreed to meet me, I don't know... I was about to give up. But even if we hadn't run into each other today, I still would've wanted the experience with you."

"Better to have lost…" I blurt out.

"Than never to have loved at all, yes." My nerves surge when he says the L-word. We're not quite ready for that kind of talk!

"Last question." I try to move the conversation along.

"Yes?"

"You're not just into me because I happened to show interest, right? I mean if it had been some other girl, would you now be in her bed, saying the same sort of stuff?"

He shakes his head, hesitating for a moment.

"I've had other girls contact me through my Fetlife profile recently…"

I fail to breathe, and just stare at him, scared to guess where this is going.

"I didn't want to meet them. Not after that night with you."

Unsure what to say, I decide it's best not to say a word. While I've been trying to move my list idea along, he's been faithful to me? This isn't helping my earlier guilt issues and yet confirms what Sally advised: he must never know about Craig.

"That means a lot," I whisper.

Fuck, I'm a terrible person. But that's my problem, not his.

I'd better do what Sally suggested. Focus on the here and now, on my feelings for him, his feelings for me. There's no doubt in my mind that he's genuine. At least I can find solace in knowing that my intentions are too.

"You up for round two?" He winks at me and pulls me into a much needed embrace.

"Always."

The kisses and caresses invite my earlier arousal to return, which is enough to almost make me forget. By the time we fall back on the bed after my release, my mind is so foggy, the guilt has almost faded. I decide I must be strong for him and not give in to my usual urges. If I need to vent about my worries, about all I've done wrong, it should be with Sally.

***

His arm weighs heavy on my chest, but I don't stir straightaway. The regular breaths tell me he's still asleep, so I keep listening. I'm glad he stayed. After everything, and despite all the confusion and worries earlier, I'm happy that we've taken our first, shaky steps towards becoming a couple.

He's scared, of course he is, as am I. This is weird

for both of us. You don't put yourself out there to be with another person every day. Especially when the stakes seem so high. Not counting the boy I lost my own virginity to in secondary school, Alex is my second real lover. At least I hope I'll still be able to call him that once this early awkwardness has passed.

I am his first. Of course all of this started because I wanted to be. But I didn't plan for it to go further than one night. I knew then that things wouldn't get much easier for him beyond that *first time*. The sex would be the easy part, and I never thought that I'd share in the difficulties to come after.

All of this should terrify me. It should make me doubt whether this relationship is even worthwhile. Rationally I realise I should be out there trying to snag myself the modern equivalent of a confident hunter-gatherer who could fight wild beasts for me, and protect me from harm. We, as women, are conditioned from a young age to want only alpha males.

Yet, I'm not scared. He has all of that in him, even if it doesn't always show. Once he gets used to the idea that we're in this together, everything has to work itself out.

I carefully use my free hand to feel around for a watch on the nightstand. Six a.m.

Turning just my head, I watch him for a while. His face—completely at rest now—is what initially attracted me the most. Shallow, I know, but it's still true.

He thinks too much, though right now his features give nothing away. Maybe I'm thinking too much now.

He twitches and turns onto his back, releasing me from his grasp. But the breathing continues at the same calm pace as before.

I wonder if I'm just awake because I'm thirsty, and slip out of bed. On the way back from the kitchen, I notice my diary and little notepad on the coffee table. I'd best tidy those things away. The diary goes into the drawer and the notepad… I flip to the page with *the list*.

*To Do:*

~~*Virgin*~~

~~*Silver Fox*~~

*Stranger*

*Threesome*

Looks like I won't be needing that anymore...

After tearing the page off and scrunching it up, I aim for the waste basket across the room and tiptoe back into the bedroom. When I'm under the covers again, he takes my arm and pulls me closer behind him.

I've missed this togetherness. Before things went south with Jeff, it had already been ages since we slept like this. In hindsight, that might have been the first sign things weren't quite right between us.

By that logic, right now, everything ought to be perfect.

Perhaps I'll be right this time...

# Threesome

# CHAPTER ONE

In one crazy day and night, we inaugurated every room of my little flat. We kissed until our lips burned bright red, and made love until our limbs felt like they were made of lead.

But now, on this first working day of the New Year, all of that must end. Normality will set in.

The hot water hits my face and runs down my body, loosening muscles wherever it passes. Today is going to be a chore. Still, at least I've got plenty to talk to Sally about. Wonder what the new place will be like though, if they're as easy-going as Craig was? I'm going to miss Craig, and our little chats over a cup of tea.

"Becky, phone's ringing. Dunno who." Alex knocks on the door to make his point and sure enough I can hear the distinctive sound of the handheld through the bathroom door.

"I'm all shampooed up, can you get it?" Who could be calling me at this hour? Sally? Unlikely, she'd message me rather than call.

I rinse the shampoo out of my hair, while still trying to relax my shoulders and neck under the jet of water.

"Um, Becky? I think you ought to get this." Alex knocks again. What the hell. I'm already not a morning person, and I can't imagine what would be so urgent that I can't even have a shower in peace.

"Coming, just a minute!"

Shutting off the water about a third shy of my

standard fifteen minute shower time, I snatch a towel and tiptoe to the door in an attempt to limit drippage. Alex, rather than enjoying the view of me barely covered in a towel, looks uncomfortable and distracted.

"Your mum." He hands me the phone as if in a rush to get rid of it. *Shit.*

"Hi, Mum, didn't expect your call this morning!" I try to sound cheerful, but I'm possibly feeling even more awkward than Alex is.

"Darling, I'm getting the feeling I'm interrupting something." Her tone grates on me. She's never been shy about voicing her disapproval.

"I'm getting ready for work."

"Ah yes, the new place. I got back from my trip last night so I thought I'd wish you a happy New Year and good luck for your first day."

"Thanks, happy New Year to you too. Hope you had fun in—wherever?"

"Egypt. Yes. It was magical."

The silence that follows is made even more awkward because I'm dreading what I know she's going to bring up next.

*Sorry,* I mouth at Alex, who still looks uncomfortable.

"Say, Rebecca—" Mum only calls me that before a lecture. "Don't you think it's all a bit soon? You've only just had your little fight with Jeff."

"Mum, that was in October. And it wasn't a little f—"

"Well, I just don't think you're thinking clearly."

I sigh. She won't listen. She never listens.

"Anyway, I was planning to visit next week. So, let's have lunch on Saturday. Bring the new boy if you must. But I really don't think—"

"Mum, I really must get ready for work, or I'll be late. Next week Saturday is fine. We'll text about where and when to meet up."

"OK. Bye, darling." Click.

Ugh. Talk about a morning ruined.

"So, your mum seems like quite a character. She called me Jeff over and over, even after I introduced myself."

"Oh God, I'm so sorry. I didn't expect her to call this early."

He attempts a smile and takes the phone from my hand.

"You really are going to get late on your first day at this rate."

"Shit, you're right. Thanks." I don't know whether to even mention the lunch plan. If the preceding phone call was uncomfortable, lunch with Mum would be unbearable. I'm not sure I can subject Alex to that, at least not yet.

He follows me into the bedroom while I rummage through my wardrobe on the lookout for that special first-day outfit. Truthfully, any old skirt and blouse combo will do though. I'd rather have them be impressed with my work than my dress sense.

"So, Saturday…" Alex says, while running his hand over his chin. "I take it you're no longer free then?"

"Lunch. With Mum. She said you could come, but I don't think that'd be… wise."

"You don't want me to meet your mother?"

"No, no. It's just that it'll be painfully awkward."

I hurriedly put on my clothes and do my hair while he continues to watch.

"Tonight I should probably show my face at home. It's not ideal, being back with my folks, but I've no choice until I get a job." Alex sounds glum. It must be hard being out of work. His parents sound easier to live with, after all he's got the whole perfect family life thing going on. But still I'm sure he can't wait to get out on his own.

"About that, I'll talk to my old boss again to see if he's willing to interview you."

"Thanks. I'll call you."

"If you don't, I will." We smile at each other for a moment, share a slightly sore kiss and off I go. He's going to let himself out when ready.

✱✱✱

"Sal!" I shout, trying to catch up with her.

She turns and gives me a warm hug.

"Becks, finally! Exciting, right? This is the first day of a new chapter of our lives." She grins and puts her arm through mine as we walk towards the large, glass-fronted building. Halfway up, large lettering in silver and blue spells the name of our new employer: Aspect Technologies.

This is indeed a change from our earlier place of work.

We make our way inside and I'm perfectly happy to let Sally take the lead. She knows where we're going, or is at the very least successfully pretending to.

When we get out of the elevator at hopefully the correct floor, she spies a familiar face and waves. The man in the perfect looking suit, with the even more perfect looking hair walks over and shakes first her hand, then mine.

"Good morning, Sally—and you must be Rebecca. I'm Mark. Lovely to meet you! And welcome."

Tall, broad and athletic, as well as impeccably dressed. I can see why Sally's kept in touch with him: he's totally her type. And yet, I'm not sure why she's continued to play the field ever since they first met. The way he looks at her suggests he likes her too. Could he be married?

"Thanks, please call me Becky. Quite a nice set up you have here," I remark and meet his smile, before his gaze is distracted by Sally's presence again. Yep, he definitely likes her.

"Indeed. I'm sure you'll feel at home in no time, Becky. My assistant, Cath, will get you two settled. I've a few things to attend to this morning."

No sooner does Mark mention her name, than a woman who must be Cath walks up to us and greets us as well. Before long, we're shown around the office floor and provided with folders with important HR paperwork and cardboard cups of tea. Or in Sal's case, coffee.

Our desks are beside each other, as I had hoped. While we figure out where everything is, Cath makes her excuses before returning to her desk nearer Mark's office. We're promised some time to read the short training manual, before someone from IT will come and set up our email. Later this morning, Mark will apparently give us a short presentation about the business and yet another colleague will give us some more training in the afternoon. There's no time for a cheeky message to Alex, nor a proper catch up with Sally until much later.

***

The first chance I get, as prescribed by our office rules, I log into my private email at the start of lunchtime and fire a quick email off to Craig asking how things are going over there. He responds immediately in his standard work style: short, no word wasted, yet professional. I'm thinking it's tough without the both of us. I suggest Alex to him as a possible replacement. Sure, he'd need training, but realistically, so would everyone else. Craig is going to think about it.

No sooner am I done, than Sally suggests we check out the local area for lunch options. Apparently Cath told her about some takeaways and cafés nearby that we might like. By the time I've got something to eat, I see that there are three unread messages waiting for me on my mobile. Alex…

*He's just leaving my place and wondering how things are going for me…*

From an hour later: *He's wondering when we can see each other next, perhaps the day after tomorrow, after I get off work…*

Another thirty minutes later: *About next week Saturday, do I actually not want him to come to lunch with Mum or what…*

I furiously tap away at a response, while Sal's busy checking her Facebook on her own phone in between bites from the sandwiches we bought. Alex sure has been thinking about me a lot, which is sweet. But it looks like perhaps he's been over-thinking as well.

Saturday's lunch plan is not something I can refuse. But if I were him I'd welcome the chance to avoid it.

*Day-after: a definite yes to meeting up! Lunch with Mum: it's up to him, I wouldn't want to go myself, except that I kinda have to.* I also let him know I had a quick exchange with Craig about him.

When I put the phone down, I see Sally watch me intently, her head cocked to one side, with a sly little smile on her face.

"So you're boyfriend-girlfriend now, eh? So sweet." Her tone suggests amusement, as well as a hint of sarcasm.

"Yeah, you should try it sometimes."

She rolls her eyes at my suggestion.

"I think I like my life as it is, thank-you-very-much." She's still smiling. In her own way I know she's happy for me, even if we'll never fully understand each other.

"So, gimme the details then. How was your New Year after you ran off with the boy?"

When I hesitate for a moment, she nudges me into

action. When she says *details,* she really does mean *details.*

"Let's just say there was nothing shy about everything we did once we got home." I sip my tea for much longer than necessary, just to torture her a bit.

Finally, I cave and tell her almost everything. There's no way Sal would let us return to office otherwise.

"He doesn't sound much like a virgin, you must've taught him pretty well." Sally winks at me and dabs the corners of her lips with her napkin, before piling it on her now empty plate.

"There wasn't much to teach, honestly. He's the most attentive lover ever."

"As far as you know."

"I can't say I've experienced the same sample size you have, but I'm satisfied."

"Uh-huh."

"Say, that reminds me. What's the whole story with you and Mark anyway? The way he looks at you suggests he really likes you... Plus, he's super hot."

Sally shrugs and prepares to get up, dodging the question with an over-the-top gesture checking the time on her watch. I rush behind her, out the door and back towards our new office.

"Seriously? Nothing? After I just gave you a scene-by-scene account of how Alex and I christened the whole apartment?"

"I dunno, he's OK I suppose. But I'm not ready to be tied down by any one man. Not yet anyway." With that, Sally is done talking.

I guess it was a predictable response. Had I asked

about his measurements and performance stats, she would've spilled all. But for some reason she really hates all the other stuff. Emotions. Strings that can get attached in awkward, painful places. I wonder if I'll ever find out why she feels that way.

# CHAPTER TWO

When I meet Alex again, it's after I get home from my second day at the office, just as agreed during our numerous messages and lengthy phone call in between. He says he's been waiting for me for 'only a minute', but I'm sceptical. I find myself flustered, staring at the bouquet of roses he brought for me, before thinking to unlock the front door.

"Do you not like them?" Somehow, less than forty-eight hours apart have made things a little weird again. Everything still seems so new and fragile.

"Love them. Thank you!" I shoot him a wide smile and lean in for a kiss which he immediately responds to. Things may be fragile, but also beautifully simple.

"Thought I should bring something. Technically this is our third date, depending on how you count these things."

"Not sure how the counting works, I've never really dated much…" And I don't recall the last time anyone's given me flowers, except on days when popular culture have made it almost mandatory.

"That makes two of us."

We retreat into my living room, for our very untraditional second or third date—depending on how you count it. Apparently he'd like to cook me dinner. It's a sweet gesture, considering I'm not that motivated myself after working all day. My head's still spinning with all the new things they've tried to teach Sally and me.

Being near him after the short time apart, catching his unmistakable scent in the air is making me want to skip straight to dessert. The weaker version of it that's been lingering on my pillow since our last "date", served as welcome company last night, making me crave him more.

"What?" he asks, noticing me stare.

"Sounds silly, but I missed you last night."

He stops checking out the sparse contents of my kitchen cupboards and faces me. He watches for a moment while I attempt to loosen the straps that secure my pumps.

"I did too."

Every time he says something sweet, I'm done for.

Even that first time, when we role-played during our first night together, and I asked what he'd say to me if he was trying to chat me up... And although he would have been just acting, still it had an undeniable effect. He has a sincerity around him, a hint of vulnerability, as if he's still worried how I might respond.

I don't doubt that he indeed missed me, perhaps even more than I did him.

When he cups my face, I can't bear maintaining eye contact. I've never felt this way, I don't think. At least I don't remember it from the early days with Jeff, which feel like they happened in another lifetime.

So involved after such a short time. And for a change, I'm the one with the secrets.

"What's wrong?" he whispers.

I shake my head and allow myself to drown in his eyes again.

"Just kiss me. It's all I want."

He flashes a grin at me, which immediately lifts me.

"*That,* I can do."

I am ready to burst, either into tears or laughter, I'm not sure. His lips are so soft, they could make me weep. The sweet taste on his tongue brings back even more memories.

He rests his hands on my waist and directs me against the fridge, pressing himself against me while devouring my neck and the little bit of skin left exposed by the open collar of my blouse. It's obvious he's as affected as I am.

I start to unbutton myself but he stops me.

"No." He shakes his head and locks my wrists together into one of his hands to make his point. Helplessly pinned in place, with my arms now held firmly above my head, I wait for what he has planned for me. He reaches around and unzips my skirt, letting it fall around my ankles. Then he runs his free hand up and down my hip and sides, exploring the different textures from my plain office tights, to the smooth cotton shirt, and underneath. His fingertips leave trails of goose bumps on my flesh, which continue to sting deliciously even after his attention has moved on.

Then, he releases me from his grasp, leaving me hanging.

"Now take it off." His voice is raw, full of need.

Our relationship may have started with me firmly in

charge, but I can't deny this new dynamic is extremely hot. So I obey, unbuttoning my shirt and discarding it on the floor while he looks on with his right hand down his pants.

I unclasp my heels and kick them aside, then I rid myself of every last bit of fabric that's still covering me: underwear, tights. His gaze wanders up and down my naked form, seemingly unable to focus. Do I please him?

It's weird being completely naked while he's still dressed, but it's putting me more on edge, so I'm not about to complain. It's warm in here, yet I'm covered in little goose bumps. Not for long, I hope.

"Put those back on." He nods at my shoes.

I bend down deeply to retrieve them, and he can't resist a feel of my taut ass. His hands cup my hips, squeezing impatiently. No sooner have I fastened the straps again, than he drops his jeans just enough and directs me against the counter.

Hanging on to the wooden edge with both hands, I wait for him to position himself behind me. There's no need for further foreplay, I'm dripping and I already saw he's swollen to an impressive length. He enters me with confidence, plunging deeply into me until he can go no further. I let out an involuntary gasp.

He threads his fingers through my hair and I brace against the counter, attempting to keep my legs straight and arse out, despite his continued thrusting. While I'm too busy hanging on, he has free reign over my body, tugging at my hair just hard enough for it to be hot, grazing my back with his fingernails.

There is nothing learnt about his actions. This isn't a cheap copy of something once observed in a porn movie. It's pure, basal instinct.

Our breaths quicken, sweat starts to tickle the small of my neck. He leans into me, reaching my aching nipples at last. I had been tired before, but now I'm heading towards that post-coital bliss that washes over you, sometimes without the need for an orgasm.

Then, he pulls out, takes my hand and leads me away from the counter.

"I want to see your face when I cum in you." He doesn't look directly at me when he speaks, except for a split second at the end, when his gaze meets mine.

A shiver rushes down every inch of my skin.

"Yes," I whisper. *I want to see your face too.*

He's still dressed, which frustrates me. I tug at his t-shirt, as he leads me around the living room in search of a suitable spot, but he ignores it.

"Bedroom?" I suggest.

He shakes his head and inspects the messy dining table in front of us. Brushing the stack of magazines and bills swiftly aside with his arm, he gives me another one of those looks: he means business. With my ass partially up on the table, he spreads my legs and enters me again. I hold on to him with both arms around his neck and enjoy how he instantly continues his earlier furious rhythm.

Alex's face is tense, with droplets of sweat collecting on his brow. My entire body seems focused on only one thing: pleasure, both his and mine. He continues to fuck me, forcing my legs apart as far as they'll go. His fingers dig deeply into the flesh of my thighs, and I can feel him growing more and more excited inside of me which further heightens my own arousal. With every push, he hits me deep inside, adding sweet fuel to the explosion we're inevitably heading towards.

"Baby, are you close?" He speaks through gritted teeth, teetering on the edge of control.

I'm ahead of him, and unable to answer at all. I freeze, clinging on with my legs wrapped around his waist, as my orgasm threatens to drown me. His movements slow my thighs lock up, aiming to keep him in place. My arms are similarly stuck around his neck. It's hard to breathe, impossible to cry out, at least at first. Then, I die a sweet, little death and wish this moment with him would last forever.

I'm still frozen in position, and riding the last seconds of my release when he lifts me up, and carries me across my little flat and into the bedroom. When I'm once again on my back, he brushes a few damp strands of hair out of my face and kisses me deeply, before resuming. He's still intent on seeing my face without even the slightest obstruction.

He doesn't take long, despite a short interruption where I finally manage to pull his t-shirt up and over his head. The last thrusts are almost calculated. His every effort goes towards hovering above me, with his arms locked into position, and keeping his eyes focused on me. He groans, and shudders. I lean upwards to meet him, my arms once more around his shoulders and let out a moan when I feel his relief.

Flopping back against the pillows, I let out a contented sigh. He carefully lowers himself on top of me, resting his head on my chest. We spend what feels like ages, just like this. With my fingers running through his hair, while both of us catch our breath. God knows what time it is, or what he'd planned for tonight other than this.

"You know what, let's just order takeaway," I suggest, after the post-orgasmic fog has lifted.

He mutters something in the affirmative.

With him still on me, I attempt a contortionist move to reach my feet, finally releasing them from the strappy heels. He gets the hint and helps me with the other one, until I have been freed.

"Would you like to stay the night?" I ask.

"If you want me to."

"Always."

While I mentally run through the takeaway options, he seems equally preoccupied.

I'm about to ask if he wants pizza when he jumps in with a question of his own.

"Becky, since we're like *together*, now…" He adjusts himself and pulls the duvet over the both of us.

"You've been in a relationship before, with… Anyway, I suppose it means we're exclusive then?"

My heartbeat surges again at the thought of all I'm keeping from him.

"I'd never cheat on you if that's what you're asking."

"Right."

"Seriously, I know how much it hurts, going behind someone's back. I couldn't do that." Not knowingly, anyway. Despite that mental caveat, I feel like a liar.

"Is that what ended it for you?"

I hesitate to bring up details, to rake up all that's happened with Jeff so early on in this new relationship. Isn't it best to start anew? Keep the old baggage locked up in the back of your memory until it fades into irrelevance?

"Becky?"

"Oh, sorry. I'm trying to figure it out. It was definitely part of it. Perhaps the relationship was already dead long before that."

"Sorry if this is weird. But better to learn from the past, even if it's not my own," Alex explains.

"I think we grew apart for quite some time. And then I found out he'd been…"

He looks so serious, leaning up on his elbow next to me with a slight furrow in his brow. It's endearing, and manages to make me smile despite myself.

"What?" Alex asks.

My earlier smile turns into a grin.

"You're so cute when you look all worried like that."

"Oh yeah?"

"I'll show you who's cute." He dives into my neck, nibbling and licking me until I'm incapacitated by a laughter fit. It didn't take him long to learn where it tickles the most.

# CHAPTER THREE

"Darling!" Mum gets up to give me a hug, then spies Alex waiting a couple of steps behind me and hesitates. Strange how quickly time passed this past week-and-a-half. After getting used to spending time with Alex, I was happy he insisted on coming along, even if it's already weird.

"Hi…" I awkwardly put my arms around her, never having been all that comfortable with her habit of greeting me in the most exuberant fashion ever, no matter the circumstances.

I can tell she's not all that into the standard hug and kiss routine either, possibly because she's scrutinising my choice of lunch date. And so she releases me, and I wish I could just turn around and avoid this mess.

"Nice to meet you, Mrs. Radcliffe." Alex stretches out his hand.

"Ah yes. Likewise. You must be…"

"That's Alex, Mum. My boyfriend."

She gives me a curt nod and attempts to stare him into submission. Alex, meanwhile, seems to be handling things a lot better than I am. I thought I even saw a little twitch in the corner of his mouth when I said the word *boyfriend*.

"I do hope we didn't make you wait too long," Alex says, while pulling out a chair for me.

Before Mum gets the chance to answer, the waiter arrives carrying two more menus. That's when I notice the empty glass towards her side of the table. She has been waiting, even though we're five minutes early.

We get settled in, order a round of drinks, and hastily try to choose our food while Mum looks on. She's had time to decide before we even walked in.

I wish she wouldn't have this ability to make me feel so self-conscious. Still, every time I glance over at Alex, my nerves calm a little. I'm glad he's decided to come.

"So, Alex—was it?" Mum leans back in her seat and looks at him for a few seconds. "What do you do?"

Of course. It's a logical first question to ask, but I wish we could skip that one.

"Currently I'm looking. It's been tough, not a lot of demand out there for new graduates."

The silence after his answer is enough for me to guess what she's thinking. She's not pleased. She's never pleased.

"But thanks to Becky—" Alex shoots me a quick smile. "I had an interview last week and I think it went quite well."

"Let's hope so. Money worries are not the best basis for a relationship," Mum remarks dryly.

The drinks arrive, providing a welcome interruption.

"Mum, why don't you tell us about your trip," I try and steer the conversation in a more pleasant direction.

"Oh, just lovely. Egypt is such a special place. Next time, you should come along, Rebecca."

I force a smile and nod.

My next encouraging question sets the course for a lengthy report of the Nile cruise she took. Apparently the place was wonderful, but next time she'll book with another company because she didn't like the tour guide. I decide it's not worth the hassle to try and explain that they probably have multiple guides so it would be unlikely to end up with the same one again.

By the time our food arrives, Alex has managed to get a few specific questions in, which hopefully should endear him to her. I didn't even realise he had an interest in Egyptology, but apparently this is something he has always shared with his dad. While poking and prodding around in my risotto, I wonder what today's lunch date would have been like, had we met with his parents instead. They sound like lovely people. I'm sure there'd be a lot less weirdness—

I'm jerked back to reality with a nudge under the table.

"What?" I look around at both of them.

Alex gives me a look I can't quite decipher, while Mum's left eyebrow is raised, and her fork raised in the air as if she was using it to conduct an orchestra.

"I was just telling your mother how we celebrated New Year's Eve together."

I swallow, hard, remembering all too well how we ended up celebrating. My cheeks threaten to turn a deep crimson.

"The concert," Alex adds.

"Yes, right. We went to a party. Sally was there too."

"Ah, how is she?" Mum asks.

I shrug. "Fine, same old. It's nice that we still get to work together at the new place."

"Such a sweet girl."

With that, Alex gives me a questioning look. *Sweet?*

"I don't think you've ever told me how you two met?" Mum asks.

"Umm… Back in November…" This time, I'm definitely red-faced; I can feel it. Damn.

"Internet dating," Alex interjects. Mum's attention turns to him again, giving me the chance to sip my water.

"Yeah, after talking some online, we decided to meet at a local cinema," I add.

"In November?" Mum repeats.

We nod.

"I thought you were still with Jeff back then."

I sigh. She knows very well that wasn't the case. I don't know what I thought would happen, meeting her for lunch. Now, I'm pretty sure we're heading for the inevitable. The thing that always happens: an argument.

"We had already broken up by then," I remind her, through gritted teeth.

Alex's face has fallen a bit. He had tried, throughout, to keep things cheery. He had been invaluable, the only reason we made it through the meal without any mishaps. I'm sorry he's had to go through this bullshit.

"Right." Mum dabs her lips, leaving stains of burgundy lipstick on the crisp white napkin, and places it next to her plate.

I push my chair back, and avoid Alex's gaze.

"I'm going to go freshen up. Care to join me, Mum?"

She nods, no doubt pleased to get a moment alone with me to give me one of her lectures.

"Excuse us, please," I tell Alex, attempting to disguise the frustration in my voice.

It starts the moment I push open the door to the ladies' room.

"I know you're not going to like this, Rebecca, but believe me I'm only looking out for you."

"Spare me the nonsense, Mother. I know what you're trying to do." I make a show of checking myself in the mirror.

"This thing with *Alex*, you're just doing this to annoy me, aren't you? You knew I wouldn't approve." She's standing behind me, her hands on her hips, I can see her reflection.

"I don't care whether you approve or not." I turn away from the mirror and we both stare at each other for a moment.

"He wasn't the reason you and Jeff…" She trails off.

"What? No! No matter how much you like to twist things, it *was* already over when I met Alex."

"It didn't need to be, and you know it."

"He was talking to his ex behind my back! I found pictures and everything!"

"He's a man! That's what men do! It's our job as women to keep them from getting bored and distracted."

"And that went *so* well for you and Dad, didn't it?" A toilet stall opens next to us and a flustered looking elderly lady steps out and rushes to the sink to flee the firing zone. I wonder whether to apologise on our behalf, but I'm just too damn pissed off to follow through.

"Mum. I'm leaving now. Alex is great, he appreciates me in a way Jeff never did. And if you can't accept that, then don't bother calling me next time you're in town."

I stalk off towards the door, while Mum still continues, trying to get a last word in.

"Of course he appreciates you, he knows you can do much better!" I try give the door an almighty slam but it's one of those dampened affairs they favour in public places. It's very unsatisfying.

How dare she?

I can't help wondering why we can't just meet up for a meal like a normal family. Just catch up, be nice to one another and not end things with a shouting match.

"You OK?" Alex looks like he's regretted the question before even uttering it. Tears are stinging in my eyes and I'm having a hard time catching my breath, when all I want to do is scream.

"Let's just go. I'm sure *she* can manage the bill."

Alex shakes his head and retrieves his wallet from his back pocket anyway, to leave our share. I wait, while eyeing the corridor leading to the toilets, hoping she doesn't come back and make a scene here too.

Thankfully, all is still clear when we leave.

"Do you want to talk about it?" Alex asks, when he puts his arm around me, in a vain attempt at battling the chilly January winds outside.

"Not really," I say. "I just don't understand why we

can't just have a nice meal together. What's her fucking problem with *everything* I do?"

He pulls me closer against him, and the first tears start to roll down my face.

"Why do I get the feeling it would've turned out quite different had we met your folks instead?"

"They'll adore you."

I try to smile through the hurt. Knowing he's probably right makes the current mess worse.

★★★

When we get back to my place, I'm still quiet, as is he.

"So, your mum. She really must have liked that Jeff guy, eh?"

"Bullshit. She never liked him while we were together. She never likes any choices I make."

"I'm sure she's just trying to look out for you…" Alex looks helpless, I'm not sure if he's trying to convince me or himself as well.

I shrug.

"Anyway, let's just forget about it."

Not sure whether it's just trying to change the topic, or a desperate demand for closeness, but I put my arms around him, and surrender when he responds. Some kisses and cuddles later, things inevitably progress onto the couch. Our shared affections soothe me, but I'm unable to put the disaster that was lunch completely out of my mind.

"Becky?" Alex's voice brings me back to earth and I pause mid-kiss, waiting for what comes next.

"You're not OK, are you?" he asks.

"That obvious, eh?" I sigh and sit back into the cushions.

"Kinda, yeah." There's an uncomfortable silence during which he continues to observe me.

"Actually, lately I've often wondered if you're fully there when we're together." He looks away, he must be worried about how I'll react.

My eyes sting again. I'd tried my best to keep it together, to not let my guilt and concerns ruin the time we spent together. But it's no use.

"I like being with you," I whisper, almost too quietly for him to hear.

He did though, and reacts with a shrug.

"Dunno, maybe it's normal. Newness wearing off and all." He runs his fingers through his hair but still refuses to look at me properly. "Unless of course you're having second thoughts and just don't want to hurt my feelings by admitting it."

*No! He cannot be serious!*

Tears start to form, which I'm sure won't help the situation and I'm at a loss regarding what to do or say to convince him. Everything inside me is knotted and confused, I want to so badly spill everything, let it all out so we can move forward, but surely he'll just be more hurt.

"That's not true!" I sob. "I really like you. I think I…"

"What?"

"I love you." Hearing these words come out of my

own mouth freaks me out. I just hope he doesn't overreact or worse, think I'm messing with him.

From the corner of my eye, I try to get a read on what he's thinking, without staring blatantly. If he wants to just ignore the L-word, that's fine. It's too soon. Today is turning out rather badly, and I can't make out what he's thinking at all.

Finally, he stirs, but rather than speak, he just puts his arm around me and holds me tight.

It's a relief, being in his embrace does tend to make me feel safe. But I can't shake the tightness in my chest and the tears keep flowing steadily. There's no way I can say anything else, without screaming out everything I've tried so hard to forget.

We sit like this for a while, with nothing more to talk about. It's just weird for the moment, things will work themselves out, surely.

When he leaves some time later, I'm strangely numb to everything. I let him go and wonder if he'll call later, but I dare not ask the question.

# CHAPTER FOUR

Five days have passed and I've not heard much from Alex. I definitely scared him off telling him I love him. There's nothing to it but to give him space. I know that, and yet it feels like the worst thing ever. What if he decides all this emotional crap isn't worth it?

This never happened with Jeff, he never ran off and avoided me, at least not that I remember. He always stuck around, until things went totally south. Why do relationships have to be so complicated?

Taking another deep breath nearly calms all the various fears that have started racing around in my head. Nearly.

I focus once again on the login screen in front of me. Fetlife. I haven't dared to look at it ever since the New Year. I didn't want to draw attention to how it all started, for fear of making him suspicious that I had had more "experiences" after our first encounter.

The page loads at a crawl and I'm terrified of what I might find. He said he'd had interest from other girls lately. It's hard not to feel jealous about that. Maybe that's why he hasn't been in touch, maybe…

The newsfeed appears and I can see a bunch of messages, friend requests I've been ignoring, and—

He's uploaded a few more pictures. They're innocent enough, compared to what was already there, but why would he even log on if he was happy with me? *Goddamnit.*

I slam the laptop lid shut, needing to get away from what absolutely must be damning evidence of where his thoughts are at.

Before I lose my last shreds of sanity, I decide I need a pep talk, from the worst person in the world to take relationship advice from. I'm going to have to do my best to keep it together for a few hours until lunchtime when Sal and I can escape somewhere more private. As nice as our new colleagues are, I'm not ready to spill all on the main office floor just yet.

*** 

Before I get the chance to broach the subject with Sally, she's already looking at me suspiciously and ignoring the tempting sandwich wrap on the table in front of her.

"Trouble in paradise?" Sally squints at me, seemingly taking in every detail of my reaction.

I sigh and shrug.

"How could you tell?"

"You've been drifting around on cloud nine lately, except this week. And today you just look like you're about to cry. What did he do? Do I need to hunt him down and kick him in the balls for you?" Sally leans back with her arms crossed, while I wonder where to begin.

"I can't decide if Jeff has made me paranoid, but I'm wondering if perhaps Alex isn't content just with me, you know?"

"But you've only just started dating. And his eyes are wandering already? Who the hell does he think he is?"

She's starting to sound annoyed too. If I'm not careful, she'll indeed do something crazy in my defence.

"I don't know... We had a bit of a—well not a fight—but things got a bit awkward last Saturday after lunch."

"Your mother could make the bravest man in the world wee himself, you know that. I didn't want to say anything, but taking him to meet her maybe wasn't the best idea."

Sal might be a self-confessed party girl who refuses to take life all that seriously, but she's always there for me when I need her. I breathe a sigh of relief that finally I can talk about all this stuff. She's correct of course, it was a terrible idea, but that's not even the half of it.

"It was super awkward, I have to give you that. And it just got worse from there. He seemed to be able to tell that something is off with me generally. It was like he could see right through me and knew I'm keeping things from him."

"Shit. You didn't tell him, did you?" Sally's eyes widen at the terrible prospect of me spilling all my secrets.

"Worse. I said the L-word."

"Jesus, woman! What, two weeks in?"

"I know! I'm a fucking idiot." I hang my head in regret.

"How did he take it?"

"He didn't say a word, just hugged me and then a little while later said he had to go do whatever and left. I don't know."

"Ouch."

"I haven't heard from him since." I hear my voice crack as this morning's horrors attempt to overwhelm me. "He's been logging on to Fetlife as well, even uploaded more pictures and stuff. I only saw this morning, and don't know what to think. I've been keeping well away ever since we got together, just because I thought that would be the proper thing to do..."

"Ah. I get it. So you think he's still playing the field, yeah? What a douche canoe. You know how I feel about monogamy, but that's my business. You deserve a guy who will treat you how you want to be treated, you know?" Sal's hand finds its way onto my shoulder and I do everything in my power to not create a scene and cry in full view of a coffee shop full of office workers.

"Yeah. Thanks." Despite my best efforts, my eyes moisten, but I swallow down the lump in my throat and take a deep breath. "It was never going to be that simple. We barely know each other."

"OK, tell you what. The last thing you need right now is some asshole to make you feel like shit. It sucks now but you'll be better off."

"I guess."

"I mean it, Becks. Do not call him! If he calls you, ignore him. You've made yourself vulnerable on Saturday, and apparently the both of you aren't on the same page. Suck it up and carry on. You can do better."

"I s'pose." She's right, I made a huge mistake. I should've never said it. And I should've insisted on doing lunch without him. What an idiot I am.

"Don't call him, you hear me?" Sal reaches over and gives me a hug. "And on Saturday, we're totally going shopping, and you'll buy the hottest dress ever, and then we have a Girl's Night Out, and be obnoxious cock teases and stay out until we're asked to leave."

I can't help but smile at the prospect.

"Let's see."

✳✳✳

The rest of the day I do my best to convince myself that anyone who would throw my love away like that isn't worth my time. At five, I almost believe it. By the time I get home, barely half an hour later, my best intentions are in tatters. The only reason I don't cave and call him to ask why he's avoiding me rather than just manning up and telling me it's over, is because the phone rings. *Shit.*

I stare at his name blinking on screen, while the *Game of Thrones* theme music continues to play on a never-ending loop. *Shit, what do I do?*

My finger hovers over the screen, ready to either hang up or pick up, but I'm still hesitating. Let's just get it over with already. The quicker this mess is cleared up, the sooner I can once again focus on healing and moving on. I pick up and bring the phone to my ear, only to be met by a weird dinging noise and then, nothing. I was too late. *Shit, shit, SHIT!*

I'm not sure I would have wanted him to, but am still disappointed not to see the voicemail icon pop up. Should I call back? I can still hear Sally's voice ringing in my ears from earlier on; *do not call him, you hear me.* But she also said I shouldn't pick up, and yet I tried to do just that.

And what does she know about relationships, anyway?

The phone buzzes in my hand and I drop it onto the floor as my ringtone starts off again. This time I rush to retrieve it and answer straightaway.

"Hello?" My voice trembles slightly with nerves. I just hope he doesn't notice.

"Hey! Sorry I haven't called these past few days, but I had some stuff to take care of at home. Would you like to meet up?"

"Uh, OK." The words escape my lips before I have the time to think about what's happening.

"Great, so, how about tomorrow at seven? Do you know The King's Head just off Bath Road?"

"Yep."

"I'll be waiting outside." Click.

I stare at my phone, the screen dark once again. Did this seriously just happen? Did I just agree to meet Alex at a pub in town tomorrow, with no explanation regarding where he's been these last few days? He sounded cheerful, as if nothing ever happened…

Well I suppose I'll find out soon enough, but there's no way I can tell Sal about any of this, she'll have me for breakfast.

# CHAPTER FIVE

Although difficult, I managed to keep my evening plans, and the phone call that lead to them, a total secret from Sally. This is something I must sort out for myself. As I take the elevator down, ready to leave work for the day and battle the cold darkness outside, I can't help obsessing about what's going to happen in a short twenty minutes from now.

Overnight, I have been worrying, unable to sleep for hours, wondering over and over why Alex might be acting so strangely. After all, he could have just continued to avoid me, if he wanted to be a coward about it. Or even just tell me to my face that I've jumped the gun. Eventually, and exhaustedly, I decided to give him the benefit of the doubt. For now.

It doesn't seem so simple anymore. Can I just show up there, smile and pretend all is well when in fact I've had to rethink our entire relationship after my faux pas on Saturday?

The pub is only a short bus ride away, apparently. I've not come this way often, it's pretty much in the opposite direction from where I and everyone I know lives.

A look at the time reveals I'm going to be slightly early. Despite the cold weather, my hands are clammy and my cheeks have burnt up. Is the slightest glimmer of a happy love life really worth all this?

When I get off the bus, the cold hits me like a knife

piercing right through the thick fabric of my coat. I shiver again when I turn the corner and see Alex standing in front of the pub already, conveniently lit up by the streetlight. In his hand he's holding a bunch of flowers that look like they're about to freeze to death as well.

"Hey," I say, trying keep my teeth from chattering.

He steps forward and hugs me. *As if nothing ever happened! What the hell!*

"What's wrong?" he asks, probably noticing that I'm about as huggable as a stone obelisk right now.

"I'm confused."

He looks at me as if he wants to say something, but just hands me the flowers.

"These are for you."

I accept the pink roses, mumbling my thanks. This was cute the first time, but back then the roses were red. Now they're pink. What does it mean?

"I have a surprise for you," Alex says, gesturing at me to come with him.

I'm a little bit disappointed we're not actually going inside the pub, because a drink and warm surroundings seem like a brilliant idea right now. But intrigue spurs me onward.

"So these last couple of days, a few things happened…" Alex starts. "But we can go into that later."

Goddamnit. An explanation about the last few days is exactly what I need the most right now!

"First…" He turns into a little alley between two

houses and urges me on with his hand on my shoulder. "I'd like to…"

"Where are we going?" I ask, finally unable to stay quiet.

"My new place," he beams.

I look around at the dark façade of something that looks like it might have been a garage at some point. Or a shed. But it's got proper windows and a door…

He unlocks the door and lets it swing open, turns on the light and beckons me inside.

"Really? How?" I look around at the blank room, which currently only contains a couple of chairs, an inbuilt kitchenette on the side, and a dark doorway right opposite.

"I got the job!" Alex grins. "Months and months of searching, I was about ready to give up but thanks to you, that old boss of yours actually hired me… Surprise!"

I don't know what to say.

"Look, I know it's not much, but I've got to start somewhere."

"It's… wow." It's starting to dawn on me that maybe, just maybe, he may have had a legitimate reason behind not calling or getting in touch for a few days, even if the execution—and timing—of this master plan were absolutely terrible. That maybe, my own fears may have just gotten away from me a little bit and made this into a much bigger deal than it actually was.

"Congratulations," I say at last, then continue staring at the room. Although it's the last thing I want, I can feel the tears coming. I'm not sure yet if I'm relieved, angry, just tired.

"Hey! It's not that bad. A few trips to Ikea and it'll be like a whole different place!"

"It's not that. Dammit I've been so worried after Saturday. I thought you'd—" I take a deep breath and try and compose myself again.

"That I'd what?" Alex asks, with a serious frown on his face.

Oh bloody hell, he's totally clueless. And I feel like a ginormous idiot right now.

"Never mind. You're right. A few bits of furniture, maybe some new curtains—" I run my fingertip reluctantly over the suspect fabric covering the window. "And it'll feel like home."

"Just you wait till I get paid! I'll prove it to you." Alex takes my hand and I instinctively thread my fingers through his.

He pulls me closer and I follow.

"You haven't even seen the best part yet," he whispers in my ear, and nods at the dark doorway.

Together we walk the first few steps, until he stays back and I continue on. I find the light switch on the inside of the wall by touch, and when the light comes on, I can't hold back a surprised giggle.

Inside the otherwise equally blank and depressing room, there's a fully made-up bed with a gift hamper right in the centre of it, containing a bottle of champagne, two glasses and an envelope with my name on it.

I go closer, knees trembling almost as much as my hands, and pick up the envelope. Inside is a card that reads simply:

*Becky, you're the best thing that's ever happened to me. I love you too.*

That does it. Now my eyes do get moist.

Alex comes up behind me and wraps his arms around my waist.

"On Saturday I realised that all of this—you and me—is quite a hard sell. In your mum's place I might not have been thrilled to meet me either."

I lean back against him, still too overwhelmed to say anything much.

"Of course I'd wanted to move out anyway, but as soon as I got the official job offer I decided to speed things along. Now at least you're no longer dating some broke loser who still lives with his parents."

"I never thought that about you." But obviously Mum disagrees with me like she always does.

Alex gives me a quick kiss on the side of my head, before letting go and sitting down on the bed.

"What do you say we crack this thing open." He picks up the bottle and gives me a questioning look.

I smile in agreement and take a seat next to him. There's so much going on in my head, I'm not sure where to start. Or if I should even say anything at all. The worst thing right now would be to ruin the moment with my usual bad timing and bluntness.

He hands me a glass and pours himself one too.

"To your new digs," I say, while raising it in his

direction.

"To being a responsible, working man," he responds, clinking his glass against mine.

The cold liquid sends a shiver down my spine, but I don't mind anymore. Despite the cold appearance, it's actually quite warm in here, he must have had the heating on.

"So when do you plan to move your stuff in?"

"Over the weekend. I plan to borrow Dad's car."

"And when is your first day at work?" I lean back on my hand and observe him as I take another sip.

"Monday." He smiles at me and reaches over to stroke my face.

My heartbeat surges and I close my eyes. I can't do this. I can't...

"Until just now, I thought you wanted to call it quits," I blurt out, and immediately wish I could vanish on the spot.

"Wait, what? Why the hell would you think that?!" Alex looks horrified.

"Obviously I get it now, but you went all awkward on Saturday, and then I didn't hear from you. I decided to give you space to figure it out. I panicked."

"You did seem quite standoffish on the phone, and then earlier. I was wondering what that was all about."

"I'm sorry. As I said, I panicked." In a way, I still am.

I stare down at the glass in my hand. In a moment, a misunderstanding, an argument, everything that we have could disappear. Secrets, even well intentioned ones, can ruin all we have. Plus I have no hope in hell of keeping my big mouth shut forever. Wouldn't it be worse if he found out everything much later into our relationship?

And what about the extra pictures I found on Fetlife yesterday morning? Do I even want to know what that's all about?

"I need to tell you something." Despite having realised that this is the best thing to do, I'm still terrified.

"Shoot." Alex puts down his glass on the floor and watches me intently.

"I haven't wanted to mention this, because I was so scared about how you'd feel about it."

"Right."

My throat snaps shut and I feel light-headed. I'm unable to look him in the eye.

"Craig…"

"Yeah, I know," Alex interjects.

"You do?"

"Well, I had my suspicions."

I'm speechless, and only partially because the jackhammer inside my chest has refused to calm down. He looks at me with an amused half-smile.

"That first time at your place, I was trying to find my phone after getting up in the morning. I came across this on the living room floor…" Alex pulls out his wallet from the back pocket of his jeans and fishes out a folded-up piece of paper. A torn off bit of notepaper. He smooths it out against his thigh and hands it to me.

*The list.*

"Holy shit," I gasp.

"Let's just say a few things started to click into place when I saw it."

My own handwriting screams out to me until the items on the list appear to be dancing on the paper. It wouldn't have been hard to put two and two together, considering I had already crossed off half of the items.

"I had wanted to throw that away. So that both of us would have a real chance together."

"You thought I would disapprove?" Alex is putting on his best poker face now, but the glint in his eyes gives him away. Unless I'm only seeing what I want to see.

I shrug in response, still unable to find the words to properly explain it.

"Remember what you said the first time we talked online?" he asks.

"What."

"That you wanted crazy experiences. I knew the deal, even if the circumstances were slightly different." Seeing my still bewildered expression finally does make him crack a smile.

"It's OK! What happened before isn't really my business, is it? You didn't owe me anything. I felt like I didn't deserve someone like you, but there you were anyway." Alex's expression grows thoughtful. "I'm already the luckiest guy in the world."

"But…" I blink a few times, wondering if maybe this is all a dream, and actually it's still Wednesday morning, and things still seem impossible between the two of us.

"I'm sorry," I say, because I can't think of anything

else.

"Don't be." He reaches over and takes my hand.

"I just wish I could've seen it happen," Alex says, his tone suddenly turning playful again.

A chill runs down my spine and fragmented memories of that encounter in Craig's office hit me again. Alex would have liked to watch?

"You wouldn't have been jealous?" I ask, still unable to quite believe where the conversation has gone.

He shrugs and plays with my fingers, picking them up one by one and straightening them over his palm.

"It's something of a fantasy of mine." He doesn't look at me as he speaks. Opening up must be awkward for him too.

*Holy fucking shit.* Of all the ways I thought this confession could go, this wasn't one of them.

"Just watching, or…?" The question escapes me before I can rein myself in.

All this time, I was thinking the fact that I was his first meant he'd be a lot more old-fashioned about sex. Although I do remember some of the stuff on his online profile hinted that this might not be the case, I somehow assumed things would be different in the context of a relationship. Could I have been so off the mark?

Alex weighs my hand in his, then closes his other one around it and looks back at me but only briefly.

"Honestly, I don't know. I'd hope to do more than just watch, but so far I've not had the chance to find out…"

He lets go of me, kicks off his sneakers and sits back against the pillows with his legs folded.

The thought of Alex watching me, whether with Craig or someone else, perhaps even joining in, is impossibly tempting. I'm trying to stay grounded in reality, but can't help imagining what it would be like. Could I share him with someone else as he thinks he could share me? I know people do this type of stuff. People much more adventurous and experienced than me. *Could I?*

Ever since we've been together, I haven't felt the need to think about anyone else. But if he was on board with it… That would change everything.

"Maybe we could figure it out together?" I whisper.

I put my glass next to his on the floor, the hamper as well, and join him after taking my own shoes off as well.

This time, now that everything's out in the open, I feel like he truly sees me for who I am, and I see him. Our kisses feel more real, every touch makes me tremble. When he enters me, I am truly his for the first time.

# CHAPTER SIX

*Be dressed up and ready by nine.*

I stare at the note, and the tiniest little black dress in the box below it.

Turning the note over tells me nothing further. I flip it back how I found it and study it some more. The handwriting is obviously Alex's. Who else would send me a dress, or any gift at all? And such a sexy number too. I struggle to think when I'd normally wear such a garment.

And nine o'clock is quite a weird time to meet up. Am I supposed to eat dinner on my own beforehand? His proposition, and the gift are intriguing enough for me to just go along with it. Whatever he's been thinking, there must be some kind of plan.

For the past couple of weeks things have been better than ever between us. Finally coming clean has been such a relief, I can hardly recall why I was so scared before. Sure, most guys might have freaked out just a little bit at the thought of their girlfriend and their new boss going at it during an office Christmas party, but I should've realised that Alex is different. Alex is—

"Hey, are you just going to stand there like a total loser or let me know what's going on?" Sal puts her hands on her hips and juts out her chin in fake outrage.

"This is private, go be nosy somewhere else." I close the box and attempt to hide it under my desk, but she's not letting me off that easily.

"If you're going to be receiving gifts at work, be prepared to have them inspected by me!" Sally smiles pretend-sweetly and snatches the gift box right out of my hands.

"Ohh... love the dress!" Yeah, of course she would.

"Not sure what Alex has planned, but…"

"Clubbing maybe? I mean, nine is kinda late for dinner…" Sally muses.

"That's what I thought."

She runs her fingers over the fabric of the dress again before handing the box back.

"You must tell me everything on Monday. Ideally before that, but definitely on Monday."

I smile and nod. We shall see.

Since Alex and I have properly confided in each other, we've also become a lot more experimental and expressive in the bedroom. In between the occasional dirty talk, he's mentioned all sorts of naughty ideas. At the time I wondered if they'd remain fantasies forever. Could he be planning something rather more real for tonight?

***

I'm ready by eight-fifteen. It would have been better had I kept busy with other stuff all evening, leaving no time to wonder about Alex's plan, but predictably the opposite happened. As soon as I got home, I simply had to try the dress on to see how revealing it would be. His choice impresses me: it's surprisingly elegant for something so short.

Choosing the right pair of shoes to go with the dress could not be stretched beyond half an hour. Add to that the slowest make-up application in the history of mankind and I'm still early.

I pace around the living room, making the occasional trip to the window to look outside. Maybe he's going to be early too. Or maybe not.

I'm all pins and needles by the time I finally see some promising movement outside. A taxi. He doesn't normally come by taxi, but sure enough, the vehicle pulls up right outside and a silhouette steps out and heads towards my building.

Just when I'm about to give up on the idea that it might have been Alex, I hear a knock on my door. *What a drama queen; he has a key!*

But I play along and open it up.

We don't say a word to each other at first, just look. He's made an effort too. A black suit I haven't seen him wear before. I don't think I've ever seen him in a suit at all, just work trousers and shirts, but never a full suit. He's absolutely gorgeous. The look on his face suggests he's equally impressed, even if he chose my wardrobe for me.

"You look amazing," he says finally.

"So do you." I smile, forgetting how antsy I had been only moments earlier.

"Happy One Month Anniversary."

I'm stumped for a moment. Has it only been a month? On paper it has, but it feels like we've been a couple forever. In a good way.

"You too," I say.

"Ready to go?" he asks.

He must have made the taxi wait downstairs. I quickly grab my coat and a simple, black clutch, and nod.

"Where are we going?"

"On a date." It sounds so obvious, yet his tone tells me it's not as simple as it sounds.

"A date?"

"Yeah. I put up that ad like I said. Someone responded…" Although he's trying to hide it, I can tell he's a bit nervous. And now, I am that, multiplied by a hundred.

"Wow, seriously?" Up until this point, his idea to post another classified ad on Fetlife had felt a bit surreal. Like nothing much would come out of it. Ridiculous, of course, we met via a similar ad after all. But he'd been insistent we should at least try to make our fantasies happen.

We walk down the stairs and head straight towards the waiting cab. Alex gives the driver a name of a hotel I've never heard of.

"So tell me about this guy, the one who responded?" I have trouble keeping my voice down, my heart feels like it's beating right in my throat.

"Well, his name is Jamie, he's twenty-eight, bi…"

"Has he sent a photo? And what if we're not feeling it?"

"We're going to meet in the hotel bar and get to know each other first. No pressure to do anything we don't want to."

I'm about to ask about the photo again, but perhaps this is all part of the game. It's not just going to be a date, but a blind one.

It takes us about twenty minutes to get there, and by the end, my hands are clammy and my knees shot.

I wonder what Jamie is going to be like. Whether he's even going to like the look of us. I also wonder how far Alex would want to go. The thought of him with another guy is… interesting. But I'm getting ahead of myself, we haven't even met the guy yet.

The cab pulls up in front of a rather nice, luxurious looking building. The gold signage, spelling out the name 'Hotel Lucille', together with the classically ornate facade promise that no matter what is going to happen next, it'll take place within a beautiful setting.

Alex pays the driver and gets out, and offers me his hand to step out after him. I love it when he does such gentlemanly things.

The old-fashioned porter gets the door for us and we step into the lobby. The interior certainly delivers on what the outside of the building had already promised: luxury and opulence. Beautiful Victorian style furniture set against rich hues of gold and burgundy on the walls, yet the odd modern, quirky accent in the decor makes it look chic rather than stuffy.

We step right across the lobby and through the archway leading into the bar, where subdued lighting and background music succeed to create a relaxing atmosphere. But I'm anything but relaxed and Alex also looks tense next to me as he scans the room.

I take a look around, noting there are quite a few groups and couples occupying the various tables near us, no single men that I can see. What if the guy didn't turn up? My throat is parched and knees still week.

Then Alex gently tugs at my arm and I follow the direction he's looking in. At the other side of the bar, almost obscured by a pillar, there's a man sitting alone with his back towards us, apparently playing with his phone. The subtle music in the background is being drowned out by the relentless beating of my heart.

*Come on, Becks, you're not alone and it'll be fine!*

"Jamie?" Alex asks, and the figure with the short cropped black hair turns to reveal a handsome face with expressive brown eyes and a wide, friendly smile.

"Hey, Alex! You must be Becky. I'm Jamie." Jamie gets up and shakes our hands in turn.

Two things occur to me at once; he's hot, and I've never been with a black guy before. He's just a bit taller than me, but not as tall as Alex. His hands are soft; he looks like he really takes care of his appearance.

"Nice to meet you, Jamie," I say, noting that he looks to be quite athletic underneath the white shirt and grey waistcoat combo he has on.

We sit down, order a round of drinks and start to chat. Mainly everyday stuff for the first fifteen minutes or so, which surprises me considering what we came here for.

"Have you done this before? Met a couple in a hotel…" I ask, eager to steer the conversation somewhere more interesting.

Jamie smiles. "Only a couple of times, I'm new to the lifestyle."

"Not as new as we are," Alex remarks, while shooting me a questioning look.

I nod in the most subtle manner I can, and he reacts in kind. We're both interested. But is Jamie?

The way he's looking at both of us suggests he might be, but I'm not sure. God, this is nerve-racking. The short silence that follows feels like it lasts forever.

"Shall we head up to my room?" Jamie asks.

Wow, he already has a room? That's some foresight.

Alex, still looking at me, nods and I do too. I quickly finish my drink, and find that although the first hurdle has been crossed, I'm still feeling a bit awkward about it. Apparently Alex notices, because he puts his arm around me as we walk out of the bar and towards the lift in the lobby. Once inside the small, mirrored space, Jamie looks at us both in turn and smiles.

"Relax, this is supposed to be fun. If you're uncomfortable with anything, just say so."

I can't explain it but there's something about him, his eyes, that makes me want to trust him.

"May I?" He reaches towards me, waiting for both mine and Alex's approval.

I close my eyes, enjoying the sensation of his fingers running through my hair. Simultaneously, Alex takes my hand and starts kissing the space between my knuckles.

"You're such a cute couple. I knew coming out tonight would be a good idea."

# CHAPTER SEVEN

The doors open with the customary *ding*, and we step out, following Jamie, who seems to know exactly where he's going: the room at the end of the hallway.

Once we get inside, Alex casts off his jacket, and takes my coat and clutch bag from me. The room looks suitably opulent, with its carefully chosen colour scheme of earthy bronzes and golds; it certainly matches the expectation set by the stylish lobby and bar. There's nowhere for three people to sit, but the massive four-poster bed, so that's where I go, while watching Jamie unbutton his waistcoat.

Alex, who returned to take his spot by my side, bends down to help with my heels. Are we getting naked straightaway? Once my shoes are off, he signals I should lie back in the centre of the bed, up against the plush satin-covered scatter cushions. I adore how the smooth fabric feels against my bare legs and arms, but it's going to take a bit more mind-control to fully relax.

"Don't worry. Tonight is all for you." He takes my hand again, resuming the kissing and caressing he'd started with in the elevator.

*All for me?* Butterflies seem to swarm my stomach, and most of my nerves are replaced by excitement and curiosity.

Jamie, who has also gotten rid of his shoes, sits down on the other side of me.

"May I kiss you?" he whispers.

The thought, plus Alex's continued affections, give me goose bumps. I swallow hard, and nod.

He kneels beside me and cups my face. His skin smells fresh, slightly citrusy. It's an interesting contrast compared to Alex's richer, sweeter scent.

The moment Jamie's lips touch mine, I'm convinced of how brilliant this idea was. If I was intrigued, but still slightly nervous before, I'm all in now.

Alex has also moved up my arm, his lips nibbling at the top of my shoulder, where the broad strap of the dress ends. With my head turned towards Jamie, tasting yet more citrus on his lips and tongue, Alex has enough room to start nibbling on my neck. My ticklish spot.

Pleasure washes over me, lighting up choice parts of my body. My nipples tense, as does my stomach; right where it matters. Of course I had fantasised, at least in passing, while writing a threesome into *the list*. But to actually experience both these gorgeous men, showering me with attention, is more magical than I could have thought.

I reach for Jamie's neck on one side, encouraging the kisses to become deeper, more passionate, while running my hand down Alex's chest and stomach, until I can untuck the bottom of his shirt. The only way the here and now could get any better is if there's more skin on display, and not just mine.

Alex, who fortunately isn't wearing an undershirt, starts to unbutton, with his other hand placed on the most infuriating spot on my thigh. I wish he'd touch me higher up. Nevertheless, I'm glad to be able to touch his chest, unimpaired by clothing.

I pull back from Jamie, hoping Alex won't mind taking over. His eyes tell me he won't mind anything right now. He dives in, aiming to outdo Jamie's kisses, and succeeds. Alex's familiar taste makes me giddy. I want him.

I want both of them, differently.

Jamie, meanwhile, takes off his shirt, to reveal gorgeous, flawless skin, too irresistible not to caress as well. He scoots down the bed and begins kissing my legs, from the calf, upwards, but not all the way. I want to scream, that's how badly I crave to be touched more directly, but they seem intent on teasing me a little more.

The contrast between the two of them is beautiful. Jamie, who's mostly hairless and completely toned, versus Alex, who's luxuriously cuddly, and sporting the sexy manfur I continue to find irresistible on him. And then there's the difference in skin tone. It shouldn't matter, of course, but it does—in a good way. They're both so perfect.

Tugging at Alex's shirt, I make it come off his shoulder. He does the rest and lets it fall to the floor. Then, two pairs of hands fondle, caress, tickle and squeeze what feels like my entire body, all at once. I lean up, Alex gets the hint and unzips me. Jamie and he work together to peel me out of my dress.

While one of my hands continues to explore Jamie's sculpted physique, my other gets busy with Alex's belt, before slipping inside his trousers and finding him rock hard and ready to go. He lets out a sigh against my lips.

The lips that had earlier left teasing kisses on my inner thigh, have made their way to the outside of my hip and up my side. All the while Alex's tongue continues to almost wrestle mine. I'm intoxicated by him, his scent, which I show by stroking him, aiming to heighten his pleasure as well. It's working, the tremble in his lips tells me. Then he pulls back and out of reach.

Jamie looks up from my stomach, those expressive brown eyes as feverish as Alex's had been just a second ago. They switch places.

Alex kneels between my legs, tracing the outline of my lacy panty ever so lightly with the tip of his finger. His fingernail lightly catches on parts of the fabric, sending shockwaves through my body.

Jamie hooks his finger through my bra straps, sliding them off my shoulders and leans down for further kisses and nibbles. My collarbone, shoulder, neck, and finally, my cleavage sing under his expert teasing.

I can't take much more of this without losing patience and control. Leaning off the bed again, I unhook my bra, and struggle out of it until I can fling it across the room.

My nakedness has the desired effect.

"She's beautiful," Jamie says.

"Yes, she is."

Alex and Jamie exchange a look, an understanding, as if I'm not really there and have no control over what's going to happen next. Indeed I feel a bit helpless, slumped against the pillows once more, hoping desperately that one or both of them will soon touch me where I need it the most, now that I'm no longer covered up. My pleasure lies in their hands, yet I must trust I'll be well taken care of before tonight is over.

Alex leans over the side of the bed, away from me and just when I'm about to ask what he's doing, he returns with a blindfold in his hand. Oh my…

"Do you trust me?" he asks. I nod in response.

He carefully places it over my eyes and I lift my head to help him fasten it in the back. All becomes black, and it's hard to fight the strange sensation of falling backwards. *Please don't make me wait too long...*

Just when I'm about to cry out impatiently for someone to touch me properly already, a hand closes over my mound momentarily, forcing another type of cry out of me. Two heads dive down, each taking position over one nipple, to tease, tickle and play with me in competition as well as collaboration. I try to focus on what each is doing, but it's too much, it overwhelms me. My eyes snap shut despite already being covered and I writhe into the mattress, trying to draw them closer to me. I run my hands over their backs, the back of their necks, feeling the different texture of their hair, while both pairs of lips continue working me into a fever.

I need to find that hand again, the one that held me earlier, but it has gone. My hips grind upwards into nothing, until one of them, I can't tell which, hooks his finger into the elastic of my panties. Rather than pulling them down right away, he grazes his finger along the sensitive skin just inside, side to side a couple of times, sending me into despair. *Touch me properly, dammit!*

Another hand moves in, yanking at the panties from the other side, and finally forcing them downwards.

I try to find where Jamie and Alex are by touch, but it's difficult to, not wanting to risk poking either of them in the face and ruining the vibe. The distance between them and me seems instantly farther, now that I can no longer see.

But I can still feel their playful affections. A finger, running straight down from my belly button and finding the fold that hides my clitoris. Another couple of fingers, travelling upwards along the inside of my thigh, until they meet my soft, freshly shaven lips, already moist and begging for further attention.

Someone hitches up my leg and lays it across a warm body part, probably his thigh, but I can't be sure. . When did he get naked? Which one out of the two is it?

Lips find mine; a now familiar taste. It's Jamie again. His hand closes around the back of my neck and holds me tightly and safely in place.

I twitch and struggle against what I assume must be Alex's hands on my thighs, until I'm kissed down below as well. It's almost too much, I cry out into Jamie's mouth, and both pull away.

I hear muffled voices, but can't make out what they say. Then I hear what must be a condom packet, torn open. Is Alex going to let Jamie fuck me? That has to be it, because Alex wouldn't have a reason to use a condom...

Someone takes my hand and places it on his cock.

Smooth, silky and impressively long and thick, the erection I've wrapped my hands around feels awfully tempting. I know exactly where I'd want it, if given the chance. Two things are certain, this isn't Alex, and yet there's no condom.

But what finds its way into my other hand does feel like him. And then, both pull away again, and I'm fighting every urge not to scream out and stop teasing me. I can't let them know they've all but won.

Only seconds later, hands caress my thighs, and the mattress between my legs seems to give way. There's someone down there, but what is he going to do this time? Further kisses, tickles, light touches?

I gasp in surprise when suddenly I'm filled. This is what I wanted ever since they started their gentle torture. And it kills me that I can't see who it is.

Imagining both Jamie, then Alex, in turn, I reach out, wanting to figure it out for sure, but my hand is intercepted mid-air and held there. The stranger in the dark starts to move. Controlled thrusts, possibly holding back as much as he can. I need to see. I need to feel him against my body and I'd know.

Is it Alex? He might've wanted to have me first. But then what was the condom wrapper sound all about?

I buck my hips to meet him, to encourage him to speed up more. Never before have I felt so desperate for release as now. The hands loosen their tight grip on my wrists and I place my arms beside me. I'll play along if it means my itch gets scratched.

Lips surround my nipples almost simultaneously. A

jolt runs through me, sending me spiralling out of control ever more. I can't help it, my hands reach for them. I must feel the rather different texture of their hair against my fingertips. I must know who is doing what.

My defiance disturbs them, and the punishment is swift. The lips pull away, just before I'm able to determine who is who based on angle and positioning. Thankfully, the fucking doesn't stop. I focus on the in-and-out. The flesh against flesh when he goes deep.

In front of my face, a familiar scent appears. Salty, but pleasantly so.

I reach out for him. Yes, this is Alex's cock. I know the taste. I know how he feels in my hand. I love him. I love how he makes me feel—tonight, as well as during all the time leading up to now.

He tenses when I run my fingernails gently over his balls. He holds back a groan when tilt my head and let him enter my mouth.

I love you. *Oh my God, I love this.*

Jamie's going at it hard, but somehow there's still a certain smoothness and control to his movements, however fast. I moan into Alex's cock with each push, eager to please him in turn.

Fingers circle my nipples, which sets off an inevitable chain reaction. I scream out, albeit muffled, and time seems to freeze, before speeding up tenfold. After all that build-up, my orgasm is almost painfully good, then just painful when both men pull back again.

"No!" I whimper.

My complaint is answered almost immediately. Alex fills me, I can tell because his body presses up against mine. A feeling I know all too well.

He fucks me harder than Jamie did, through the pleasure, the pain, the confusion, until there's yet more pleasure to come. I'm helpless, swallowed up by pillows, and pinned down by my lover. He groans with pleasure, and marks me as his. With his final shudder, I erupt again, and tears stream down my face.

A long few seconds later, the blindfold is removed, and it takes me a moment to adjust my sight.

"Sweetheart, are you OK?" Alex's voice is a concerned whisper, as he wipes the moisture from my cheeks.

I can only smile and nod. *I love you.*

In the background Jamie, who somehow looks even more beautiful now than before, has finished himself off and shoots a smile my way before turning to Alex.

"Maybe next time, you and I can have a go together." The twinkle in his eye that makes me giggle, even if I'd seriously love to see that.

Alex, who's gone from complete stud to sheepish in about half a second, has no comeback. It does look like perhaps he's more interested than he's willing to let on.

Both lie down beside me, we're all in need of a little rest. Just because the main course is over, doesn't mean we can't have dessert. Arms surround me, soothing my spent body until my heartbeat has all but settled. This moment possesses a beauty of its own.

I'm not sure how much time passes before Alex stirs

and checks his watch on the night table beside him. It's time.

Not sure if we'll ever see Jamie again, that's something to figure out later. Hopefully we will, because our parting feels bittersweet. While we put our clothes back on, Jamie orders some room service. I'm sad to go, but excited for the chance of being alone with Alex. So much to discuss and think about. Tonight will stay with us forever.

We say our goodbyes, without surprises or arguments. This must have been agreed beforehand.

"It's been wonderful, thank you," I say, while offering Jamie my hand.

He kisses it gently and grins.

"The pleasure was all mine." Then he turns to Alex and nods in a way only he can understand.

* * *

"Wow, that was amazing," I whisper, hoping the cabbie doesn't overhear us.

Alex gives me a grin and squeezes my hand, before releasing it to locate his wallet. He pulls out the familiar piece of paper—my list—and a pen from his breast pocket and hands them to me.

"I suppose tonight covers both?" he suggests.

I smooth out the list against his shoulder and read through once again. A stranger and a threesome - he's right. Although he kind of knew Jamie beforehand, he was a stranger to me. After crossing out both, I hand *the list* back to Alex.

"Now what?" I ask.

He puts it back into his wallet and leans against the seat and I scoot closer, into his outstretched arm.

"How about… we make our own?" he says.

"Our own what?"

His smile tells me all I need to know.

"Do you have any ideas yet?" I ask.

"I've always wanted to make a video," he says.

"Brilliant. A video will be number one on the new list." I smile at the thought. "Hey, you seemed rather taken with Jamie yourself, do you think there's something else there to explore?"

Alex shrugs, and only answers after a significant pause. "I got nervous."

"Maybe next time you won't be."

"I love you," he whispers.

"I love you too."

We're soon lost in thought, at least I am. This is going to be so much fun!

I rest my head on his shoulder while continuing to hold his hand and realise I'm happy in a way I haven't felt very often: I'm truly, deeply contented. Tonight we were free, wild, and a little bit insane together. Tomorrow we'll do regular couple stuff: watch some TV, enjoy a lazy day at home. Or perhaps even do a bit of shopping to make his new place more liveable. And on some evenings, or weekends, we'll experiment with more craziness as a couple. Perfect.

The contrast makes me smile. As long as we keep this up and remain honest with one another, I know we'll be wonderful together. I love him, and he loves me. But that doesn't mean we have to restrain ourselves.

We're adults, we have fantasies and dreams beyond couplehood, and that's OK. The potential for our experimentation is limitless. Even if we involve other people in our bedroom activities, our priorities are set: *us* before *them*. That's what commitment should be.

***

# SALLY

# CHAPTER ONE

Working for one's fuck-buddy is a funny situation to be in. One moment you're trying to be professional, then, you see them, or as in this case, get a suggestive message from them, and all propriety goes out the window.

Today is no different, judging from the words that have just popped up on my phone, while I was supposed to be working on a spreadsheet of sales stats.

'Tedious management meeting. Can't stop thinking about the other night… M'

Neither can I. Mark, who has got to be the sexiest man I've ever hooked up with, ordered some takeout for the both of us, allowing us to enjoy a not so quiet night in without the added hassle of cooking, or heading out for food. We tried watching a movie, but were quickly distracted by each other's company.

It's impossible for me to be near him without my hormones going haywire, and the feeling is mutual.

By the time the end credits rolled along, he had me bent over the edge of his bed and given me an orgasm I'll remember for the rest of my life. We finished the evening in the bath, letting the hot water calm our taxed muscles, while still unwilling to keep our hands off each other. All in all, a perfect night in. I went home before things got awkward for either him or me.

I respond with 'Likewise, perhaps we can do it again sometime ;)', and put my phone away before anyone comments.

My affair with Mark is common knowledge in the office, but luckily I haven't had to deal with jealousy as such. If anything, a few of them seem to feel sorry for me, or so they say, for getting involved with a guy who's never had a steady relationship in all of the five years he's worked here.

They don't realise that it's perfect how things between us are. I don't do steady relationships either.

***

"Is Sally Irving in?" This simple question, spoken by a familiar voice, rudely drags me out of my daydream and back into reality. *It can't be!*

Despite the years that have passed since I last heard this voice, and the fantasy I had just been absorbed in, there's no way I would make a mistake identifying this ghost from my past.

"You're looking for Sally?" I can hear Cath's clear soprano respond. As Mark's assistant, she's the one who usually deals with the occasional visitor to our floor. "How exactly did you get in here?"

I peek over my PC screen across the office towards the man with the bunch of tulips in his hand. He has his back turned towards me, not giving me much to go by, except the long-ish dark brown hair, broad shoulders, and faded brown leather jacket. Fuck.

*Fuck, fuck, fuck, FUCK!*

"Psst, Becks," I whisper shout, but Becky next to me, is so focused on her computer screen that she's completely oblivious to the disaster that's about to unfurl around me. The furrow in her brow tells me she's probably struggling with Excel again, which means she might as well have blinders on. She finally looks up when I throw a paper clip at her.

"What? Can't you see I'm in the middle of-" The irritation sounds through in her voice. I know she hates interruptions, but this is an emergency, damnit!

"Shh!" I slink back into my chair and gesture at her to keep her volume down. "There. That guy Cath's talking to. Please be a dear and get rid of him. Tell him I'm off sick or whatever. Or dead. Tell him I died last month. Try to make it convincing." My heart is hammering in my throat, making it hard to keep my voice from cracking and I'm starting to feel faint like all the blood has drained out of my head.

Becky takes a moment, scrutinising my face, before checking out the figure in brown leather. *Please, don't argue!*

"Fine. I'll do it, but only because I love you. Don't think you can get out of this without providing some sort of explanation later!"

I put my head in my hands and shrug. "Whatever. Just please, make him leave."

I hear her roll her chair back, followed by the click-clock of her heels against the shiny office floor.

"Cath, I'll take care of this, thanks." Becky's voice sounds suspiciously upbeat as usual when she's *handling* someone.

"So, who are you?" She asks the man. I half hope he's just some random person who shares some familiarities with who I'm thinking of. Maybe a courier, who happens to have a voice that sounds just like-

"Gareth Doyle. Sally and I go way back." Fuck. It *is* him. Gareth. Now there's a name I've tried so hard and nearly succeeded to banish from my memory. Gareth fucking Doyle.

"Right, Mr. Doyle." Knowing Becks, and hearing the ridiculous tone she's using to address him, I have to assume she's enjoying this role a bit too much. Fine, as long as she does the needful. "Well it's terrible timing, Sally's actually on holiday at the moment."

"Oh. When will she return?"

"Not for a couple of weeks I'm afraid."

I lean up just enough to catch another glimpse, ignoring the risk of him turning around at some point and spotting me. At least from behind it seems he hasn't changed too much, even the hair is almost the same as I remember.

"Oh well, not sure they will last that long, but perhaps you can tell her I came by and left these for her." Gareth hands Becky the colourful bouquet.

"I'll let her know. Thanks." She keeps standing there, flowers in one hand, her other on her hip, waiting for him to make a move.

I breathe a sigh of relief, when after a few seconds of

indecision, Gareth does indeed walk out the door. My hands are shaking, beads of sweat collecting around my hairline. *What the fuck was he doing here?*

And why am I so affected by him, despite everything that's happened? It's totally ridiculous, bizarre even. I'm panting, as if the atmosphere has thinned out and I simply can't get the oxygen I need. *Jesus.*

Becky returns to our desks, and I can't face her. All I want to do is curl up into a ball and vanish. My stomach is all twisted up, confused and achy. If I'm not careful, I'm going to be ill right here.

"So. These are for you." She drops the flowers on top of my IN tray and sits down.

"Hey… Hey, Sal, are you OK?"

I once again cover my face with my hands, unable to wrap my head around what just happened.

"You didn't tell him I was dead. He's going to come back. I need to-" I can't finish; my throat feels dry, and I'm no longer sure what I was going to say anyway.

"What's wrong? You eat guys like that for breakfast, what's with this one?" Becky puts her hand on my shoulder, but I shake it off.

"I can't. Gimme a second." I get up and rush off towards the exit. *God, please make it so he's not lurking out in the hallway. Make it so I don't get caught!*

Luckily, the coast seems clear and I make a dash for the facilities. I need some alone time. No questions, no talk, just time.

The knot in my stomach is tighter than ever. Before I know it, I'm forced inside a stall, and faced with what's left of my lunch inside the bowl. Sadly, that doesn't do much to calm me down, just makes me angrier at myself. How dare he just drop right into my life while things are going exactly how I want them to? How fucking dare he?

My phone buzzes inside my pocket and I fish it out, with shaky fingers, managing to narrowly avoid dropping it into the mess in the toilet. It's Mark.

'Meeting just finished but you weren't at your desk. Let's go out, somewhere nice. French food maybe, or anything you like.'

Clutching the phone in my hands, I sink down to the floor, with my back against the stall door.

Taking a deep breath, I type out a typo-littered response. Sure, dinner would be nice. I guess. Ugh, I don't know anymore...

I was happy, dammit. Things were going pretty well with Mark, who seems to understand me in a way most guys don't. And now, all I see are complications.

I hate complications. That's the main reason I don't date, never have, ever since...

Why, of all times, does Gareth have to turn up now? It's been eight years, and only the latter half of them were worthwhile. After the hell he put me through, it took a whole four years to find my way back to normality again. Now, within seconds of seeing him, it's as if years of progress have been wiped away.

I thought I was over all this. I thought I was over him.

"Sal?" Becky's voice echoes against the tiled walls.

Shit, can't people get a hint? I decide to ignore her, but she knocks on my stall soon after.

"Sally, are you OK? Don't make me bust the door in."

"Yeah, I'm fine," I snap.

"Alright." Becky doesn't sound convinced, and predictably I don't hear her walk away either. "Then why are you sitting on the floor?"

Fuck, she's right. I take a deep breath, trying to focus my attention on the task at hand. Pass for normal, get the fuck out of here and think later. Or ideally, don't think at all, I've got dinner with Mark to survive without losing my shit.

"There, happy now? I got up," I say, after getting up and flushing away any evidence of my breakdown. If I'm going to make it to dinner, I'd better brush my teeth first.

"Sal? Who was that guy?"

"Didn't you hear him? His name's Gareth. Just some guy I used to know."

"It seems like there's a lot more to that story than what you're letting on."

"Whatever." I shake myself off, breathe deeply another few times to let my nerves settle, and open the door, attempting to act normal.

Once outside, I blank Becky and walk straight to the mirrors along the wall to fix my hair. Well at least I didn't cry. He didn't manage to break me completely. It's hard to look and feel halfway normal, with makeup smeared all over your cheeks.

"You know you can talk to me, right? You don't have to be some kind of lone crusader in all of this, it's OK to let people in sometimes." Becky is right, but I can't face her or anyone right now.

"Mark is taking me somewhere nice for dinner, I should probably finish off for the day and pack up my stuff."

Becky's reflection in the mirror shrugs and turns towards the door.

"If you change your mind, you know where to find me. Anyway, I have a date with Alex tonight too, so..." Her use of the word *date* grates at me. What Mark and I have planned is so not a date, and I intend to keep it that way.

When the door shuts behind her, I breathe a sigh of relief.

Her barging in here and insisting to check on me served its purpose as a distraction, but talking it out means releasing everything I've worked so hard to bury for years. I can't risk that.

# CHAPTER TWO

As soon as five o'clock rolls along, I head out and across the street from the big shiny building that is Aspect Technologies and straight towards the little local supermarket for a toothbrush, followed by a quick smoke. Knowing Mark, he'll be a little late, giving me enough time to eliminate any evidence of my earlier meltdown.

Thankfully Becky didn't bring up Gareth anymore after I escaped her interrogation in the ladies' room, she was too busy making plans with her man, Alex. Those two are at the height of the icky in-love phase most couples seem to go through before things inevitably fall apart. It's both kind of cute as well as tiresome to observe.

As I head back in after finishing my cigarette, Becks passes me with a spring in her step uncharacteristic for the gloomy January season, which would see most sensible people brace themselves before heading outside. She, however, can't wait to get out into the cold.

"Later!" She flashes a wide grin, earlier questions clearly forgotten.

I give her a wave and head into the facilities once more. Time to transform myself as well as my mood, just in time for my non-date with Mark. One of the main pillars of my affair with Mark depends on keeping things light and airy. No suffocating emotions, no bullshit, no drama. It's imperative I leave my baggage behind.

After brushing my teeth, I redo my lipstick and add a few extra touches of eyeshadow and liner, just how I know Mark likes it. If he's still in the same mood as earlier today, I'll come around in no time as well. Hopefully.

No sooner am I done, does my phone alert me of a new message. Sure enough, just one word from him: 'Ready?'

I check the mirror one last time, seeing my reflection smile back at me through deep red lips. *There, that's better.* Just as I head out the door and across the hallway, he exits the office floor and greets me with an infectious, much more genuine smile than the one I had just practised.

"Oh, there you are." He obviously checks me out, making my skin tingle with anticipation. "Have you given any thought to where you'd like to go?"

I shrug, and lean in for a quick hug, enjoying the feel of his athletic body wrapping itself around me. It'll be at least a couple of hours before we enjoy more of those intimate pleasures, and I cannot wait.

"French sounds lovely." And in any case, I intend to focus more on him all evening than on the food. Nothing like the undivided attention of a catch like Mark to make you feel alive.

✳✳✳

"Wow, this place is amazing," I remark, looking around at the tastefully decorated restaurant. Everything, down to the earthy palate and subdued lighting aims to create an intimate atmosphere. It succeeds, too.

"Yeah, Cath told me about it. It truly is a gem." Mark gives me an intense stare across the table and the hairs on the back of my neck stand up straightaway. In this light, his eyes stand out deep black against his symmetrical, flawless face. As far as men go, he is quite something. Gareth would have nothing on- *What the hell is wrong with me? Why am I still thinking about Gareth?*

"Something wrong?" Mark reaches over to take my hand, the gesture matching his suddenly softened features.

I shake my head, trying to rid myself of those stupid, lingering memories. *Get back on track, woman!*

"No, I'm sorry. I guess I'm just hungry and it's made me light-headed. Would you mind ordering for me?" I push my chair back and grab my purse for a quick trip to the ladies' room.

He nods in agreement and starts studying the menu. Halfway towards the facilities, I wonder if I should let him know I don't do snails, but figure it doesn't really matter either way. For a change I'm OK to go with the flow if it means I'll get a moment to collect myself.

I continue on and find myself staring at my own face in the bathroom mirror. It might be just the light, or my imagination, but I look like I've aged five years in the last few hours.

*Chill, it's just in your head...* After dabbing some water

on my cheeks and forehead, and practising a bit of deep breathing, I'm ready for the world again, or so I hope.

By the time I reach our table again, a bottle of red wine and two glasses have appeared, along with a basket of bread.

"Here, this ought to take care of the lightheadedness." He offers me a piece, pre-buttered, and I gladly take it.

"So what's the occasion for all this? Have something to celebrate?" I ask while nibbling on the bread.

He smiles and sits back.

"What makes you say that? Can't I take you somewhere nice just like that?"

"Just like that, huh. Not that I'm complaining, but our usual M.O. has been to just take each other, wherever." I wink at him and take a sip of wine. Lovely, perhaps now I can relax.

His smile turns into a grin, flashing his perfectly white teeth at me.

"There's still time."

Studying his face, with the high cheek bones and sharp jaw, and especially those lips that manage to distract with just the right amount of fullness… I'm reminded of that first time I noticed him.

I was out one cold October night at one of my regular hangouts, a nightclub where unusually I was not having much luck with the male of the species. Of course a few were biting, as they usually do. But they were either too drunk, too obnoxious, too creepy…

When I decided to give up and call it a night, Mark

was outside, waiting for a radio cab. He caught my eye immediately. It was like a scene from a sappy movie; the handsome hero, with his jacket collar pulled up, finding shelter from the incessant drizzle against the wall of the building. We shared a cigarette, and some small talk, when he asked where I was headed.

Sensing the changed dynamic of the evening, I suggested his place would suit me just fine. A pause and a meaningful gaze later, he answered with a smile.

When the cab arrived, he offered me dry passage, protected by his jacket. The ensuing night was long, sleepless, featuring much naked acrobatics and multiple orgasms. Unusually for me, I stayed until he gave me breakfast and his phone number in the morning. Both were very welcome indeed. Neither of us asked what any of it meant, it was understood.

There's a distinct difference between a date, and a prolonged hookup. A date holds certain promises, expectations, complications. A hookup simply happens; there's no pretence.

Although we've met up with each other off and on since then, I know he's been seeing other women, as I've been open to the odd flirtation with other guys. Though it's been a while since I actually went home with someone else, not that I'd ever admit it. After Mark, most guys I ended up flirting with never seemed quite interesting enough.

We've never openly talked about these things, which is probably for the best. Familiarity, contempt, and all that jazz.

"So I was thinking, Paris would be nice despite the February weather…" Mark's soothing voice makes me smile.

"Paris?" Wait, what is he talking about?

"Yeah. It does fit the theme."

"Theme?"

"For Valentine's, silly. You must be really hungry. I'll ask how much longer it'll take."

While Mark waves over the waiter, I wonder what the preceding conversation was all about. It's so unlike me to daydream much at all, especially not in the company of others.

Then I spy the envelope on the table. How did that get there?

"Five minutes, apparently." Mark turns to face me again, then slides the envelope over.

"I have it all figured out, you just need to turn up with your passport on the day."

Looking inside reveals a pair of etickets and a booking confirmation from a rather fancy sounding hotel.

"Wow, just like that, huh?" I'm as yet unsure how to respond. Would I like to spend a long weekend in Paris with Mark? Sure. Do I like the connotations of celebrating Valentine's Day there together? *Errr..*

I shoot him a tentative smile, hoping to understand where his head is at.

"What's made you so romantic all of a sudden?"

He shrugs, and sits back.

"Relax, I'm not proposing. It's only a trip. A bit of

fun." His eyes are glued to mine, and although he is sort of smiling, his lips are tense.

"Although, I would love for us to move forward together."

With that, everything about tonight changes. Everything about *us*, every assumption I had made about what our relationship entails, is altered. I hate it when this happens.

"You know how I feel about stuff like that." I remind him, struggling not to sound defensive.

"Look, I know you're not ready to settle down. And that's fine. It doesn't have to be *that* formal."

It sounds like he's also having a hard time maintaining his composure. I wish he'd never brought this up.

"You say that as if it's all me." My earlier dreaminess has vanished, what's I'm left with is the cold, hard reality. All isn't how it seemed.

"At least I'm trying." *Oh no, he didn't!*

Something inside me boils over and claws at every inch of my being to give him my full, uncensored opinion.

"Trying, my ass!" I exclaim under my breath. "Don't think I didn't notice the frilly panties in the laundry at your place. Or the fake nail that made its way onto the passenger foot well of your car!"

He looks away, and refuses to comment.

"I don't care if you're fucking other people, just as long as we're clear this isn't just a one-sided issue." I cross my arms and wait, but he just shakes his head and doesn't say a word.

When the waiter arrives with our food, all we can muster is a mumbled thanks, before resuming our silent stand-off.

Admittedly the food is lovely, but the evening has been thoroughly ruined, so we rush through it and skip dessert. Ever the gentleman, he does drop me home, but I don't ask him to stay and neither does he insist. We part ways with little more than a nod.

***

What a fucking day. The mess with Mark overshadowed today's earlier shock, but only while in his company. Now that I'm back home, all of it hits me in full force.

Gareth.

I hadn't allowed myself to think about him in years. What he did to me was inexcusable but it did make me into who I am today. For that, I suppose I should thank him: I'm stronger now.

The eighteen year old me, who was so certain she knew what love was, no longer exists. I was such an idiot back then. Today, I know it's just a fairytale. A convenient plot point that adds the saccharine sweetness to every other Disney movie. The original German fairy tales had it more figured out: love, as well as life, equals suffering.

Nobody lives happily ever after, to think otherwise is risky. It opens you up to a world of pain and disillusionment.

And Mark? Jesus, what a hypocrite. I thought he was

different. His carefree attitude towards relationships had been the topic of many an office discussion after Becks and I joined Aspect. When a few of our new colleagues tried to warn me, when all they succeeded at was to make me like him better.

Is that really how it's going to go from now on? Even when I'm sleeping with the biggest manwhore in town, my magic pussy manages to effortlessly turn him? Many women might crave such a talent. To me, it's a curse.

I would've gone with him to Paris, had he not made that final remark before everything went south. It would've been fun: see some of the sights, enjoy amazing food, wine, perhaps a spot of shopping. And at the end of the day - or even during - retreat to the hotel and do what we tend to do best. Give the other guests something to be envious about.

After hyping myself up all over again, it's going to be impossible to just go to sleep. I opt for a hot bath and a nightcap instead, just when my phone dings and a message from Becky turns up: 'Don't think you're off the hook for today.'

Oh God, she'll be insufferable in the morning.

# CHAPTER THREE : MARK

When I caught a glimpse of the guy, Gareth, leaving the building, and then noticed the bunch of flowers on Sally's desk which Cath and some of the others were excitedly gossiping about, something in me snapped. For too long, I've been complacent, simply going along with whatever our relationship or lack thereof entailed. I didn't figure I could ever date traditionally anyway so it's been convenient that she hasn't made too many demands.

I knew she'd been seeing other people. Obviously she assumed I'd been doing the same. But for some reason I thought that she and I shared a certain magnetism that meant that we'd continue to circle around each other indefinitely. Now, I'm not so sure. That guy showing up at work for her threw me off balance.

She doesn't owe me an explanation, she's entitled her secrets as I am mine. I don't believe in full disclosure, especially in relationships. Some things are simply too private to be shared, to be opened up to judgement. But I couldn't stand by and watch while the best thing that's ever happened to me runs off into the sunset with some loser with 80s hair and bad tattoos.

I remember the first time we met so clearly. Like it happened only the other night, not months ago.

This girl I'd been seeing, Leila, and I had a big row

that night. It was the type of thing you can't recover from. Rather than stay over at her place, as I'd done so many times before, I called myself a cab and got out of there as quickly as I could. I waited by the main landmark of the region, *Luminous*, a nightclub that had seen better days. Braving the drizzly October skies had seemed a lot more cosy than hanging around Leila's place, where hell threatened to freeze over.

Sally came out of the club, managing to look fresh and radiant despite the ungodly hour, and we got chatting. She was quite something. Her mannerisms were deliberate and confident, yet everything she did from lighting a cigarette to checking her phone had a certain elegance to it. She almost seemed feline. Beautiful, with a hint of danger. She looked like she belonged somewhere more metropolitan, like London or New York, not in our quaint little corner of the world.

Her athletic frame was protected by an expensive looking woollen coat with a furry collar, her gorgeous dangly earrings promised that whatever was hidden underneath would also be stylish and chosen with one goal in mind: to complement her natural beauty. Her choice in fashion has always been like the expert cut to an already flawless diamond. For the effortlessness of it all, I envied her and felt drawn to her at the same time.

Before I had the chance to consider whether flirting with her would be overly ungentlemanly considering the situation, she had already begun.

Of course I wanted her to come home with me. Of

course I'd pay for the cab. Obviously, I'd make her breakfast, pleased to no end that she decided to stay the night. A few weeks later, naturally I'd offer her and her friend a job. Sally isn't the sort of girl you say no to.

She got under my skin and made me forget for a moment how complicated my life was and had been for the past couple of years. We clicked between the sheets as well as during those moments when we needed a little break. Only with Sally could you get into a passionate discussion about the plight of Indie musicians, mere seconds after flopping back on the pillow, out of breath with sweaty locks still stuck to our brows.

Today, when I saw that Gareth person, I forgot how I had sworn to myself I'd keep my relationships simple. I instantly knew couldn't let her get away. After casually asking Cath for a restaurant recommendation, I started to work on a rushed plan to try to show her I could be more than just a cock in a suit.

I should've known the Paris idea would backfire so spectacularly. She wouldn't have had a problem with it on any other date, but I had been an idiot planning a trip for Valentine's. In my hurry, I had thrown every possible cliché into the mix. You don't sway a girl like her with heart shaped balloons and cheesy greeting cards.

All I can hope for now is that that Gareth fellow gets the same response. But considering how distracted she was all evening, I'm not liking the odds.

Perhaps it's best to forget the whole idea. Bury the possibilities I suddenly saw, despite myself. Perhaps it's time I let her go.

She'd found some panties in my laundry bin and a stick-on fingernail in the car. How careless.

Of course she doesn't trust me. I wouldn't trust me either. Best I start looking out for my own survival rather than chase silly dreams which aren't meant to be.

With that in mind, I log on to the chat room where I've spent so many sleepless nights over the years. I'm not sure what I'm after, support to cut her loose or encouragement to try again, but it may just be nice to find a sympathetic ear.

# CHAPTER FOUR

"Sally and you are close, so what do *you* think the story is?" Cath asks.

"I dunno, she hasn't let on," Becky responds. "She doesn't exactly share stuff, you know."

*Fuck, here we go.*

Both have their backs turned towards me, but Elaine, who's so far just been listening in has spotted me and started shuffling uncomfortably from one foot to the next.

"Don't mind me, I'm just going to do some actual work," I remark and nod at them, just as the two busybodies turn with guilty expressions on their faces.

"I'm sorry, Sal. But you're being so mysterious that we can't help ourselves." Becky plops down next to me and repeatedly tries to push a lock of her stubborn hair behind her ear, to no avail.

"Whatever."

"He was hot though, that Gareth guy."

I shrug, trying to block my old memories of him. As disinterested as I am in those fragments of the past, I care even less to find out how hot or otherwise he is currently. Deep breaths. *Some asshole from forever ago cannot hurt me anymore!*

"Elaine seems to have a thing for tats. Kept using the phrase 'the hawtness' so often it almost became tiresome," Becky says, then pauses for a moment before patting me on my upper arm. "Anyway, screw that. Have you seen Mark around? He asked me to pull a report first thing this morning, and now he's nowhere to be found."

"No flipping clue." Who am I, his minder? "Why don't you ask Cath."

"Already did, but she hadn't seen him either," Becks responds.

I turn on my PC, and shuffle around the papers on my desk in an attempt to look busy, but Becky's eyes continue to burn into me.

"OK, Sal. I won't ask what's wrong because you'd rather choke on it than tell me, but you're not fooling anyone."

I sigh and rub my temples. Goddamn Becky and her habit of always saying exactly what comes to mind. Shame she doesn't know when to let things be.

"I'm glad you're not going to ask."

"Alright then."

She pulls her chair closer to her workstation and pretends to be productive for a few minutes as well, before coming back towards me.

"Hey, shall we make a plan to go out? Just the two of us, no boys? I promise not to bring up anything you don't want to talk about." Her eyes have lit up and it's hard not to get swept up in her sudden mood swing.

A smile forms on my lips too, despite myself. Perhaps a girls' night out is just what I need. It would certainly beat sitting at home, driving myself crazy wondering why Gareth is trying to get in touch all of a sudden. Becky and I will have a few rounds, chat for a bit, be silly like we used to be. If only she can stop being so nosy and just focus on having fun.

"OK, sure."

"Sally, my office?" says Mark, who turned up behind us out of nowhere. "Nice flowers."

"Right." I confidently push my chair back, hoping I at least come across somewhat normal. Wonder what he wants.

Becky's eyes meet mine when I get up, but she somehow manages to contain herself and her quick tongue. The last thing I need today is her smart-ass remarks making an awkward situation even worse.

"Yes?" I ask, unable to decide whether to enter his office fully, or if this is something that can be gotten over with quickly.

"Please close the door," Mark says, trying to sound casual. Still, my pulse starts racing immediately. I hope and pray that this isn't a follow-up from last night, because I'm dangerously close to losing it again.

Still, I do as he says and wait in front of his desk until he finishes scribbling something on a notepad. He gestures at me to sit down, which I do as well.

"I wanted to apologise. I was out of line yesterday." No shit.

"I'm sorry too. It's a tricky subject for me."

"Hopefully it won't affect us working together?" He looks me straight in the eye, and yet I can't tell what he's thinking. It freaks me out when people act so guarded.

"Not at all." I shift uncomfortably in my seat. "It

need not necessarily need to affect anything else either."

There's no change in his expression, no twitch or blink. He gives nothing away.

"Thanks, that's all then."

Stunned, it takes me a few seconds of staring at him writing more nonsense scribbles onto his notepad to realise I've been excused rather abruptly. *Well, fuck you too then.*

Back at my desk, I decide to inspect the bouquet Gareth left yesterday, which had already attracted Mark's attention earlier. It's in a vase, with water and all, probably thanks to Becky.

I would've binned it.

The mixed blooms are colourful, cheery, and very out of character for the Gareth I used to know. All those years ago, he would've been more likely to buy me some spiky body jewellery, rather than *girly flowers*. There's even an equally girly card attached. Knowing Becky, she's probably read it already… I might as well…

*Dear Sally,*
*What I did was inexcusable. I am so sorry.*
*Please allow me this chance to explain. The past eight years have been rough, for you too I imagine, and I'll understand if you never want to see me again after this.*
*But I must try and do my bit to make amends.*
*Yours,*
*Gareth*

Fuck.

Rough, eh? For the first few years, that would be the understatement of the century. Lately, things have of course perked up considerably, and it's hard to imagine putting all that at risk to give him a chance to explain fucking dumping me on what was meant to be the best day of our lives.

I ought to ignore him, avoid him, never speak to him again. Do to him what he did to me.

It's childish, I know it is. And it wouldn't be satisfying because the current scenario isn't nearly as emotionally loaded as how things were when he let me down. What the hell is wrong with him? To think that after abandoning me when I needed him the most, I'd just welcome him back with open arms to let him *explain why?*

He's got to be delusional.

It occurs to me that my current state of mind is a lot more productive than yesterday's shock. Maybe hearing him out wouldn't be so bad, if I can remain sufficiently angry throughout. Telling him where to shove his explanation might bring me closure.

I stuff the card back into the little envelope and hide it in my desk to prevent anyone else from accessing it too easily. Just when I close the desk drawer, Becky turns up with two cups: tea for her, coffee for me.

"Thought you could use this," she says, while putting it down on my desk.

"Cheers."

"How are things between you and *the hair?*" She puts extra emphasis on her favourite nickname for Mark, who indeed has the most perfect hair I've ever come across in the wild.

Goddamnit, here we go again. If being asked about Gareth was uncomfortable, an interrogation about Mark and I would be a close second. Especially since I can't figure out why he's made a complete U-turn since last night.

I can think of only one way to derail this conversation: relying on Becky's complete inability to contain her own happiness whenever prompted.

"Fine," I respond. "Say, how come you're just squeezing me for gossip lately. Why don't you tell me about your own love life for a change?"

Becky blushes slightly and stares down into her drink while taking a sip.

"Things are great."

"Uhuh."

Her eyes dart back and forth between me and the rest of our colleagues, who are far away enough that they couldn't possibly overhear. *That was easy.*

"Alex and I are planning to-I probably shouldn't tell you this." Becky tries to keep a straight face, but soon a coy smile breaks through anyway. *Score!*

"Don't be a tease. Spill."

"Well I told him I quite like the idea of doing it somewhere less private… Somewhere with more fresh air if you get my drift." She fidgets with a lock of her hair while speaking. The innocence of that gesture is hilariously out of whack with what she's just said.

"You want to go dogging?! That's insanely awesome.

Are you planning to get people to watch?" I can't suppress a grin myself. Former good girl Becky continues to surprise me; she truly has undergone an insane transformation these past few months. What's even more of a shock is Alex's willingness to accept the new her. Most men would baulk at some of her ideas.

"I dunno… But a change of scenery would be exciting."

I lean back, warming my hands on the hot cup.

"Sweet. I'm proud of you, Becks. Hope you don't mind me saying you were a bit dull earlier, when you were still together with Jeff."

"I know. That's all in the past now." She sniggers to herself and puts her mug down, with that same smile still playing on her lips.

"Good for you."

I'd never admit it to her in so many words, but at times I am glad for her how things turned out with Alex. Obviously I had plenty of reservations before, which I've been vocal about. The biggest problem I saw was that whole disaster that happened a few weeks ago after they had lunch with her Mum and he seemed to drop off the face of the earth for almost a week.

His reasons were solid, but the poor execution would have made it near impossible for me to forgive him, had I been in Becky's shoes. She's a better person than I am.

"So, how about tomorrow night? Just you and me?" Becky says.

"Are you sure you don't need to ask for *permission* first," I tease. "After all, your man might have different ideas."

"Don't be a cow."

"OK. It's a plan."

# CHAPTER FIVE

Another day, another bouquet on my desk.

As I walk towards my spot, I note that the all too familiar gaggle of colleagues has already formed. I'm sure they'll know the circumstances of how the flowers ended up here already. In fact I'm sure people on other floors whom I've never met before know all about my stupid fucking flowers.

Becky is spinning back and forth on her chair, while talking to Cath and Elaine with a thoughtful, all-knowing look on her face. As I get nearer, she finally spots me and shoos them away before I can overhear.

"Morning," she chirps.

"Meh." I let my handbag drop to the floor beside my desk and eye the flowers.

A different florist than the others, and their colours are more coordinated. The last ones looked like Gareth tried his best and did something totally out of character. With these, however, it seems like he had expert help.

"I haven't read the card," Becky remarks.

"You'd better hope you haven't."

"Read it! Come on, you know you want to!"

Goddamnit. I might as well, just to shut her up.

The tiny little envelope matches the dark purple of some of the whatever-type-flowers. My name is written on top in a vaguely familiar, neat handwriting.

*Sally,*

*I realise yesterday's apology was anything but. If you let me, I'll do better this time. I prefer a life with you in it, on your terms. Perhaps we can talk it over tonight?*

*Mark*

I casually pop the card back into the envelope, and drop it into my handbag, before anyone else gets their grabby hands on it.

"So? Did the hot guy with the tats from yesterday not believe my story?" Becky asks.

"Gareth? No, these are from Mark."

She breathes in through her teeth and scrutinises my face.

"Cath had mentioned he's been acting weird. Do you think he's jealous?"

"I don't know what he is." I turn towards my PC, signalling that the conversation is over.

Indeed, I'm not sure what to make of this. Has Mark accepted my stance on relationships or is this just an opening to try again? I do wish we could get back to how things were earlier: uncomplicated, but extremely satisfying booty calls along with a seemingly endless supply of intelligent conversation. And laughs, lots of laughs. Men like that don't grow on trees and I really did enjoy his company, no matter what we ended up doing.

Whatever he's thinking though, I've already made plans with Becks tonight. If there's one thing I won't do over this, it's cancelling an existing commitment. No matter how many flowers end up on my desk.

Realising he probably expects some kind of reaction, I do a quick scan of the office, noting that the door to Mark's office is ajar, but there is no movement in sight. Cath is nowhere to be seen either. Perhaps there's a meeting going on.

So I get my phone out, to get this over with quick.

'Hey. Thanks for the lovely flowers. Tonight I'm going out with Becky already, how's tomorrow night for you? S.'

That'll do. I put my phone away without waiting for a response.

*  *  *

"OK, so where shall we go?" Becks looks up while putting her things away. Her wide grin betrays her excitement at tonight's plan.

"Hadn't thought about it. Somewhere nearby? I need a drink."

"Sure." She glances at her phone one last time before slipping it into her handbag as well. "You're not going to be texting with Alex all night, are you? You two have practically been attached by the hip."

Becky sticks out her tongue at me and pats her bag.

"You're just jealous. My phone stays in here, just in case."

As if.

We head downstairs and out the door, where Becks offers me her arm. Together we stroll off, braving the wintery elements, towards a rather promising looking neon sign some distance down the road. Any old pub will do for me tonight. And any old pub it turns out to be.

Beyond the rustic wooden doors and fogged up windows I can just about make out a few dim lights and some silhouettes of others with similar evening plans. This isn't a place you end up when you're after sophistication and fine dining. This is where you come to drink.

"So, red or white?" Becky asks, with the barman waiting impatiently for her instructions. As if he's busy, I snort internally at the thought.

"Whatever you like, we can share a bottle."

Becky turns to order, while I scan the room. An old fashioned looking pub, with heavy wooden furniture and the obligatory old guy in the corner who's staring out the window while sipping his Guinness. His tweed jacket is about the same greenish brown colour as the curtains and the carpet. Funny, how every pub seems to have at least one of these characters. Hell, at least the drinks are cheap.

"Let's sit by the window." Becks nods at a grouping of leather arm chairs somewhere halfway between the door and the fireplace.

"Sure."

We discard our soggy coats and rest our feet. Although a good few feet away, the fire manages to quickly warm us up while we start sipping the fruity red Becky had picked out. Though not quite of the same calibre as what Mark and I enjoyed at the French restaurant last night, it's still rather nice.

"So, Mum's been asking about you," Becky remarks and puts her glass on the round table between us.

"Oh yeah?" I'm afraid to push, considering the dark expression on her face.

"I often feel like she considers you more her daughter than me."

I can't withhold a snort.

"If she knew me, I mean really knew me, she would think otherwise."

"Yeah well, tell *her* that."

Becky puts one leg over the other and observes me for a moment, as if contemplating what to say next.

"She hates Alex."

"She hated Jeff too," I respond.

"Apparently now that he's out of the picture, he's an angel."

I lean over and pat her on her arm.

"So the solution is simple, tell her you've dumped Alex. She'll be singing his praises in no time, then you can have a joyful reconciliation and everyone will be happy."

"That's not funny."

It is precisely these issues that make me glad I don't have to deal with such nonsense. No attachments means no drama. Or at least that was the plan until everything went to shit a couple of days ago.

"You know I'm not the best person to advise you here. Your Mum is a peculiar character."

"That she is." Becky sighs, with a stubborn frown on her face. "Or Alex and I could run away together and not leave a forwarding address."

I give her a stare and she looks back at me, until we both start giggling.

"Tell you what, you should sign her up on some dating site for oldies. She just needs a good lay." I grin.

Our giggles turn into full-on laughter.

"Oh can you imagine? My Mum on a blind date with some stranger off *the world-wide-web. You know there are too many perverts on the world-wide-web.*" Becky's impression is pretty close, but I daren't tell her for fear of freaking her out. Her worst fear in life has got to be the idea of turning into her Mum.

"God forbid if his shoes and socks clash, she'll have that sour expression on her face like he pissed in her entree."

We pour another glass of wine each and sit back, quiet once more. I feel for her, nobody should have such a complicated relationship with a parent, and without a proper reason. Becky is too sensitive, always has been, and her mother too set in her ways to see how she affects her.

"Do tell me more about your dogging plans though," I try to steer the chat into more cheerful territory. "Is it like a plan plan, or are you still on the fence?"

Becky blinks a few times and focuses down on her glass of wine.

"I'm all for it, but I do have some concerns of how it would really work, you know?"

"What do you mean, you go somewhere and get it on, what's so hard in that?"

"Yeah, but what if we like get caught?"

"Isn't that the whole point?" I wink at her.

She starts giggling again and shrugs.

"Well it's anyway not going to happen until the weather warms up."

"Unless you get a car…"

"Mhm."

Around us, the pub is starting to fill up, though not by much. A couple more regulars have sat down next to lonely Guinness man, and a group of broad shouldered manly blokes are standing by the bar, commenting on the sports playing on the telly.

A glance at the clock tells me it's nearing dinner time, but I'm not in any mood to get up.

"Are you hungry, shall we just eat here?" I ask Becky, who simply nods, while rummaging around in her bag, no doubt checking for messages from Alex.

I am compelled to check mine too, and am strangely excited to see there's a response from Mark. Tomorrow night, his place. Becks is still busy, her frustrations from earlier about her Mum seemingly forgotten while furiously typing a lengthy message. He does seem to make her happy, that Alex, which is nice. Some people simply aren't cut out to be on their own, and Becky is one of them.

I decide to respond to Mark as well, and whether it's the wine or something else, something makes me wish that we can get things worked out somehow. I'd rather have him in my life than out of it. He makes things more interesting, more fun somehow. And it helps that he's absolutely gorgeous.

When we're both done, we study the specials on the chalkboard above the fireplace.

The offerings are a perfect reflection of the rest of the pub: not very sophisticated but they'll have to do. And anyway, it's been a while since I've had Shepherd's Pie. We order our food at the bar and sit back down with another bottle of wine.

"You know, I've never told you this, but I wasn't always like this," I say.

Becky looks up while zipping up her bag.

"I wasn't always so - cynical." I rest my head on my hand and take a deep breath. Perhaps it's time she knew.

"Oh yeah?"

"I was supposed to get married… It feels like a different life now, but there it is."

"Shit, I had no idea!"

"It didn't happen of course, but-"

"Gareth. He was the guy wasn't he?" Becky's eyes are about the size of saucers as she leans over and takes my hand. "That's why you were so upset when he came into work."

I nod. After half a bottle of wine, it's somehow easier to let go of some of those so closely guarded secrets. They still hurt though. I still have to fight the prickle of tears in my eyes thinking back to it all.

"I was 18, he was a couple of years older. Our parents knew but didn't approve of course, not that they could do much about it." That's as much detail as I'm willing to divulge. She knows I'm not in touch with my folks, this should be enough of an explanation why.

"What happened?"

"Honestly, I don't know. Everything was supposed to be simple, just the two of us, we didn't share the specifics with anyone. The day we were supposed to meet at the Registrar's office together, he never turned up and his phone was off too. Like he'd vanished."

Becky's face has fallen about as much as it could. For once, my chatty best friend has run out of questions.

"Fucking hell." She leans back in her armchair and shakes her head.

"Yep."

"What an absolute douchebag."

"Yep."

"And now he's come weaselling back looking to make amends? The nerve on that guy."

"I know."

For the rest of the evening, the topic of Gareth doesn't come up, instead we focus on other people's lives for some much needed gossip.

# CHAPTER SIX

"I was worried you wouldn't want to come over," Mark evades my gaze, instead looking down at his hands, in a rare showing of weakness. It's completely out of character for him, and actually kind of endearing.

"Well it's only fair we figure this thing out." I observe him, as he starts to chop the onions and garlic, in preparation for the feast he's promised me. Apparently he's making some kind of seared duck breast in a red wine something, I wasn't quite listening and anyway I'm not that much of a foodie.

"Indeed. Well, I've done a lot of thinking lately."

"Oh?" I awkwardly smooth down my grey pinstripe shift dress and take a seat on the stool opposite him at the breakfast bar. I can't help but miss the good old days when things between us were so much simpler.

"It wouldn't be fair to lie to you in order to keep the peace. I really did mean it when I said I want to move forward together. As a couple."

I'm about to protest, but he raises his hand signalling he's not finished yet.

"I know. You prefer the status quo. But I can't help feeling that what we share deserves more than the odd shared meal followed by sex."

"Great sex," I mutter under my breath, omitting the caveat that great sex tends to get ruined by labels and responsibilities.

His eyes squint slightly, betraying his amusement at my remark, yet he moves on.

"The thing is…" He leans across the breakfast bar and takes my hand, running his thumb over my knuckles in a way that makes me a little weak and hence uncomfortable. Yet I daren't pull away. "I really care about you, Sally. And I respect your side in all of this…" His voice trails off and we're left in silence, staring at each other.

I don't have the energy for another argument, if he truly does respect my opinion, hopefully he will soon drop it.

"What if…" He squeezes my hand gently before continuing, his gaze averted for the moment. "It doesn't have to be so rigid, so restrictive. So monogamous?"

His eyes flicker up and there's a flutter of something odd in my stomach. I can't tell yet if I'm about to have another meltdown or I'm just affected by his touch, his scent in the air, the memories of what else we've used this work surface for in the past.

"I don't get it." My voice sounds hardly more than a croak. How is it that his presence makes me weak, even when I want to do nothing more than to blow up and make him shut up about the relationship crap already? I must be losing my mind.

"I mean, how about we take baby steps. How about an open relationship?" He seems so boyish, vulnerable. For a change, the great Mark Lloyd, with the perfect hair, flawless bod and impeccable dress sense is completely out of his element, because he's not the one in charge. Strangely I don't feel in charge either.

I'm not sure what to say, I'm sure this offer, this compromise, was hard for him to suggest. I can tell by the look on his face. He's not excited about the prospect of an open relationship, he's just hoping for something more than what we've had so far. Our dinner together the other night made it clear that what he actually hopes for is only a lick of paint away from a white picket fence.

But he did suggest it. And he's not been faithful to me either, despite how he was trying to play it.

That must mean the offer is actually on the table?

All day at work I've been wondering, going back and forth on what Mark possibly wanted to discuss tonight to make things work out. I just want things back where they were. I need to forget about all the unwelcome drama of this week, and the best way to achieve that would be it's a good hard session of what we tend to be good at together. Dirty, nasty, sticky sex which in no way, shape or form comes close to the term "lovemaking".

I force a smile, and squeeze his hand for a moment before letting go. This is way awkward.

"Would it be OK for me to think about this?"

"Sure, sure." He retreats again, and starts rubbing the meat with some salt and spices. His expression is guarded but at least it doesn't seem like this will be the start of another battle.

"I mean, so much has been going on lately, it wouldn't be fair to answer without thinking it through properly," I mumble and continue to observe him.

He wipes his brow and continues to focus on the task at hand. The food. It's all a tad domestic for my liking, even if it's not the first time he's cooked for me. And I'm not even counting the attempts that evolved into hungry sex before the ingredients had even made it into the pan.

I wonder if all of this has only come about because he is indeed jealous of whatever he imagines Gareth means to me, like what Becky suggested. If only he knew the whole story. But telling Becky last night had already felt like pulling teeth despite the wine we'd shared, and I'm not ready to let Mark in on it. Not now, not ever. It's all way too raw still.

"So what's for afters." I try to sound cheerful, but to my own ears the bittersweet undertones are still obvious in my voice.

"Mousse au chocolat." He focuses his attention downwards after answering, and turns on the stove.

I consider my next move, observing him as he organises the utensils he's going to need. Something's gotta give, I can't stand this glum atmosphere any longer.

"I hear that tastes much nicer when it comes with a side of nipple."

He stops mid-movement, the duck breast hovering about a foot over the pan on the fire, and gives me a sideways look.

"A side of nipple, eh. I'll have to remember that."

The sight of him, distracted from the recipe he'd

painstakingly followed earlier, makes me smile. *Please, please, let things be more normal now!* Let's forget about relationships, open or otherwise, let me just enjoy his company for as long as I'll still have it.

The look we share, which seems to last forever suggests an understanding. Little by little, his guard comes down and he checks me out more like how he used to, before things got complicated.

Finally, he does put the meat, skin down, into the pan. It sizzles violently and we're almost instantly surrounded by the appetising aroma of duck. I sigh deeply, noting his changed demeanour. Perhaps tonight won't be so bad after all.

He picks up a bottle of red from the counter, and grabs two glasses, putting them next to one another in front of me.

"I hope you like duck pink on the inside, because I'm not sure I have the patience to cook it for too long." Mark removes the cork with a swift movement of the corkscrew and pours until my glass is half full. I think I see yet another glimmer of the old Mark in front of me, and decide to test the waters.

"Patience has never been your strong suit when it comes to female company, or so I hear," I tease, accepting the wine he hands me.

"Is that so? What else have you heard?" After filling his glass too, he raises it, clinking it to mine. Definitely, there's a bit of a smile hidden in those dark, brooding eyes.

"It's only rumour, of course, but I heard you prefer it

when female guests arrive for dinner already prepared for what is to come later. With as few *barriers* as possible in the way, if you get my drift." I take a sip, feigning innocence, but I sense his eyes burning into me, seeking evidence that I've indeed arrived *prepared.*

The richer scents coming from the stove break his focus on me for a moment, prompting him to step around to flip the meat. But then, he's back with a vengeance.

"You seem to know me very well." He takes my hands into his and gives me an intense stare.

I shrug and continue to play coy.

"I like to think I know your type."

He moves in closer, running his fingers over the back of my hands, and up over my arms. With me still seated on the high stool, our height difference is practically gone. We have perfect access of one another, but I continue to hold back.

I catch a hint of his cologne, which previously had been disguised by the range of other scents in his kitchen. He does smell perfect as well, always does, even after we've worked up so much of a sweat that I feel filthy myself, he somehow manages to remain enticing.

He leans in, almost touching his lips against mine, but then pauses in that most infuriating way, as if to make me beg.

I won't.

I can't.

But I must do something.

"Something's burning," I say. My throat has gone

dry, making my voice sound hoarse.

"Food's fine." Mark doesn't bother to check the stove, he's that confident.

"Right." I blink a few times, trying to fight the urge to give in to him. It's frustrating how much I want him, even though we seem to exist on completely different planes of reality. Why isn't this enough for him?

He makes the first move, bridging that final fraction of an inch until our lips meet. My reaction is instant; eyes snap shut, even though I wish to see more of him. I'll get that chance shortly, I'm sure. For now, I focus on the sensation of our tongues, touching only slightly at first in a playful dance which is teetering on the edge of control.

I wrap my arms around him, exploring the outlines of his shoulder blades underneath the smart light grey shirt he wore to work today. Although I know what awaits me, for some reason I haven't get gotten bored. Mark couldn't be boring if he wanted to be.

His lips have worked their way down the side of my neck, and his hand reaches around to unzip the back of my dress just enough to give him access to my collarbone which had so far been hidden underneath the high neckline.

"I'm not hungry, let's skip dinner," I breathe, and try to direct his mouth back to my neck.

"Give me a minute, I'm confident you'll change your mind." His breath against my skin tickles and gives me goosebumps.

He pulls away, leaving me vulnerable and wanting.

After bridging the distance to the stove in long, rushed strides, he switches off the gas and covers the pan with a lid and returns equally quickly.

"Now, where were we?" He offers his hand, which I take gratefully before sliding off the bar stool.

"We were having dessert."

His strong, toned arms surround me and before I can do or say anything he lifts me up, bringing my mouth up to his level. I wrangle the bottom of my dress up over my hips, allowing me to wrap my legs around his waist for added stability.

He kisses me and things seem to fall into place again. This is how things are supposed to be between us. Less talk, less drama, more physical connection.

While still in the midst of that initial frenzy which overstimulates the senses when you finally reach that moment you've been longing for during days apart, he somehow still manages to navigate through his lounge and towards the sofa.

I fall back into the soft cushions, and rid myself of the top of the dress at least, letting the bodice fold over and fall down on my stomach. He leans down, and kneels over me, pulling the whole thing down over my hips and all the way off my legs. Sitting on the armrest, he takes first my left foot into his hand, unzipping my ankle boot and discarding it on the floor, followed by the right.

"Indeed, you are prepared," he remarks, running his finger down along the centre of my stomach, from between my exposed breasts, towards where my panties should have been.

Thank God for hold-ups, because pantyhose would have made this little stunt uncomfortable, if not unmanageable.

I shiver, as his fingertip brushes over the narrow triangle of neatly trimmed hair which crowns my folds. Mesmerised, the only change in his expression comes as he licks his lips in anticipation. I know what's about to happen and I cannot wait.

"Don't. Go. Anywhere," he whispers, and withdraws his fingers again. "And close your eyes."

He sure knows how to tease… Still, I obey and wait for an agonising few seconds, unable to make out what the noises in the background are meant to signify.

Then, with a gasp, I'm startled, as something so cold it might as well be frozen hits my flush skin. My eyes snap open, to find Mark, leaning over me with a serving spoon and a bowl, after depositing a generous mouthful of chocolate mousse right in the centre of my cleavage. He lowers the spoon again, painting a line straight down the middle of me, a treasure map of sorts.

As cold as the dessert felt initially, it warmed to my flesh quite quickly, making each movement of the icy spoon almost as intense as the last.

He stands back, admiring his artistry and puts down the bowl. *Come on, dive in, I cannot wait!*

Sure enough, he kneels beside me on the carpet and starting at the top, licks the chocolatey mess off my skin, making it a point to indeed add a bit of nipple action. I writhe into the cushions, impatient for him to finish with my stomach and move lower down.

*Please, please don't be gentle with me after this!*

I moan, closing my eyes again, and gather all my willpower not to grab a handful of his hair, directing him to where we both know he must end up eventually. If only he wasn't so damn good at this, at whatever he sets his mind to, I may not even have turned up tonight. And even if I had, I may have left after he brought up the relationship stuff again.

But it's hard to go without this, this sweet torture he's putting me through.

"Good girl," he whispers in my ear, leaving my skin painfully unkissed once more. "Open up."

I obey, opening my mouth to the velvety taste of chocolate. Rich, with a bitter hint coming through that's just enough not to make it overly sweet. Perfect.

After the first spoonful, I open my eyes again to find him naked. His sculpted, though slim body is an image of perfection to match everything else about him. I signal at him with my finger to come closer, which he does, and then to turn around…

He understands me perfectly, when I move onto my side, allowing him space to lie down in the opposite direction next to me. Spreading my legs, he reaches back for the spoon one last time, depositing a dollop of mousse right where it matters.

"Ow!" I cry out, startled by the cold, then am forced to repeat the same outcry when his hot tongue follows almost immediately.

I thrust my hips into his face, while diving into his

crotch myself, taking his solid length between my lips. The slight saltiness of him is rather pleasing to the palate, how it cuts through and complements the richness of the chocolate he'd fed me earlier.

Meanwhile his movements between my legs deepen, his tongue burrows into my folds as he laps up every last hint of chocolate from my wet pussy. I can't help myself, twitching and wriggling so much he has to hang on with both hands to prevent me from throwing us both off the sofa.

And yet somehow, I manage to focus on the task at hand, sucking him with all I've got, deeply, but letting go every so often to slow down and lick the head of his cock like how I know he likes it.

His reaction is quick, the tremor in his tongue instant when I run mine over the slit right at the top. He pulls away slightly, and moans into my swollen, excited lips, before dipping in again just enough to tease my clit, causing me to react similarly. We're both running on autopilot almost, doing what we know best, pushing, goading the other further, in a fevered competition towards the finish line.

"Enough," he grunts, releasing me.

I smile as he gets up, knowing that I've all but won, even if he's taken my favourite toy away for now.

He gestures at me to get up, then grabs me around my thighs and swiftly flips me over his shoulder. It continues to be a surprise me how strong he is. Before I know it he deposits me right-side-up on the bathmat in front of his shower.

I shiver at the slight chill in the air when he turns on the water, which takes a moment to get up to temperature. Then, he leads me inside and I'm surrounded by the soothing warm stream, as well as his arms which have me pinned in place against the tiled wall.

Behind me, he spreads my legs to allow him access, and releases me except for one firm hand on the back of my neck. Then he plunges into me, filling me with that sweet sensation I'd been craving for days. He continues to hold me steady, with his other hand on my hip, while pushing against and into me, repeatedly.

His impressive girth, stretching my aching pussy makes my knees weak. Or perhaps that's still due to my conflicting emotions. But it feels so good I wouldn't want him to stop or hold back.

I'm grateful for the wall in front of me, or the intensity of his thrusts would have me wobbling about on my feet. Instead though, I brace myself against it, keeping a strong footing and meet his strokes with the resistance necessary to make it count.

He speeds up, intensifies the grip on my neck, before releasing me only momentarily to hang on to my wet hair. I struggle against his grip, willing him to pull at my hair a bit harder. As he continues to fuck me hard against that wall, I can't tell if it's the hot water misting up the shower cabin, or our combined efforts. Possibly a bit of both.

"Go on, finish it," I cry, causing him to go into overdrive, hitting all the right spots to send me into a tailspin of sensations.

I'd been close before, on the sofa, thanks to the expert treatment of his tongue, but now, it's becoming unbearable. He lets go of my hip, wraps both arms around me again and kisses and bites into my neck and shoulder, making me moan even louder. Yet somehow, he manages to continue the same rhythm, until I find sweet release and my knees threaten to buckle from underneath me. He's all but carrying me, pushing into me a final time and groaning into the back of my neck, with his arms still locked around me like a safety harness.

When his loosened grip allows me to turn around, I take the shower head out of its holder, and use it to massage both our spent muscles until our breathing has stilled to a more normal level.

"You were right," I remark, while getting out of the cabin to pick up some towels.

"Mhhm?"

"I am indeed hungry now."

He grins at me and gladly accepts the towel.

"Told you so."

# CHAPTER SEVEN

Once again, I'm home and confused. Although in the end Mark and I had a nice evening together, I couldn't shake the earlier awkwardness completely.

I like spending time with him. I think I might even like him as a person. But I don't like being forced into things.

Men have an awful habit of making you feel like you owe them something. Isn't it enough that I choose to spend my time with him more regularly now? Why does one always have to *move forward*. What's wrong with being content with the here and now?

I drop my stuff on the floor next to the sofa and sit down, letting the plush cushions envelop me. Home sweet home. At least here I'm free to do whatever the fuck I want.

Closing my eyes for a moment, I try to clear my head, but it's not working. Restless, I sit up and note a blinking light originating inside my handbag on the floor. My phone. *Now what?*

I scroll through the notifications and nearly choke on my breath when I see it's a Facebook friend request from Gareth. Fuck. For years I've enjoyed myself without answering to anyone. Now all of a sudden not just one, but two guys are after me, demanding my attention.

In a moment of weakness I allow myself a quick

glance at his profile. He hasn't changed one bit, except perhaps that the brooding expression that I remember him with has been etched into his features a little deeper than before. Eight years will do that to a person. Neither of us are getting any younger.

There are a couple of familiar names in his friend list, people we used to know, whom I've since lost touch with. It strikes me as weird that he has seemingly popped up from nowhere, after disappearing on me almost a decade ago, but his profile suggests that I'm the odd one out and he's never been away.

After poking around in his life for a few minutes, I check my messages, seeing that he's been in touch here too. Flowers, cards and messages, whatever will be next?

*Dear Sally,*

*If/when you see this, I hope you'll read on rather than delete this straight away. Please allow me the chance to explain things face-to-face. I can't face another eight years without you.*
*Gareth*

I want to throw my phone across the room. What fucking nerve, to come back begging, in a way putting the blame on me for his pathetic, lonely existence. What an absolute wanker!

That's it. I decide to break my self-imposed rule of never smoking inside my flat and light up. But not even the familiar taste of my Marlboro Lights can soothe me tonight. I get up and put out the cigarette again, discarding it in the ashtray by the tiny balcony in frustration.

The view from up here was one of the main draws of this flat, despite the slightly iffy locale. I normally enjoy the sensation of being so high up and far away from whatever nonsense goes on at ground level. Tonight, my special place to escape it all seems inferior and all I end up doing is pace around the lounge, arms folded, trying to analyse the mess in my head.

If Mark wants things to work out, he's going to have to back off a bit.

If Gareth wants to *explain things,* his reasons have got to be bullet-proof, or he'll wish he never found me. That is, if I give him that chance. Should I?

And what about the whole open relationship thing with Mark? How would that be different from what we do now? Aren't things open already, why tag such a heavy term to the end of it. Does he expect me to disclose who I want to go out with and when? What's to guarantee he won't end up being jealous?

I can't agree to anything like that, especially not with this Gareth bullshit hanging over my head. My instincts may tell me to run from it all, but perhaps it's time to face things head-on.

Best to sleep on it, and think of a solution in the morning. Provided I can get to sleep, that is.

Still restless, I pack a few essentials into the shoulder bag hanging behind the door.

It's times like these I'm grateful for the 24 hour gym around the corner. At this time of night it'll be blissfully quiet; I'll probably be the only person in there. I'll work up a sweat until my mind goes blank, then rush back and crash into bed for a much needed few hours of rest.

★★★

*I'm surrounded by a heavy blanket of fog, allowing me only to see about ten feet ahead. Someone is holding my hand, looking over I see that it is Dad, his eyes smiling even if the rest of his features remain straight. He's happy for me, in his own way.*

*The guests come into view on either side of the aisle. Softly lit, cheerful faces appear in the mist, applauding as I take one step after the other, balancing precariously on white satin heels which threaten to sink into the damp ground.*

*My heart beats faster as I move forward, staying in tune with the band in the background playing* 'Here Comes the Bride'. *It'll only be a matter of minutes before I'm reunited with my soon to be groom.*

*Towards my left, Mom grabs my hand and gives it an encouraging squeeze. The tears gathering in the corner of her eyes tell me how proud she is today.*

*Two, three steps up and I'll have reached the front of the wedding party. Dad lets go of me and stands off to the side, while another hand slips through the crook of my arm, coaxing me closer to the right. The fog has thickened though, so I cannot see his face, only the outline of his broad shoulders, dressed in a dark tailored suit.*

*Instinctively my left hand finds rest on my stomach, which hides a new life I have only just found out about. Nobody knows, I haven't even been able to tell him yet because we've spent the past two nights apart with our respective parents.*

*It's unnerving, not knowing how he will react, but something inside me has awoken, the desire to see our child grow from an infant into a toddler, and onward through the years. We'll recognise ourselves and each other in her, creating a permanent bond that cannot be broken. Surely, he can't object to something so beautiful?*

*Gareth's dad steps up in front of us, holding a bible, which is weird, since neither of us are religious. He starts to speak, but my head is swimming with so many hopes and thoughts that I can't focus on what he's saying. His words merge into the background noise, of people, chatting and laughing.*

*I'm dizzy, it's probably just morning sickness, but I must soldier on without creating a scene in front of everyone. Still, I'm unsteady on my feet and sway to keep my balance. His hand catches me, propping me up.*

*"Here, this should take care of the lightheadedness," Mark whispers in my ear.*

*My head snaps to the right, where he's offering me a basket of bread, which I gladly accept. He's so handsome, of course I'd realised that many times before, but today, on our special day, it's even more apparent.*

*Gareth's dad acts like nothing has ever happened, furiously speaking some gibberish as the guests look on, mesmerised. Minute after minute passes before I can finally decipher some of what is being said.*

*"Will you, Sally Irving take Gareth Frances Doyle to be your husband…"*

*Looking over to my right again, Gareth smiles warmly at me.*

*"Sorry I slipped away for a moment there, but I had good reason to."*

*"Well?" his dad asks expectantly. "What will it be?"*

I jerk up, bathed in sweat and with a jackhammer going off in my temples. *What the fuck was all that about?* It takes me a while to realise where I am, safely back in bed with the curtains drawn tight to keep out the streetlights down below. In the corner, the alarm clock flips to 4:00.

After breathing a deep sigh of relief, I fall back into the pillows. It was only a dream.

My hand is still resting on my stomach though, as if trying to protect what's left of an old, hopeless fantasy. I know there's nothing there. No life, no hope.

All that fizzled away a long time ago, before I became me.

# CHAPTER EIGHT

"Morning." Becky smiles, before continuing to unpack her lunch, ready to go into the staff fridge.

I try to respond, but nothing much comes out, except a cough. After surviving most of the winter without so much as a sniffle, today my body decides it would be funny to develop a cold.

"You look like shit." She takes a step back and cocks her head to the side.

"Thanks, I feel so much better hearing that." My voice has returned, though way more hoarse than normal.

"Thank fuck it's Friday, eh?" Becky gives me a pat on the back and heads to the kitchenette. I hope she's going to bring coffee. I could kill for a cup of coffee right now.

While she's gone, I try to snap out of my fuzzy-headed trance. It's like someone has placed a metal torture helmet over my head and is now putting the screws on tight.

Perhaps I should've stayed home. But calling in sick is not my style, because normally, I'm never sick.

Dazed, I sit down at my desk and switch on my PC, but I'm not quite sure what I'm meant to be doing. My To do list from yesterday still has plenty of unfinished items, but I can't focus on either one of them and so I just sit and stare at nothing.

When Becks finally returns she's trying to carry three cups at a time, and nearly spills everything on the ground.

"Here, I found some pouches of Cold & Flu medicine in the kitchen."

She puts two of the cups in front of me, one smelling suspiciously of lemon, and the coffee I desperately crave. She all but swats my hand away when I try to pick up the latter.

"Have the meds first. If you had bothered to look in a mirror on your way in, you'd understand why."

I grumble something mean and unintelligible, and do as she says. She's probably right, even if I don't like to admit it.

"Don't make a face, you grumpy git, drink it!" she orders.

I can't help it though, the stuff tastes hideous, but somehow I manage to force the rest of it down. My struggle lasts for a painful few minutes, before realising it's starting to take effect already.

If my pounding headache and achy throat aren't enough, I'm having a lot of trouble ignoring the crazy dream I had at night. I've never subscribed to dream interpretation, rejecting it as a rather New Age concept, but this time clearly it meant something.

Guess I've been so confused with stuff lately, that even my subconscious can't decide which way to go. I was going to figure out what to do this morning, but I'm not quite up for it.

Hopefully Mark will be patient enough, letting me

think things through this weekend. I don't think we should meet up until I work it out.

As for Gareth... No matter how hard I try not to go down that rabbit hole, it's impossible to resist.

The dream... We were going to be married- though not at all like how it was going to play out in reality of course. But I was so happy, the dream only reminded me of how I felt when I still thought things would work out between us. I haven't felt that hopeful in ages.

I caught a glimpse of the old me, and now that she's out, it's hard to put her back in her box.

How lovely it must be to go through life like that, like how Becky still is to some extent: despite a failed relationship or two, she still has hope that things will work out in the end. For me, cynicism wins in the end without fail.

Looking over at Becky's desk, I see she's texting as usual, her expression calm and content.

I wish I could have that kind of faith.

Across the office, the odd sniffle and sneeze breaks the silence. I guess I'm not the only one who's infected. Everyone is at their desks, either enjoying their first cup of whatever of the day, or quietly working away at those tasks that were meant to be finished already. You never truly can catch up and stay on top of your work in a place like this. But then you're not expected to.

Thankfully though there isn't any chatter today. I wouldn't have the patience to deal with it either. Apparently, losing one's temper is frowned upon in a professional environment.

Mark stalks out of his office, and towards Cath's desk, holding a bundle of paperwork. He looks magnificent as always, whereas I would like nothing better than to vanish today. No baggage, no bullshit, that's our M.O. Being a red-eyed sniffly mess definitely counts as both.

After he's done talking to Cath, he gives me a wave and nod, which I return rather bleakly.

*Please don't come over here, or I'll cough on you.*

Thankfully, he returns to his office and closes the door. Fridays tend to be busy for everyone, especially him.

My headache lifts slightly further, I like to think it's due to finally being allowed my much needed coffee, and I randomly pick one of today's pending tasks to start with: put together a sales forecast, oh joy.

The morning passes by rather slowly, mainly because my condition seems to be worsening again. By lunchtime, I decide I've had enough and knock on Mark's door.

"Come in," he says.

"Hey…" I'm suddenly torn between wanting to come across all perfect for the Mark I share my bed with, as opposed to needing to play up the miserable sick angle for Mark, the boss.

"Are you alright?" He gets up and lifts my chin towards him.

"Not really, you might want to keep your distance if you don't want to catch it," I say, backing away.

"Don't be stupid. Do you need anything? You

should probably go home and rest. I can come by after work to check on you." His voice sounds so warm and inviting, it's making my chest feel tight.

After spending most of the morning feeling sorry for myself, I hate to admit that I really could use some TLC. Just a hug would be nice even. But I can't accept his offer, if I did, it would mean I'm agreeing to something else also. I can't do that, my mind is racing again and I'm almost suffocating with more than just a congested chest.

"Uhh no, that's the other thing I wanted to say. Perhaps it's best we have some distance while I figure everything out."

His expression falls, and he backs away, sitting down on his chair again.

"If that's what you want."

"That's it, I don't know what I want. Except a nap. I really want a nap right now."

"Just let Cath know on your way out and get Becky to take over any urgent accounts."

It stings, the realisation that I've basically shot him down while he was trying to be nice and caring. I'm no good at letting people care for me. They inevitably let you down when you need them the most, so it's best not to rely on anyone.

"OK thanks, Mark," I mumble, while letting myself out of his office.

I don't know how we'll ever be OK again.

***

By the time I reach my place, I feel deflated and empty. It occurs to me I should probably have lunch before crashing into bed, but I can't be arsed to do anything about it. My cupboards are pretty much barren, as is the fridge. Who the hell even delivers takeout at this time of day?

I grab a bunch of sweets leftover from Christmas and get cosy under the covers.

For hours I'm drifting in and out of sleep, until I finally get up at nine, starving and aching all over.

Now I really wish I hadn't told Mark to stay away. If nothing else, he would've brought food or could've made me something. But it's too late for that now, and a quick check of my phone reveals he's not on chat either.

Plus, it's not like I could do or say anything to him now to make things better. He'll be pissed at me, and with good reason too.

Just when I want to put the phone away again, something makes me open up Gareth's message from last night again. Would it be so bad to meet him once? Now that he's haunting me in my dreams again for the first time in years, I've got to do *something* to make it stop.

He broke me once, and I have to believe I'm stronger now.

Once he says whatever it is he has to say, I'll know why things turned out the way they did. I'll understand why he left me.

And then I can tell him to fuck off in person.

*OK fine. Come to the White Hart on Bath Road. Monday, 7pm.*
*Sally*


I hit send before I have the chance to change my mind.

# CHAPTER NINE

I reluctantly wait by the pub entrance, scanning the crowd for Gareth. He better not have stood me up this time, after practically begging to meet! I'm in a good mind to turn around as it is.

A figure, in the same old leather jacket I spied at the office earlier this week turns away from the bar, holding two drinks, and I'm stopped in my tracks. *Fuck*. There he is.

He shoots me a tentative smile, and nods over at some empty seats by the window, away from most of the commotion in the place. I cut across the room, as does he, until we meet on opposite sides of the round wooden table.

"Hi," he says.

I just nod. I may have drugged myself heavily with various over-the-counter concoctions to get here, but I'm not yet convinced they'll have worked on my voice. Only two hours ago, I sounded barely any better than a creaking door. Perhaps I should have cancelled, after all I suggested tonight thinking I'd be better by now. Then again I'm just keen to get it all over with.

We sit down, not knowing what else to do and stare at each other for a moment. This is so weird. I want to be angry at him, ask him what the fuck was wrong with him to let me down so badly eight years ago, but suddenly I'm more intrigued than pissed off.

And awkward. Mainly I'm feeling super awkward.

"You look great," he remarks, finally.

"Thanks." Thank fuck, my voice works again.

"I got you a rum & coke. You always used to like those." He slides one of the two identical tall glasses towards me.

I don't say anything, just nod, no point telling him now that my tastes have developed a bit during our time apart. But he still seems the same. I spent years trying to reinvent myself, assuming it's a process everyone goes through growing up. Perhaps I was wrong.

The bit of stubble on his chin, messy brown hair, the blue piercing eyes which could see right into my soul - or so I thought when I was a stupid teenager - he's exactly how I remember him. Even down to the jacket, paired with faded jeans and biker boots. No wonder Elaine was so taken with him after he came to work, he does still have that bad boy charm around him. *But I'm so over all that!*

I don't know whether to cut right to it, or let him lead the conversation for a bit. Being in his presence again after such a long time is making me unsure of a lot of stuff.

"So… how have you been? Had a good holiday?" He smiles again, awkwardly, and we clink our drinks together before taking our first sips.

"Fine. Very well actually. Things have been great." I don't think that sounded convincing, but somehow, I really do want to make it a point that I did just fine without him, or anyone. "You?"

"Yeah… No, I can't say the same. It's been a rough few years." He fishes the lemon wedge out of his drink and squeezes a few drops of juice out of it. That old habit of his used to annoy me even back then, but I don't comment.

"So to what do I owe this sudden pleasure?" I say.

"It took me a while to track you down. You'd pretty much vanished after… " I stare at him, daring him to finish that sentence. I pretty much vanished, after he fucking vanished first, but still, I bite my tongue.

"About that, I have been curious how you managed it. I've not kept in touch with anyone from back in the day."

He smiles briefly, then averts his gaze.

"It's all a lot easier nowadays, with the internet and all."

"Uhuh." I get the feeling there's something he's leaving unsaid.

"Well anyway, I just wanted to let you know that I never meant for things to end the way they did. I was in a bad place back then." He runs his hands through his hair, something he always used to do when nervous.

I press my lips together, trying to prevent any rash remarks from passing through.

"Neither did I, and yet, they did end." *And who's fault is that?* I take another, bigger sip this time, glad that he at least ordered me a double.

"You know, that day-" He pauses, stares down at my hand on my glass.

"What about it?"

"I got arrested. That's why I didn't turn up." His eyes flick up at me, and for the first time I think I see regret.

"Right." *That's the big reason? What a load of shit.*

"They got me for that time I was out with Roy and Luke and we nicked that car off old Mr. Teesdale and went for a little drive around town. We intended to park it back in its place, but by the time we had had our fun, there were cops everywhere so we dumped it and ran."

I take a deep breath, and rub my temples. My fingertips are nearly frozen from holding on to the cold drink. I don't know if it's my cold, or talking to Gareth after so long, perhaps both, but my head is swimming again.

"You couldn't have called? Sent someone to let me know? I was waiting around the registrar's office like a total idiot, until finally they took pity on me and made me a cup of tea..."

I remember the thing with the old guy's car. As soon as I heard about it, I had wanted to lop Gareth over the head with the nearest blunt object. Those two assholes he chose to hang out with had always been trouble.

"I tried to, I called Karen, but she told me to piss off and that you'd be better off without me anyway."

With the mention of my cousin and our mutual 'friend' Karen things start to fall into place. That sounds like her, the meddling bitch. As I recall, she always had a thing for him, so obviously she would welcome the chance to break us up. But to think that it actually worked is too much.

"So that was that then?" I hate this sinking feeling in my chest, like I'm being let down again when I had tried so hard not to go into this with any expectations whatsoever. Perhaps, if only subconsciously, I had hoped for something more. That the worst day of my life would have been caused by something a bit more substantial.

"I figured she was probably right."

"And my opinion didn't matter anymore, yeah?"

"By the time I realised I made a huge mistake, you were nowhere to be found. I've regretted it every single day."

Even though the last part sounds genuine enough, and he's put his best guilty face on, I can't contain my frustration. My cheeks glow and my breathing has turned ragged as a result of the anger burning up inside my chest. I can't believe I suffered so much pain because of something so stupid.

"Should've thought of that sooner." I push my chair back, take another two big gulps from the drink, suffering severe brain freeze as a consequence, but I don't care. I've had enough of this shit and need to get away. Suddenly the pub atmosphere is not cosy, as probably intended by the landlord, but instead it threatens to suffocate me.

"Wait, Sally!" He jumps up as well, and tries to squeeze through some of the chairs blocking him in, but I don't stand around and wait. I make a beeline for the exit, nearly hitting into a group of girls in skimpy dresses, much like the type I would wear, before I hit my mid-twenties and discovered that I could sense the cold after all.

After that near-accident, nothing stands between me and the door. I need air.

Outside, I get out my packet of cigarettes, noticing the unwelcome shakiness in my fingers. Never in the past eight years have I let anyone affect me like this. But all this old shit being dragged back up is making my defences crumble at every instance. That's why the awkwardness with Mark has been so rough as well: I'm totally off my game. It's unacceptable.

I light up and inhale deeply, waiting for the nicotine to do its job.

Gareth has finally made it out as well, and notices me quickly enough. I'm in a good mind to run, but he'd catch me. And I guess I do have to finish this conversation somehow.

"Hey! I thought you were going to up and disappear again." He leans against the wall next to me and observes me as I take another drag. If he says a word about how I never used to smoke, I'll put it out in his fucking face.

"You didn't expect that once I listen to that story of yours everything would be forgiven?"

"Uhh, no I guess not. But how things ended between us has really bothered me and I couldn't just leave things as they were." It *really bothered* him? That's the best he can come up with?

"I gave up everything to be with you, to make a life with you. And you threw it away for some shit Karen said?"

"I…" He shifts uncomfortably from one foot to the other. "She did make a solid point. There I was, being held for stealing a car - which by the way they never did catch Luke or Roy for, only me - meanwhile you were giving up on going to university for me. Without me, you could make something of yourself. I didn't even know whether I'd be looking at being locked up or just a warning or what."

Put like that, I suppose I can see where he's coming from. But if he had wanted to somehow save me from what a life with him would entail, wouldn't it have been better to give me a choice in the matter?

"You have no idea what you did that day." I throw the cigarette butt down and stomp on it repeatedly, releasing some of my anger, until everything down to the filter is destroyed and mushed into the moist pavement.

"Clearly not. They let me out the following day and I went looking for you, went by your folks where your Dad nearly beat the shit out of me. They thought you'd left with me as planned. Nobody knew where you were."

"Of course they didn't! What was I supposed to do? After weeks of arguments, I had packed my shit, emptied my savings account and left, leaving only a note. I couldn't very well turn back and say '*Oh, things didn't work out with Gareth, just like you said they wouldn't, can I move back in now?*'" I snort in outrage. "And after they obviously welcomed me with *open arms*, I'd add: '*By the way, Mum, Dad, I'm pregnant.'* That would've gone down *so well* with them."

Throughout my rant, I hadn't noticed the tears streaming down my face.

I hadn't told a soul the whole story of what happened that day. After waiting all day I ran, not to London like we'd agreed, instead I boarded the first train I saw. In the end I wouldn't have known where I ended up but for the sign at the final station: Newtowne, a bland 1970s commuter town which has nothing much going for it. Mainly, I wanted to get away from everything I guess. Everything and everyone. And I couldn't imagine anyone would think to follow me *here.*

Gareth's expression is one of utter shock. His mouth is half open and eyes are about ready to pop out.

"So it's true," he finally says, blinking a few times.

"What?" I'm doing my best to dry my eyes, but it's no use. All my defences have finally crumbled.

"Karen said-" I shoot him a mean glance through wet lashes at the mention of that backstabbing bitch but he ignores me. "Fuck. You really were pregnant."

"I never told anyone, especially her."

"She guessed it, anyway, that's not the point. Where is it? Where's the child?"

I can't stop the flow of tears, and try to hide my face which must be streaky and hideously patchy by now.

"How could you let me down like that? I had nobody else but you, you know that. It was supposed to be us against the world." Hearing those words spoken in my own voice opens the floodgates for deeper, more desperate sobs.

He grabs me by both my arms, his warmth piercing starkly through the surrounding cold and I start to shiver uncontrollably. For a moment, I'm swept up by the thought that perhaps this is one of those stupid, crazy reconciliations you get at the end of a romance novel. That just maybe, through his touch which I had so intensely craved for years, I could overcome all the pain he's caused me. Still, I'm a puddle of overwhelming emotions and lean into him slightly, trying to reclaim my balance.

"Where is it?" he repeats.

I look up, trying to blink the watery haze away.

"Where's what?"

"*My* child." His features have hardened, and his fingers are digging in harder now. The deliberate emphasis in his demand gives me pause.

"There is no child." I sniffle, and try to reach up to check that my nose isn't starting to drip, but he refuses to loosen his grip.

"What do you mean, you just said you were pregnant." Both his eyes have narrowed, he's getting annoyed.

"I miscarried a few months later," I stammer, taken aback by the sudden change in his mood.

"Fuck." He lets go and balls his fists hard enough I can hear his knuckles crack.

"Is that what this was about? You tracked me down thinking I had your baby?" I take a step back, and wipe my face dry once and for all. *Enough*. I've had enough of the drama, enough of the stories, the fucking emotions. How dare he?

"Answer me!" Again, I've got that sinking feeling of not only disappointment now, but betrayal.

"What do you think? I'd find out about something so major and not investigate? Karen said-"

"What's with Karen this, Karen that? You two seem to be awfully chummy!"

He throws me a cold glance. I understand now.

"You've been fucking Karen ever since, haven't you? That's why you never tried to come after me until now." I take a deep breath, aiming not to let the growing rage inside my belly boil over. I'm shaking again, but not due to cold or painful memories. My muscles tighten with a sudden surge in adrenalin.

"We've been an item, yes."

"And for whatever reason, she told you I had your baby? Jesus fucking Christ. You really are a dumb shit, Gareth!"

"Keep your voice down, I'm telling you!" he spits through gritted teeth.

"You don't get to tell me a fucking thing, Gareth! As far as I'm concerned all this shit is done and over with. Why don't you run along home to *Karen*. You two deserve each other."

He steps forward to grab me again, my own rage reflected in his eyes.

"Bitch, I didn't come all this way to be humiliated in public by some whore, who thinks it's below her to give people a chance. Who just cuts and runs at the first sign of trouble and leaves behind all those who care about her." His hand locks around my wrist again, so tight the blood flow to my fingers is starting to slow.

"Oh hell no! This shit may fly with my cousin, but you're not laying a finger on me!"

From the corner of my eye, I see some bystanders shuffle around uncomfortably, uncertain whether to intervene. I look towards the door of the pub, wondering if their bouncer has started his shift yet, but there's no sign of anyone who fits the bill. He takes a step forward until his face is mere inches away from mine. I wonder what he's going to do next. Gareth has always had a temper, even back then. But I refuse to let him faze me.

"Let go of me or you'll regret it." I stare straight at him, into those blue eyes that used to mean something to me, which now just seem empty and unimportant.

He doesn't react, not instantly, until out of nowhere, a hand, adorned with a couple of oriental silver rings and bright red nail polish wraps itself around Gareth's throat.

"Get your hands off her," a familiar voice threatens, as Gareth stumbles backwards.

*Holy fucking shit.*

# CHAPTER TEN : MARK

The first time I saw the guy, my understanding of what I felt for Sally changed. The second time, it changed my understanding of who she was, really.

Not only was she infuriatingly independent, to the extent that she pretended not to need a soul around her. This part I had already understood before, which had pretty much made me give up on trying to win her over. She also had a softer, vulnerable side which I'd never seen before.

When she basically told me to piss off on Friday, I was in a good mood to shut her out of my life completely. If she wanted things to be like that, I would tolerate her at the office somehow, then get on with life on my own. For years I've hidden a significant part of myself from the world, which has made me a good liar. I'd learnt to lie to myself pretty well too.

I had tried to show what I could offer her. If it took more than a traditional relationship, then I'd find a way of sharing her with other people. But I needed to put a label on it. I needed to reassure myself that she wouldn't just up and leave without so much as an explanation. I needed a commitment.

If any of my exes knew about this, they'd find it hard to contain their laughter. I had never wanted a commitment before Sally.

But to see that creep threaten her in public made me

see red. I forgot that I was angry at her. That I had vowed not to let her get under my skin again because we had no hope in hell of making it work. I threw caution in the wind, and followed my instincts.

I even forgot that I was wearing stiletto heels and a cocktail dress.

When I realised, it was too late. Sally's mouth hung open in shock, and she could not stop staring at me while I held Gareth in a headlock.

I totally fucked up.

That's when the cops turned up and shoved her and me into one of those fortified vans you often see parked around the town centre at night, before stuffing Gareth by himself into the back of their car.

"Umm…" Sally breaks the silence inside the dark mobile holding cell.

I don't respond, but keep on sitting there, with my head in my hands. Holy hell, this is awkward as awkward can be. In all the years I've allowed myself the occasional night out fully dressed up, I've always been super careful not to go near where I know people from work hang out. Despite living in a relatively small city, with few places to go, I'd never been made.

There are a few noises, some shuffling around at the far side of the van where I know she is, followed by footsteps.

"I'm really sorry," Sally says.

I flinch when her hand rests on my shoulder. Her touch always has caused me to react intensely, but now that the game is up, it's not arousal that I feel but shame. It's a lot easier to convince yourself you have nothing to be ashamed of when nobody you know has seen you femmed up.

"He didn't hurt you, did he?" she asks.

I shake my head. Gareth tried to get a few punches in while I tried to pry him away from her, but the only casualties in this fight were a couple of my fingernails.

There's more silence between us, it's painful to wait through it for what I know will come next: awkward questions or remarks. If I'm lucky she'll assume I was going to a fancy dress party.

She sits down next to me, so close I can sense the warmth of her thigh radiate against mine.

"So…" she pauses.

I sigh, waiting for the inevitable.

"What's your name?"

I look up, confused. Is she in denial? Surely, she must have recognised me.

"I mean - and I may be way off - but I thought perhaps you'd use a different name. When you're dressed like this I mean." She blinks nervously, then looks away.

Though this is obviously uncomfortable, she seems more intrigued than put off.

"Melody. I tend to go by Melody."

"Nice. I like it." She smiles briefly, without making eye contact, then fidgets with the buttons on her coat. "It would've been weird, calling you Mark. That would sort of ruin it, wouldn't it?"

Recognising her question as rhetorical, I remain

quiet. Anyway, I'm not sure what to say to her. This whole situation is way too similar to many nightmares I've had, which inevitably end up in humiliation. I'd never seriously considered coming out to someone I know. Perhaps if I'd given it more thought, I would have prepared a few lines. While in my job I could steer any conversation in exactly the direction I want, this is completely beyond my skills.

"Love your shoes," she says.

I look down at the buckled black leather boots on my feet. My favourites for this time of year.

"Thanks," I mumble. I feel like telling her I've always loved her choice of shoes, clothes, whatever. I want to respond that it means a lot to have her approval, but it would only sound desperate, so I keep quiet.

"I wonder how long they'll keep us in here. Clearly it was all *his* fault." Sally leans back, sighing and rubbing her forehead with the back of her hand.

Earlier, when I came across the both of them, she was staring him down despite the obvious imbalance in size and strength: he was a good foot taller than her.

Perhaps when facing off with him, she felt there was nothing more he could do to her, like she had nothing to lose. Perhaps it wasn't the first time he'd been violent with her and she'd had enough? The thought infuriates me again, causing me to tense up. I'd tried to stay composed, and only do the needful but if pushed, I would have been capable of inflicting permanent damage on the guy. Still am.

"I probably owe you an explanation, huh?" Sally

leans forward again, resting her elbows on her knees.

"Not really. It's none of my business."

"I know you were jealous when he turned up at work, but there's nothing going on between us, at least not anymore…" She rubs her hands together, and attempts to blow some warmth into them.

"I wasn't-"

"That's not what Cath said." Hell yeah I was jealous, who wouldn't be? It just seems impossible to admit now.

I glance over, and she returns my gaze. She's so different than the Sally I thought I knew. Of course I never truly got to know her, which is possibly my own fucking fault, but still. She seems smaller, more fragile than I'd ever seen her before.

"Gareth and I were together back when I was just a teenager. It didn't work out."

I wonder whether to ask questions. Like whether she'd left him because he hit her, but it really does seem like I'm better off not knowing.

"Actually, that's not the whole story. He practically left me at the altar - registrar's office - same thing. This whole business with him tracking me down… I dunno…" She sniffles and rubs her forehead again. "He said he wanted to explain what happened, to apologise. But I think it was bullshit, all of it."

"Was he always such a tool?" I wonder out loud.

"I've been asking myself that too." She lets out a half-hearted chuckle.

I reach over, covering her hands with mine. They're

freezing, of course. Putting on the fucking heating in this van would've been too much trouble for the noble protectors of the law who put us here.

Her fingers thread through mine, and for a moment there, it doesn't seem to matter what happened tonight, or over the past few weeks, or even ages ago between her and Gareth. If we ever get out of here, I just want to take care of her as long as she'll let me, even if I only get to be a friend.

She leans against me, her head on my shoulder, until we're interrupted by some commotion outside.

"Alright," a gruff voice barks right outside the metal doors at the far end of the van. "Mrs. Doubtfire and the girl can leave now." A couple more voices snigger at his remark.

We share a look, while the locks creak and groan and the door opens, letting in a waft of even colder air.

"After making further inquiries and interviewing witnesses of the incident," the skinny policeman who initially held us says, "we could confirm that you were indeed acting in self defence against a-" He nods down at his notebook. "Gareth Doyle, who has a history of violent behaviour including assault resulting in grievous injury." The cop puts his notebook into his coat pocket and steps aside to let us exit the van.

"You're free to go."

"Thanks," I grumble, while getting up.

Sally doesn't say a word, just holds on tightly to my hand. I note she's begun shivering violently, so I put my arm around her shoulder and pull her against me while we walk off towards the nearest taxi stand, leaving the bemused policemen and various bystanders behind.

# CHAPTER ELEVEN

What a fucking night.

I should have listened to my gut and not met Gareth. Then again, if I hadn't, I wouldn't have ended up here at Mark's place tonight. Or should I say Melody's place? Over towards the open plan kitchen, I can see him - her - zipping back and forth from counter to stove and back to the fridge, the black flowy fabric of her dress, exaggerating every movement.

The moment we reached back, I was consigned to the sofa, where I was to stay under any circumstance, under various warm blankets. Apparently this is how you catch pneumonia: by going out on a particularly frosty January night and ending up in an unheated police van. Although I'm still sceptical about the dangers of getting a little cold while having the sniffles, I was shivering so badly, I wasn't able or willing to argue.

I wonder how many people have stories like this to tell; tonight had started off so seemingly normal as well.

The room is starting to smell rather lovely, and I don't recall eating anything proper all weekend. To be fair I don't know how I actually survived those two days, and today at the office, consuming mainly Paracetamol and caffeinated liquids.

"Have this while I make the soup," Ma-Melody says, putting a steaming cup of herbal tea on the coffee table in front of the couch.

"Thanks."

It's all a tad surreal, finding a six foot amazonian brunette come to your aid in an escalating row with an ex you haven't seen in years. It's even more surreal recognising said brunette as your on-and-off lover and full-time boss. Thinking back, it's obvious Mark had secrets. I just thought they came in the form of *another person* with a penchant for lacey underwear and long fingernails. It's funny how life turns out sometimes.

I pick up the cup, coughing profusely when the steamy fumes hit my nose. Fucking hell. I hate being sick.

"If it tastes weird, add some honey," *Melody* says.

I wrinkle my nose at the thought, I'm more of a black coffee kind of person, but apparently I'm in need of the benefits of this particular concoction of greenery. Mint and echyna-something. I never could pronounce that one. And anyway, flowers aren't food in my mind.

Fine. If it makes *Melody* happy, I'll drink the stuff. If it makes me feel better, that'll be an added bonus.

The pounding headache that worsened after we got almost-arrested is starting to subside. Tonight generally has been an overdose of emotions and surprises. Gareth can so fuck off right now. And when he gets there, he can fuck off some more...

As I confronted him about all the shit I went through after he basically abandoned me, I started to realise that for years I haven't truly allowed myself to feel. I hadn't dealt with the negative shit, and as a result, couldn't appreciate the positive either.

During that little moment of weakness when I thought I craved his touch, actually, he wasn't who I was yearning for. I did want a connection with someone. When *Melody* turned up, and we were put in that metal box together, I finally understood that I wasn't the only one with secrets.

I was hiding a past, in which I honestly believed I could create a family with an asshole like Gareth, only to be crushed when things didn't work out quite how I had hoped. Mark had been hiding an entire side of his current self.

As scared as I had felt, opening up my weaknesses even to Becky, who I trust despite our vast differences, I couldn't imagine how he must have felt. I couldn't have known of course, but I felt ashamed that I'd brought up those little details I found, that evidence of his other life, during our argument last week.

I unknowingly poked around in something I didn't understand, something so private he wasn't ready to share. Just like how I hadn't been ready to share my secrets with him.

Yet all that stuff was forced out into the open, for better or for worse.

*Melody* is now rummaging around in a cupboard, retrieving two bowls and a tray. I watch her as she moves with a certain elegance Mark doesn't normally display. Or perhaps it's only my perception that has changed.

I had wanted to say that I was OK with it, back in the van. But it didn't seem like the right time, so I just tried to act cool.

"Here." Melody puts one bowl on the table in front of me and the other nearer the armchair towards my left.

"Thanks. That smells amazing." I smile, grateful for the chance to put the suspiciously green herbal tea back down.

"Nothing fancy, it's only chicken soup."

"I couldn't cook chicken soup to save my life," I remark.

She nods at me, a knowing grin on her face.

"Yeah, that's pretty obvious."

I smile back at her, marvelling at the transformation that can be achieved with a bit of makeup, a wig and a nice outfit. She's beautiful, not *OK-for-a-dude-in-a-dress*, but genuinely so. Meanwhile, I spent a good part of the evening looking like a scarecrow with Kiss style face paint on. It was a relief to be able to ask for makeup remover once we got here. Funny, how natural it is to act as if I'm at a girlfriend's house all of a sudden.

"If I had known you have so many nice things." I nod at Melody's handbag on the table. "I might have asked to borrow some of them."

"Perhaps then it's a good thing you didn't know." She winks at me, and starts eating her soup.

Although I never actually said anything to cut through the tension, things seem more relaxed now. We're alone, away from prying eyes, free to be ourselves.

Yet I can't take my eyes off her, although I'm trying

not to stare. Suddenly aware, Melody looks up from her bowl, wearing a concerned frown.

"If it's too weird, I can - you know - change..."

*Shit, busted!* I quickly shake my head, aware that unusually, I can't afford to play coy. There is too much of a risk for misunderstandings right now.

"No, no, it's not that." I glance down at the steamy bowl for a moment, nerves surging. Shit, how do I put this? "I just think you look really beautiful."

Her expressions changes, but only subtly, as we maintain eye contact. A bit of a smile plays on her lips, but it's too faint to be certain, while my heart hammers away inside my chest.

"Thanks." She blinks, trying to hide the beginnings of tears in her eyes.

I sit up straighter and put my soup down. It's hard to find the right words, when it seems like so much depends on the here and now. No wonder first dates are meant to be so difficult. You go into the situation hoping for the best possible outcome, at a time when things are at their most fragile. Why is it so damn impossible to find the right thing to say?

"So you don't think it's weird?" she asks.

"Not really. It's certainly different, seeing you like this," I say, regretting my phrasing as soon as she frowns again. "Shit, that didn't come out right. I mean, it's like that being with two people, rather than just one. Does that make sense?"

"I suppose so."

We quietly finish our soup, after which she collects

the dirty dishes and leaves them in the kitchen. I wonder if I fucked up and ruined what little progress we'd made so far.

It's only nine, too early to turn in for the night, though both my health and today's exertions are still catching up with me, exhausting me.

When she's back after filling up the dishwasher, Melody leans over and touches my forehead with the back of her hand. I close my eyes, trying to will my heartbeat to slow down but it's no use. Although I've often felt giddy in Mark's company, that was nothing compared to what's going on now.

"Don't think you've got a fever," she remarks. "But it would be a bad idea for you should head out into the cold anyway."

I breathe a sigh of relief. Although things are still pretty awkward, I have no wish to leave now. The only way through this weirdness is forward.

"I'd like to stay with you if that's OK."

She smiles at me.

"Of course."

I wonder if my intention shone through: I didn't mean on the couch. Her hand still lingers on my forehead, and I take it, searching for agreement in her eyes. She gently closes her fingers around mine, causing the hairs at the back of my neck to stand up. I hold my breath as I caress her with my fingertips.

"I'm so sorry I've been such a bitch lately. I hope you'll forgive me?" I ask, more desperate than ever for things to be OK between us.

Melody sits down on the armrest beside me, and I lean up against the cushions, waiting for her response.

"It's fine. It's not like I've been totally upfront." She hesitates, as if wanting to say something more, but then just reaches out and plays with a lock of my hair.

I rest my head against her thigh, noting how she flinches slightly again, like when I first touched her shoulder in the police van. But neither of us pull away, and soon, her hand finds more locks, caressing and untangling them, while I continue to hold her other hand.

If my nerves are anything to go by, how must she feel?

"I don't want to infect you with my germs…" I say. *But I really want to kiss you.*

"I don't care."

I half-turn, and find her already staring down at me. The tension between us is so intense, it's incomparable with anything I've ever felt before, whether with Mark or anyone else.

"May I?" I ask, reaching for the side of her face.

Melody closes her eyes and nods, and I let my thumb brush over her lower lip. I cast aside the throws and blankets and get up, only to kneel on the sofa, facing her.

Neither of us want to wait any longer. Her fingers thread through my locks, guiding me closer, and my lips hungrily meet hers. Our lips part almost instantly, allowing our kisses to deepen, and some of the uncertainty from before to fade. But there's still this tension, this growing need inside me to go further.

I want her with all my being.

The frantic dance our tongues have entered into tells me she wants the same.

I stare into her eyes to find that they're open again, naked and honest in amber. For once I understand when people say they can tell just from a look what the other person is thinking. Maybe I hadn't been looking hard enough, or I wasn't ready to see what was there all along.

Finally, I know all there is to know. I can plainly see her for who she is, and can't stop the urge to drown in those eyes.

"Come closer," I whisper.

Melody slides off the armrest, and kneels right in front of me, our bodies as close as we can manage. I start caressing her, exploring the contours of the body I thought I knew so well. Her toned shoulders, which I'd thought quite strong and masculine before, now seem fitting with her new persona. She's certainly not a dainty female, her height has made that an impossibility, but nothing is out of place. Her physique is more akin to a warrior princess whereas I'm weak and insignificant in comparison.

Her sides seem to curve like one would expect on a woman, even if her hips aren't as rounded as mine. I reach around, feeling for the zip of her dress, while she unbuttons my skinny jeans.

Once I manage to open it, she hesitates for a moment, searching for confirmation in my eyes, but finally lets the smooth black fabric slide off her to reveal what looks like a plain black sports bra.

This is the secret, what makes Melody Melody. The cup size she's chosen is again perfect for her athletic frame.

Leaning in, I cover what bare skin I can find with kisses, before running my fingers over the swell in her bra. Melody holds her breath, closing her eyes again. I continue to tease, explore and play, like how I would want it. I know how to treat a girl, it's not the first time. I wonder if it's the first time for her?

"You're beautiful," I mumble, while nuzzling her neck and nibbling gently on her skin. It must tickle, judging by how her head snaps to the side, almost trapping me, but she does not protest.

"You're not just saying that?" she whispers, between the short staccato of her excited breaths.

"Hell no." I try drown out any further concerns with further kisses lavishing her lips.

"I've never… you know… while dressed," Melody answers my unspoken question.

Where earlier I had felt feverish and lethargic, I'm filled with a renewed energy. What I'm doing here, to her, is special. And because of it, and our changed dynamic, I'm beside myself with desire.

"That's about to change, if you want…" I say.

She smiles into my kisses, and responds by removing my top. That's all the encouragement I need to get on my back, and wriggle out and discard the rest of my clothes.

How different things are, compared to the last time we found ourselves here on this sofa. Different and so much better.

Running my hands down her flat, toned stomach, I reach the lacey edge of her panties. The soft stretchy fabric is straining to contain the one thing I do know very well about her. I cup the bulge gently, and circle around, ever inwards with my fingernail.

"Tell me how you like it, Melody," I say.

Her eyes light up, as her breathing stocks with every movement of my fingers. I'm about ready to burst myself, and the same seems true for her.

"Gently," she mouths, almost inaudibly.

I take her by the hand, prompting her to turn 90 degrees until her stockinged legs are resting on those gorgeous heeled boots on the floor, and straddle her. Something tells me she wants to keep her panties on, so instead of undressing her further, I slip her solid cock out from the side. Taking it in my hand, I wrap my fingers around and massage, gently, but firmly enough to have an effect.

All the memories I have, of fun-filled nights involving activities much like this pale in comparison with the passion that has grown inside me. I could scream, not out of pain or frustration, but out of joy, I'm that grateful for how things have turned out.

But before I voice any of that, it's time to take the step: to take Melody's virginity.

I lower myself onto her, enjoying the familiar sensation of her length filling me. The fabric of her panties, though noticeable, does not detract from the experience. Instead it rubs my clit just right.

She moans softly into my ear, her hands close around my hips until they've stopped trembling.

"This… is so perfect." Melody runs one hand up all the way over my back until it reaches my neck and she pulls me in closer.

"I agree. Perfect," I respond.

I rock back and forth, gently as requested, my hands continuing to enjoy the softness of her breasts, which are surprisingly realistic. Until I can't hold back anymore, and speed up, coaxed along by her hold on my ass. Our bodies are joined, entwined, like they've never been before. Like I know when to push down, when to flick my hips to heighten her pleasure, along with my own. She digs her fingers in deep into my flesh, moaning almost continuously, as my own release is so achingly close I can almost taste it.

I fight the lethargy that threatens to return, struggle through the weakness in my aching limbs, focus only on her breaths and gasps and the sweet tickle in the bottom of my abdomen.

Two, three thrusts more, and I've nearly reached the summit, yet I power on to take her with me.

Sweat starts to collect on my brow, a sign of my continued efforts, and I'm dangerously close to the point of no return when she joins in, arms wrapped around me tightly and hips twitching feverishly upwards into me. I cry out, and try to hang on in a vice-like embrace as she finishes us both in an explosion of sweet relief.

I collapse on top of her, lost for words as well as breath. All I can think to do is just to hide my face in the crook of her neck, enjoying the tickle of her hair on my cheek. She holds me in her arms, caressing my hair until we've both calmed ourselves.

Time passes, but we don't stir. I don't want to give this up, this moment, and this closeness. Now I understand how very dear she - he - is to me. It's been hard-fought, us coming together like this. A lot has happened, we've both been hurt, and needed mending first. I hope this is the first step of many, to make things right again.

"I feel like I've met you for the first time tonight," a voice that sounds deceptively like Mark says.

He takes off his long wig, as well as the pretty earrings I had admired earlier. I lean up, finding him already staring at me. My heart skips a beat, though I'm not quite sure why.

"I know the feeling."

His eyes soften, as he lets his gaze linger on me a bit longer before continuing.

"You never told me you like girls." He winks at me, like he often does when he's trying to tease me.

"You never asked." I take a deep breath, forcing myself out of character, to add something more heartfelt. "Plus it would seem that Melody isn't just any girl, but someone rather special."

Mark pauses for a moment, then brushes a few strands of my damp hair out of my face.

"How about I get changed, and you finish that tea and get into bed. At this rate, you'll really catch something nasty."

I press my lips together, trying to hide my disappointment that he noticed I didn't finish my cup of whatever herbal nonsense. The look he's giving me, so full of concern is impossible to ignore though, so I decide to play along.

"Let's hope you don't catch the same thing," I mumble, while struggling up and reaching over to retrieve the half full cup. It's barely luke-warm by now so I neck it, trying to ignore the taste.

Behind me, the rustle of fabrics suggests he's getting up and gathering our various clothes. Then unexpectedly, his arms reach around my back and the back of my knees and I'm lifted into the air before I can do anything about it.

"I mean it, off to bed with you. You're not going anywhere until you're well again."

I feel like arguing, want to say I've done just fine on my own for the past few years, thank-you-very-much, but I bite my tongue instead and wrap my arms around his neck. He can have this one. Right now, there's no place I'd rather spend the night than in his bed.

# EPILOGUE

I wrap myself tighter in my fur trimmed coat, the one I wore the first time Mark and I met, and gaze up at the magnificent sight of the Eiffel Tower ahead of us. Mark steps up behind me, and rests his arm around my shoulders, which I gratefully lean back into.

Despite darkness already having set over the city, there are so many lights, so much to see. The entire tower is tastefully lit up as well, serving as a shining beacon against the crisp, starry sky.

"If you want, we can take a lift all the way up and have dinner in the panoramic restaurant."

The prospect makes me smile.

"That would be amazing, but I'm sure they'll be full. Plus I'm not quite dressed for the occasion."

"It's the middle of winter, what do they expect?"

"Some Parisian woman with legs all the way to her waist, in a designer dress with minimum coverage that perfectly matches her Christian Louboutins?"

A gust of wind reminds me that even though I'm in jeans and a sweater underneath the heavy coat, it's still not quite enough to counter the elements today.

"They can go to hell if that's the only way to get in. Let's see if we can get a table." He pulls me tighter towards him as we walk off to the base of the tower, narrowly avoiding the odd souvenir salesman trying to flog us his wares.

This trip is already special enough, I don't need a shiny golden Eiffel tower replica to remind me of it later. As far as mementos go, I've got the best one already: a sketched portrait of us, done by an artist we came across in Montmartre yesterday.

When we asked for another addition to the scene, showing him a picture of *Melody,* he simply shrugged and added her without saying a word. I'm sure he's had weirder requests in the past.

I wait off to the side from the lift entrance, while Mark makes his enquiries regarding the restaurant. It'll be a fucking miracle if he manages to get us in tonight, on Valentine's day. But sure enough, the doorman nods, and Mark gives me a little wave.

"Let's go. It'll give us a chance to warm up."

As I walk past, the doorman ticks off an entry in his notebook. Clever. Trust Mark to pre-book everything, yet present it as a spontaneous idea.

"Good job you didn't cancel everything, huh?" I ask, elbowing him gently in the ribs while we wait for the lift to come down.

He shrugs, giving me a sideways look.

"It was all non-refundable anyway, would've been a waste of time."

"Plus you could have always brought one of your other girlfriends…"

He grins for a split second, then leans over and gives me a peck on the cheek.

"Indeed, that's always an option."

The doors slide open in front of us and we step in.

There's a uniformed attendant, just like in the movies, who presses a button to take us all the way to the top. When we get there, an equally smartly dressed waiter shows us to our seats, right beside a large window. The view of the city down below is breathtaking.

"Wow," I say, unable to think of anything better.

"Yeah." Mark leans across the table, taking my hand. "Happy Valentine's day."

I respond with a smile, still speechless.

I would've never thought I'd be here with him, like this. With everything out in the open.

Ever since that night when the shit with Gareth happened, we've spent almost every spare moment together, getting to know each other. Although sometimes it's difficult not to panic and fear the worst, I can honestly say that I trust him now.

We've made a vow to not keep any more secrets.

And I fully intend to keep that promise.

***

# BONUS STORY:

# JUST ANOTHER HALLOWEEN

*'Just Another Halloween' features familiar characters from The Rebound List and Just Another Day at the Office but can be enjoyed independently.*

"Are you ready?" Alex sounds impatient, but pulling off the perfect naughty witch makeup is no laughing matter.

"Gimme a minute!" I shout, and stand back, inspecting the upward swoops of eyeliner applied to my lids. Do both sides match? After blinking at my reflection a couple of times, I decide it'll have to do. The black and purple pointy hat that came with my costume completes the look.

I grab my bag just before heading for the door; a plush toy black cat which is both hilarious and a little creepy in how convincing it looks.

"Let's go." I wave at Alex to get a move on, but he's taking his time checking me out.

"That looks way hotter on you than it did in the picture."

The look in his eyes confirms his statement and simultaneously I must admit that I'm quite partial to his costume as well. The deep red velvet 3 piece suit and top hat is formal enough to be hot as well as classy. Powerful would be the word, like a warlock ought to be.

When Cath handed me the invite to her party a couple of weeks ago, I had my reservations. I wasn't entirely sure how seriously everyone would take the fancy dress aspect of it, and whether it would be weird to go all out and buy matching costumes. Now, I'm convinced it was a good decision. These will be worn again, even if it's just in the privacy of our bedroom, before being quickly discarded.

I tiptoe to reach around his shoulders and give him a peck on the lips, carefully, so I don't transfer too much of my lipstick.

"You're not so bad yourself, handsome."

He tips his hat at me, offers me his arm and off we go. I'm curious whether our efforts will fit in or stand out, but glad we took the time anyway.

***

Cath's place is quite easy to find: the bus stops right outside her front door. I feel just a tinge of envy when I see the brass house number on the facade of one of the long row of Victorian terraced houses. What a lovely place to live. She couldn't be much older, and I didn't think she makes that much more than me either, despite working in Aspect Technologies a couple of years longer. Still, the difference between her home and my own is striking.

Supposedly scary decorations greet us as we walk up the pathway through the small front garden. Pumpkins, fake spiderwebs and candles adorn the entrance.

"What a place, eh?" Alex remarks, speaking my mind

completely.

"U-huh."

Just when he lifts his hand to ring the bell, the door opens by itself already, revealing Cath; paler than usual, except for the bright red lips and heavy eye make-up.

"You made it! Come on in." Cath smiles, showing off a pair of fangs that fit her so perfectly, they might as well be real.

I introduce Alex, and Cath calls out for John, her man, to meet us as well. Introductions happen in a blur, while I'm still eyeing the house, which despite the cheesy decorations still looks charming and stylish on the inside as well. I do note John and Cath have not gone for matching outfits, he's dressed as a medieval monk rather than another vampire. And he looks familiar, but I can't place where I've seen him before.

Beyond the door to the lounge, I hear the buzz of a party already underway. Voices I know, mixed in with ones I don't recall hearing before. My earlier curiosity about whether our costumes will stand out has been satisfied by seeing how much of an effort Cath made herself. However, I still wonder just how well we'll fit in otherwise. It can be weird socialising with coworkers outside of the usual office environment. At times people behave so differently, as if they wear a mask to work…

I hope Sally turns up soon. At least her I know as a best friend first and colleague second.

"Cath, sweetheart? I can't find the ladle to go with the punch." A cheerful sounding male voice shouts from the lounge.

She flashes a quick smile at us and excuses herself. Alex and I follow John inside shortly after, while the two of them continue to exchange pleasantries. They seem to get on well, which is a relief since Alex knows even fewer people here. It's interesting to see how similar they are, in terms of build as well as character.

Moments later we're on our own, mingling. We greet a handsome, if slightly camp gladiator, who introduces himself as 'Jason, but everyone calls me Jase' and boyfriend, who's wearing a toga. Clearly, someone's been watching *Spartacus*…

Next there are a couple of zombies whose names I can't make out because they're taking their roles too seriously. I wave at the only other familiar face, Elaine, across the room who's talking to a tall 1920's gangster looking guy I've never seen before.

"That fairy over there, that's Elaine. From work," I whisper to Alex, who nods in her direction as well.

The rest of the people, about half a dozen of them, are too preoccupied with the buffet of snacks. Just as well, because Sally has just arrived with Mark.

In what can only be described as complete couple's coordination, the both of them have dressed up as each other. It strangely works, Mark in a blonde wig to match Sally's usual style, a short dress and heels I would have trouble walking on myself. And Sal in the perfectly cut black suit with a shirt and tie combination Mark often wears to work. It's mind bending as well as hilarious.

"Hey, you! I was wondering when you'd get here. Let's get some snacks, what do you say?" I give Sally a hug and we wander off towards the tables lining the side of the room.

Looking back, I see Alex and Mark chatting awkwardly. Well, Mark looks fine, it's Alex who seems taken aback. Hopefully the weirdness will soon wear off.

Off to the side, Jase the gladiator starts fiddling around with the music system next to the snacks until it comes to life, producing familiar sounding beats. It's something popular that's playing, but I can't put my finger on what it's called.

Sal hands me a glass full of peculiar fluorescent pink liquid. I'm suspicious of it, but she chugs half her glass in one go and looks at me daringly.

"Don't be a coward. How bad can it be?"

Unconvinced, I sniff at the contents of my glass. It reminds me of one of those strange, limited edition flavours of Pimm's. The type that seem innocent enough until you're three drinks in and nauseous.

"I have a very sensitive stomach when it comes to these things."

"Shut up, it was your idea to get punch." Sally softly elbows me in my arm and I shrug, even if it wasn't my idea at all. Whatever.

The drink tastes a lot nicer than expected, so I decide to get a glass for Alex as well. One or two can't hurt...

On the way back to the boys, we come across Elaine and Cath.

"Lemme have another look. Oh my God, girl, I'm so happy for you!" Elaine's voice is shrill with excitement as she continues to stare at Cath's hand. Specifically, she's gawking at a ring.

"Oh wow, when did he pop the question?" Sally buts in.

Cath looks up, her cheeks turning crimson despite the pale makeup.

"Just last night. He surprised me with dinner and got me a box of my favourite chocolates. The ring was inside."

"Congratulations, Cath, that's so awesome!" I say, though I can't help being reminded of a year ago when I thought I was going to be in a similar position. Before Alex. It feels like another lifetime when I was still together with Jeff.

"Thanks guys. I totally didn't expect it, though in hindsight I knew something was up. John's terrible at keeping secrets from me usually."

Just at that moment, John walks by carrying a couple of bottles of beer. The look Cath and him share is enough to melt even the most cynical heart in the room, Sally's in this case.

The three of us stand around, smiling sheepishly at the happy couple, who enjoy a quick kiss on the lips before wandering off in opposite directions. They really are trying to be good hosts.

"He seems nice. Why does he look so familiar? Did he perhaps pick Cath up at work once and that's when I saw him?" I whisper at Sal. She sighs and shakes her head.

"You're kidding, right?"

I shrug and quasi-innocently bat my eyelids at her.

"John works on the second floor," she explains.

"No shit, I had no idea!"

She shakes her head at me almost in pity.

"Maybe if you spent less time texting Alex all day, you'd notice these things." She prods me in the side to make her point and grins.

"That's not an option." I scan the room to find that by now Alex and Mark seem a lot more comfortable in each other's company. From afar it looks like they're in passionate agreement about something, while Gladiator Jase is standing next to them shaking his head.

I remember I'm still holding Alex's glass, so I make my way around a priest who's sweet talking a fake Marilyn, flowy dress and all. Then I pass by the zombies, who have broken character to eat finger food.

"Here. It's not as bad as it looks." I hand Alex his punch.

"Cheers," Alex says, flashing me a grin. I'm so relieved things are going well so far.

"You'll never guess the latest," Sally tells Mark while handing him his glass.

"John proposed to Cath."

"No way!" Mark says, his voice sounding a lot more effeminate than usual. Clearly he's also taking his costume very seriously.

"Check out the rock on her hand if you don't believe me."

I take the last sip from my glass and put it on a shelf next to us. Considering Sally's guarded nature, I wonder what she's really thinking about Cath's engagement. It wasn't so long ago that she rejected the idea of relationships completely...

Jase, meanwhile, did well with that music, it has changed the mood of the entire room. One couple nearby is already dancing when Alex, very unlike himself, offers me his hand and stops my speculation about other people's private lives. Time to focus on our own.

We start moving, tentatively at first, until the beat takes over. And boy, does it take over. In seconds, it's as if I'm not the one doing this, but an invisible force has taken control.

Sally, playing her role as the man perfectly, invites Mark to dance beside us. I look around and it strikes me that everyone in the room has joined in at almost the same time. Nobody is left standing still. From one moment to the next, the restrained party has turned into a miniature rave.

"Do you see the music?" Alex remarks I my ear.

I release him just enough to get a good view of the room and realise he's right. The air is buzzing and pulsating with the sounds playing on the stereo. Weird. Perhaps it's a music activated strobe light, but that's not the only thing that's strange.

"Can you hear their thoughts?" I respond.

He tells me yes, but his lips don't move.

We both turn in Sally's direction, distracted by the filth that's going on in her head. If this is what her thoughts are like normally, I'm surprised she gets anything done at work.

*What was in that punch?* Alex thinks. I shrug, *it's hot, what Sally's imagining.*

We're allowed a look inside Sal's bedroom activities, uncensored. She's more than happy to share the mechanics of what she gets up to in conversation, but the Sally I can see in my mind right now is different: sensitive and caring. And it's all thanks to Mark.

Alex and I share a smile. This telepathic communication is ours alone, nobody can pick up on it. We would have noticed if they could.

I wrap my arms around his neck, rest my face against his chest, and try to focus just on us. It's easy to get swept away in the thoughts around us. Most of the crowd paired up when the music started to take effect. Or maybe it was the punch that did it, I'm not sure. Either way, the lust that's starting to grow all round washes over us, sweeping us up in its powerful currents until we're equally afflicted.

Behind me I can feel a prickly, sweaty tension build up. Rather than dirty, it's… tempting. Alex has located the couple, Gladiator Jase and his boyfriend, sharing the first kiss in the room. I can see them, although foggy, through Alex's thoughts. Something tells me more couples will follow suit.

Next to us Sal and Mark are staring each other down with only one thought between them: who will move first? My money is on Sally.

*This is a dream, isn't it?* Alex wonders. It's a better explanation than what I've got.

*Yours or mine?* I look him in the eye again, but our

island of quiet in the madness of the party is invaded by another outside influence. Something warm, soft, wrapping itself around my ankle. A black cat, unmistakably mine, with the strap still attached to its back. I knew there was something about that bag: it seemed too real when I spied it at the fancy dress shop last week.

*How does it matter whose dream it is?* Alex smiles at me, and I know he's right. I throw a scrap from a discarded plate towards the cat, which races off with it immediately. Hungry little bugger.

*I wouldn't mind some more punch…* Before I'm able to complete my thought, I notice the glass next to me has filled itself. As if by magic. We share a sip each and make our way past the priest I noticed earlier, whose female companion is rhythmically swaying to the music, wearing much less than I recall. Fake Marilyn is less Hollywood and more pin-up now. What kind of party is this exactly?

*Bedroom or sofa? - Bedroom.* The moment I think it, our surroundings melt and morph into a room I've never seen before. Alex chuckles at the sight ahead making me realise we're not alone.

John, oblivious to us, has been tied up to the metal headboard of the bed, using the rope belt that came with his monk costume. Cath, who's straddling him, runs her fingernails over his naked chest, causing him to writhe against his restraints. The similarities between John's physique and Alex are not lost on me and neither is Cath's adoration of what she sees in front of her. She leans back, exposes her fangs and dives back down at John's neck. *What the… she's actually feeding on him!*

*That means…* Alex takes my hand protectively, as we back up against the wall where the door must be. *She's an actual vampire? Holy shit.*

My initial shock at the bloody spectacle in front of us wears off when John's thoughts enter my mind. Rather than fearing for his life, he's enjoying himself. The bite in his neck just fuelling the fire Cath had lit up earlier. And it's so hot to be able to watch.

*Scorching,* Alex responds.

*You don't think they'll mind if we join in?*

*They don't need to know,* Alex suggests. *It's our dream; we could be invisible.*

He's right, and so we are. John and Cath will never realise we're here. This is a first, even for us: to get it on in a room with another couple who don't know we're there. The realisation that this isn't real takes away any guilt we might have felt otherwise. There's nothing wrong with any of this: it's just a dream.

I turn to present my back zip to Alex, who opens it swiftly. Then I remember we have the ability to skip past the boring bits and make our clothes vanish instantly. *That's better.*

Pacing around him, while sneaking peeks at the bed next to us every so often, I caress his naked torso. We've done so much, together as well as with other people, yet I always come back to this. Alex is the one I want.

*You're the one I want too.* I smile at his reaction, how

weird it is to have him in my head. Weird but good.

*Promise it'll stay that way?* I run my hand down Alex's treasure trail and wrap my fingers around his already hard manhood.

*Always.*

Pushing him gently against the wall, I drop onto my knees in front of him. He has full view of the bed, and I have full view of him. Seeing his mental image of the coupling that's unfolding mere feet behind my back is better than any porn I've ever seen. Cath moves with immense speed, almost too fast to see but pauses every so often to allow us, and John, a better look.

I take Alex into my mouth, and he gasps with pleasure. He rests his hand on my head, then grabs a fistful of hair.

With my eyes closed I can focus better on pleasing him while enjoying the visions he's broadcasting into my consciousness.

"You guys in here? Open up!" A voice shouts outside, followed by fists banging against the wooden door.

Cath looks up, blinking and letting out a sigh before wiping the blood from the corner of her mouth. She reaches the door - fully clothed - in a split second.

"What is it? We're in the middle of something." She peeks out to find a distressed looking Elaine, her fairy wings flapping frantically as she hovers about a foot above the ground.

"We've got a situation downstairs."

Cath shrugs and follows her down the stairs, while

Alex and I - still invisible - sneak up behind them.

Even from the top of the stairs, the mood downstairs is obvious. Everyone downstairs is still acting on their most primal desires... The only difference is which desire each person has chosen to focus on. Among the love-drunk couples, two characters are not playing along. The zombies.

Cath gasps in disgust. Alex and I transform so we're no longer invisible nor naked.

*What the hell?* The zombies are different from the other partygoers. Not only are they trying to satiate an immense hunger with whatever they can find - mainly each other - they also seem to have no other thoughts we can pick up.

*So everyone has turned into their costume?* Alex wonders. *Now what?*

"We've got to hit them over the head with something, that tends to work in the movies," Elaine concludes.

"But they stink!" Cath interjects.

I shake my head, they're wrong. They don't realise there's another choice; of course they couldn't have, they can't hear us think.

"I have an idea," I say.

Alex takes my hand and squeezes in agreement. We can do this.

"What's that, Becky?" Cath asks, while staring at me with her piercing red eyes.

"We could turn them back into normal people."

"And how exactly are you going to do that?" Elaine

narrows her eyes and crosses her arms.

I smile, *because it's our dream.*

Alex, who's remained silent so far, steps forward and pulls one of the decomposing figures off the other. Strangely, I would have thought that they'd eat other people, but thankfully they have developed a taste for zombie meat only. Both of them snarl, the woman on her back, surrounded by blood and guts wriggles but is unable to get up. The male, struggles desperately against Alex's firm grip.

We both close our eyes, and the right words enter our thoughts all by themselves. We repeat strange mantras and chants, in a language I can't understand, again and again.

When we're done, I turn and look at Cath and Elaine, who are stuck in place. In fact the entire room is frozen in time; only Alex and I can move. The general consciousness of the party has turned to silence.

*Did we do this?* Alex wonders as he lets go of the man's shoulder. What had earlier been just a rancid collection of bones and soggy tissue has been transformed. He looks well now, normal, except for being suspended a foot above the ground.

*Let's undo it.* I smile at Alex, and everything jerks into action again. *And I've had enough of this weird party, let's go.*

Behind us, the former zombie stumbles onto the ground next to his partner, who is no longer half eaten. But the thump of his landing can hardly be heard over the music that has switched back on. Except for Cath and Elaine, nobody noticed that anything was even going on.

"That's strange, I could swear I just saw them cannibalise each other," Elaine mumbles.

Cath, speechless, takes a moment to regain her composure before deciding to head back upstairs to finish what she'd started with John earlier. Within the blink of an eye, she's gone.

Alex offers me his arm and makes his apologies to Elaine, who still looks flummoxed. *Let's go.*

Instantly, the room shifts and changes again, before the colours and shapes rearrange themselves into somewhere altogether more familiar. My flat.

After willing the curtains to close, I turn my head to find Alex already undressed and in bed, waiting. The next second, I'm on top of him, feeling his hands on my hips and his face nearing mine.

*It's good to be home.*

He leans up further so his lips brush past mine.

"Tonight was crazy. But I'm glad it was you I shared my thoughts with."

*Likewise.*

Funny, how this closeness can put me in the mood instantly. Only with him.

We kiss, satiating a hunger that had been building ever since that dance. Much time can't have passed in between, my alarm clock only indicates eleven. But so much has happened…

His hands, brushing over my naked back, send shivers down my most intimate regions. I gasp, enjoying him nudge at my entrance. *You tease.*

He chuckles, before kissing me once more, exploring my tongue with his in a familiar dance that somehow never manages to become dull.

I lower myself onto him, moaning with contentment when he fills me. This is just right, the perfect ending to a crazy dream.

He grinds up at me, while I start to rock back and forth, finding a relaxed rhythm. In his arms, I simultaneously feel at ease and on edge. I can't decide whether to slow down, drag it out, or aim for something more intense. He chooses the latter for me and I feel us lift off the bed momentarily. We're suspended, inches above the mattress for only a second before he flips me and I land on my back. These newfound skills of ours are convenient indeed, and such a turn-on.

"This way I can see you better while I make you scream," Alex whispers through gritted teeth.

His tone gives me goosebumps and I surrender.

After taking in the view of me, hair fanned out over the pillow and feverish with lust, he covers my neck in kisses. They grow progressively firmer, with the odd nibble thrown in, and push me up towards the edge of what I can take.

I dig my fingers into his sides, encouraging, no, *making* him speed up. He knows how I love this: being taken on my back, quick and dirty.

Still, he's not ready for the final sprint yet and slows. His lips move downwards, over my collarbone and chest. I close my eyes and let his thoughts take over while his tongue explores my aureola. He's remembering our first night together, a memory that's very dear to me too. *I was so nervous and still it was magical. How you bared all for me, without even knowing my name. You took my hand and gave me the greatest gift ever: you made me feel like a man.*

His side of the story makes me smile and teary-eyed at the same time. He's a lot more chatty in his thoughts than what he normally says out loud. I wince when he finally takes my nipple into his mouth and sucks, flicking his tongue over it just like how I like it.

*How could I refuse, you were and are perfect. From the moment I saw you waiting for me at the cinema, I knew I had to have you, so I did.*

He straightens his back again, and kisses me on the lips before thrusting into me, hard. I cry out and hang on for the ride.

Much like Cath earlier, he speeds up so fast I'm having trouble focusing. Magic is a wonderful thing.

Faster and faster he moves, with little breaks in between to find a unique rhythm that pushes me to the point of no return. I scream, just as he likes, and nearly draw blood with my fingernails on his back. He shudders and groans in what becomes the perfect simultaneous release.

"I love you," we whisper in unison.

★★★

The buzz of my phone wakes me from a deep, comfortable slumber. I struggle to open my lids, which are still unwilling, and try to loosen Alex's protective embrace.

A new message. I blink a couple of times to lift the fog on my brain.

'Fuck, that was some party. No idea how I got home. And I had the trippiest dream,' Sally writes.

I put the phone back on the bedside table without answering. *Party? Oh right, Cath's thing. Did we ever go?*

Just as glimpses of the previous night return to me, and I try to decipher the parts that were real and those which were just imagined.

That *was* a trippy dream, she's right. I wonder if someone slipped a little something into the punch.

I lie back against the pillow, enjoying how Alex instinctively wraps his arm around me again. Warmth surrounds me, luring me back to half-sleep, until the cat's hungry meow interrupts the silence. She jumps and I can feel her land softly on the duvet next to me, before complaining some more.

Then, my eyes snap open with a startling realisation: I don't have a cat!

***

# AUTHOR'S NOTE

Thanks for reading *Undateables!*

In the first book, The Rebound List, newly single Becky tries to celebrate her freedom by exploring her sexual identity. While her best friend and colleague, Sally, cheers her on, she discovers that although there's more to life than the weekly missionary position with the same guy, being single isn't just fun and games. She's reluctant to jump right into the world of casual, no-strings-attached sex. Like many of us, Becky isn't the most confident person in the world. She's definitely no femme fatale accustomed to turning heads wherever she goes. But with a bit of trial & error, and help from modern technology, she starts strong on her journey down the list.

I suppose a lot of books contain characters based more or less on the writer themselves. *The Rebound List* is no different. In her shoes, I might attempt to break the chains of normality, and try something new and crazy like she does. Certainly, the list mirrors some of my interests and fantasies. But, would I really do it? Or would I chicken out? I'm happily married, so I may never find out.

Unlike in some of my other stories, *The Rebound List* does also contain a hero who was modeled sort of on someone I once knew. I don't want to make things awkward for him (or me), so I'll be a total tease, and leave it at that. But it was utterly fascinating to think about what could've been, in a parallel universe, if we were all slightly different (and yet very similar) people. God, I hope he never reads this book, I would die of awkwardness.

Come to think of it, I hope my former boss never reads it either. Still, at least I remembered to rename the character in question before publication...

*Sally* is another title which is a bit of a weird one, even for me. But I'd like to think it's unusual in a good way.

The idea for this story came when while writing *The Rebound List*, which features a lot of the same characters (if you haven't read it yet, you may want to check it out). It wasn't relevant to the story at the time, but I couldn't help but wonder why Sally was so cynical about love. What had happened to her to make her so suspicious? Well, that question has now been answered.

Mark's reason for not settling down came up later, and it was a bit of a surprise to me at the time. But then, why not? It's a diverse world out there, and I like to think that the revelation that Marks enjoys dressing up as a woman at times works for his relationship with Sally on multiple levels.

I wanted to highlight that not every guy who cross-dresses is gay (actually, perhaps most of them are straight), and give both of them the chance to make it work despite everything. Mark gets to let go of the life of secrecy he had consigned himself to, and be accepted for who he is. And after finally getting closure on an event from her past which has had such a massive effect on who she is, Sally gets the chance to be in a relationship again. Not just that, her relationship with Mark is set to be just a bit more exciting than having only one person to be with forever. Plus, those who've read The Rebound List, already would've known that Sally does like to play with girls occasionally. It's a win-win.

When Sally and Mark first hook up, nobody could foresee just how far their relationship would go, least of all Sally herself. There were just so many things standing in the way, making a happy ending an unlikely outcome. That is why I've left the story at the point I did. For two characters with so much baggage, it wouldn't be likely that they'd get a happily ever after in what is essentially just a week. But worry not, I'd like to think they'll get there eventually.

Weirdness and lengthy explanations aside, it's still a privilege, being able to write whatever comes to mind; to explore scenarios which are normally best left to the imagination. It's even more of an honour that I get to share these glimpses into my imagination with you, the reader.

If you got some pleasure out of it, feel free to connect or get in touch via email or social media; I do my best to answer every message I get as soon as possible!

Love, Lorelei

- ❖ Lmoone.com
- ❖ Lorelei Moone on Facebook

By the way, I also write Paranormal Romance as Lorelei Moone. If that's also your cup of tea, then please take a look at loreleimoone.com.

www.ingramcontent.com/pod-product-compliance
Lightning Source LLC
Chambersburg PA
CBHW070429170726
48291CB00002B/422